Harry G. Richey

Richey's Guide and Assistant for Carpenters and Mechanics

a work of practical information, giving almost every geometrical and practical

problem likely to arise in the work of the carpenter, and quick and easy methods

for their solution

Harry G. Richey

Richey's Guide and Assistant for Carpenters and Mechanics
a work of practical information, giving almost every geometrical and practical problem likely to arise in the work of the carpenter, and quick and easy methods for their solution

ISBN/EAN: 9783337369149

Printed in Europe, USA, Canada, Australia, Japan

Cover: Foto ©Andreas Hilbeck / pixelio.de

More available books at **www.hansebooks.com**

RICHEY'S

GUIDE and ASSISTANT

FOR

CARPENTERS AND MECHANICS.

A work of practical information, giving almost every geometrical and practical problem
likely to arise in the work of the carpenter, and quick and easy methods for
their solution.   The use of the steel square, etc., tables showing
strength and weight of materials, methods of
framing, useful recipes, etc., etc.

By H. G. RICHEY.

Illustrated by 201 Engravings.

NEW YORK:
WILLIAM T. COMSTOCK,
23 Warren Street.

PUBLISHER'S PREFACE.

In bringing out a new book on carpentry the publisher has been influenced by the fact that nothing new, except unimportant publications, have been presented for a number of years. In fact the books that are now most largely in demand are those that were old and well known ten years ago. While the general principles have not changed and they will ever be controlled by immutable mathematical principles, yet the change of habits and customs of mechanics and the general advancement of every calling is such as to demand the production of new works from time to time. A general review of these pages will make evident to the most casual observer that while the author has adhered to those mathematical rules that must ever be the same, yet he has in many cases shown methods that are more in accordance to modern practice than those laid down in earlier works on the subject. It has not been his purpose to carry his readers through long abstruse problems, but to give them simple methods of doing every-day work, and, while he has recognized that carpentry is but one of the many practical applications of geometry, he has made its study entirely subservient to his purpose, and has given the method of drawing lines rather than the theory on which they are drawn. He has also supplied a large amount of practical information by tables and otherwise, such as is called for in a manual for the every-day use of the carpenter and builder. The work is intended, as its name implies, as a guide to the artisan, not a philosophical dissertation and demonstrator of general principles.

THE PUBLISHER.

New York, February 6, 1891.

INDEX.

GUIDE AND ASSISTANT
For Carpenters and Mechanics.

CHAPTER I.

Laying Out for Excavating—Stonework—Brickwork—Table to Find the Number of Bricks in any Wall—Names of Brick—Sills—To Find Length of Sills for Bay Windows—To Find the Lengths and Bevels of Hip and Cripple Rafters—To Get the Top Bevel of Hip Rafters—To Get the Cuts and Lengths of Hip, Valley and Cripple Rafters of Roofs of Different Pitches— To Get the Lengths and Cuts of Hips and Cripples of a Square Roof—To Get the Lengths of Rafters—To Find the Back Cuts of Cripple Rafters Without a Diagram—How Much Shorter to Cut Cripple Rafters for Quarter, Third And Half Pitch Roofs.

1—Laying Out for Excavating.—In measuring over the surface of the ground, always keep your pole or tape-line level, using a plumb to give the point on the ground as shown in Fig. 1; *a* represents the pole or tape line, *b* the plumb and *c* the grade of the ground. After we

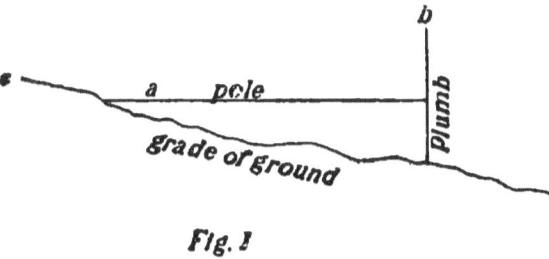

Fig. 1

have the lines all run, the next thing is to see if it is square, which is done by measuring 8 feet from the corner on one side and 6 feet from the same corner on the other side, then take 10 feet on the pole, and if the distance from the point 8 feet to the point 6 feet is 10 feet, then it is all true. But care must be taken in measuring to keep the pole level. If the excavation or building be square, then you can true it by taking the

distance from opposite corners, and if the diagonal both
ways are alike, then it is square. The next thing is to

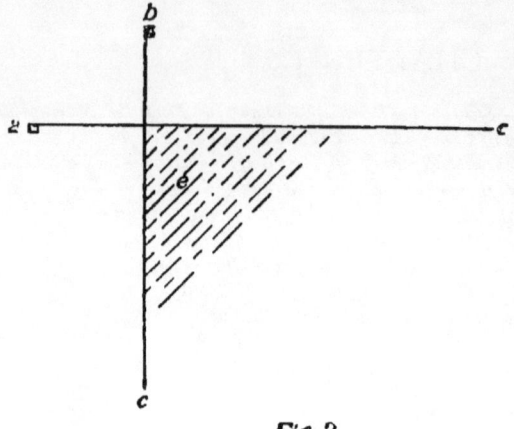

Fig.2

place the pins for
the line so they
will not be dis-
turbed when the
excavating is be-
ing done. As
shown in Fig. 2,
a and *b* are the
pins, *c d* the lines
and *e* the excava-
tion.

To find the con-
tents of an excava-
tion find the area
by multiplying the length by the breadth and this answer
by the average depth, which is found by adding together
the depth at the several different corners and dividing
this by the number of corners. Excavating is generally
done by the yard, which is 27 cubic feet.

2—Stonework.—Stonework is done by the perch, which
is 24¾ cubic feet, or, as is more convenient, 25 feet.

In measuring stonework always measure from the outside, thus measuring all the angles twice.

All walls under 18 inches are counted same as 18 inches.

One and one-quarter barrels of lime and 1 yard of sand
will lay 100 feet of stone ruble work.

One man with one tender will lay 150 feet per day.

One and one-quarter barrels cement, ¾ yard sand, will
lay 100 feet stone ruble work.

3—Brickwork.—Brickwork is counted by the thousand.
One and one-eighth barrels of lime and ¾ yard of sand
will lay 1,000 bricks.

One man with one tender will lay 1,800 to 2,000 bricks
per day.

One thousand bricks closely stacked occupy 56 cubic feet.
One thousand old bricks cleaned and loosely stacked
occupy about 70 cubic feet.
Six hundred bricks 1 cubic yard in wall.
Bricks absorb one-fifth their weight in water.

TABLE OF NUMBER OF BRICKS REQUIRED IN A WALL PER SQUARE FOOT FACE OF WALL.

4 inches	$7\frac{1}{2}$	24 inches	45
8 "	15	28 "	$52\frac{1}{2}$
12 "	$22\frac{1}{2}$	32 "	60
16 "	30	36 "	$67\frac{1}{2}$
20 "	$37\frac{1}{2}$	40 "	75

TABLE TO FIND THE NUMBER OF BRICKS IN ANY WALL.

Superficial feet of wall.	NUMBER OF BRICKS TO THICKNESS OF WALL.					
	4 inch	8 inch	12 inch	16 inch	20 inch	24 inch
1	$7\frac{1}{2}$	15	23	30	38	45
2	15	30	45	60	75	90
3	23	45	68	90	113	135
4	30	60	90	120	150	180
5	38	75	113	150	188	225
6	45	90	135	180	225	270
7	53	105	158	210	263	315
8	60	120	180	240	300	300
9	68	135	203	270	338	405
10	75	150	225	300	375	450
20	150	300	450	600	750	900
30	225	450	675	900	1,125	1,350
40	300	600	900	1,200	1,500	1,800
50	375	750	1,125	1,500	1,875	2,250
60	450	900	1,350	1,800	2,250	2,700
70	525	1,050	1,575	2,100	2,625	3,150
80	600	1,200	1,800	2,400	3,000	3,600
90	675	1,350	2,025	2,700	3,375	4,050
100	750	1,500	2,250	3,000	3,750	4,500
200	1,500	3,000	4,500	6,000	7,500	9,000
300	2,250	4,500	6,750	9,000	11,250	13,500
400	3,000	6,000	9,000	12,000	15,000	18,000
500	3,750	7,500	11,250	15,000	18,750	22,500
600	4,500	9,000	13,500	18,000	22,500	27,000
700	5,250	10,500	15,750	21,000	26,250	31,500
800	6,000	12,000	18,000	24,000	30,000	36,000
900	6,750	13,500	20,250	27,000	33,750	40,500
1,000	7,500	15,000	22,500	30,000	37,500	45,000

EXAMPLE:—Find the number of bricks in a wall 8 inches thick 5 feet high and 10 feet long ; five multiplied by ten equals 50 feet of wall 8 inches thick. Under 8 inches and opposite 50 you will find 750, the number of bricks in the wall.

4—Names of Brick.—1. All brick not hard enough to stand in the outside of buildings are known as "salmon brick."

2. All brick hard enough for the outside of buildings but not selected or graded are known as "hard kiln run."

3. All brick set in arches or benches which are discolored, broken or twisted in the burning are known as "arch brick."

4. All common brick selected for the outside of buildings are known as

Front brick. { No. 1. Light burned.
No. 2. Medium   "
No. 3. Hardest   "

5. All brick used for sidewalks are known as "sidewalk brick."

6. All the brick in the kiln not strictly soft taken together are known as "merchantable brick."

7. All brick that are set in the kiln when burned are known as "kiln run brick."

8. Bricks moulded either by hand or machine in rough, coarse sand and repressed without rubbing, so as to give the brick a rough, sand finish, are known as "stock brick."

9. All brick other than square are known as "ornamental brick."

All brick made either by the repress or dry press process and selected for the fronts of buildings are known as "press brick," which are: No. 1, light shade; No. 2, medium; No. 3, dark.

5—Sills.—We illustrate a few different styles of sills, of which Fig. 3 is the best. Take a 2 or 3x8 and bed it solid on the wall and frame your joist back 2 inches from the 3x8 so as to receive the outside piece; put your plate on top of the joist for the studs, which makes a solid frame. It is often noticed in houses, after they are up a few months, that the floor drops away from the base. This is caused by the drying and shrinking of the joist.

This style of sill overcomes all this, as the whole house is set on the joist. In the case of houses framed as shown in Figs. 4 and 5, all the weight of the house comes on that part of the stud running down onto the wall plate, and when shrinkage occurs, the flooring drops away with the joist, whereas in the case of Fig. 3 the studding and floor are affected equally.

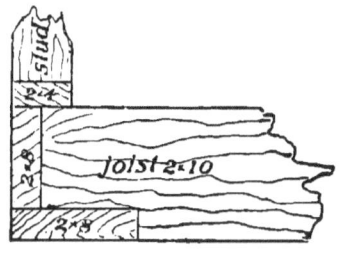

6—To Find Length of Sills for Bay Windows.— Following is shown a bay window, Fig. 6. Sometimes it is very hard to get the length of

Fig. 3

the sills. Now we have the length of the side and end sill as if they ran straight through, as shown by the dotted lines, but what we want is the length from points 1 and 2 to points *e* and *a*. Now the width of the bay is 10 feet, which divided by 2=5, the distance from *c* to *d* and *c* to *b*, which makes *a*, *b*, *c* and *c*, *d*, *e* triangles, of which we have the base and perpendic-

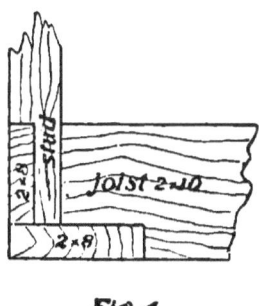

Fig. 4

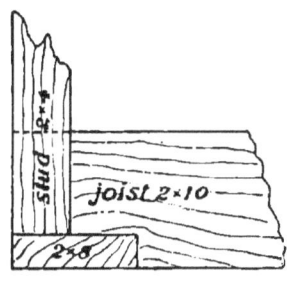

Fig. 5

ular and want to find the hypotenuse, which is done in the following way : Take the square of the base, which is 5×5=25, and the square of the perpendicular, which is 5×5=25 ; add these two answers together, which is

25+25=50, the sum of the squares of the two sides, of which we take the square root, which is 7.07 feet, the distance from *c* to *a* and *c* to *c*, which, taken from 34 feet, the

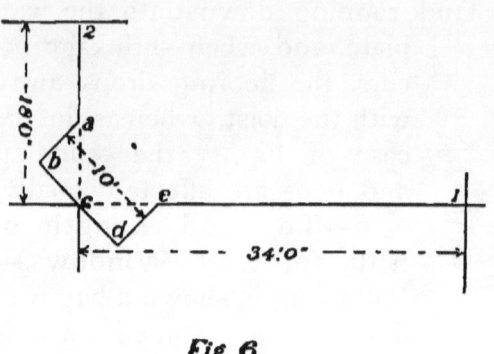

distance from *c* to 1 = 26.93 feet, the length of the sill from *c* to 1; and 18 feet, the distance from *c* to 2, less 7.07, the distance from *c* to *a*, =10.93 feet, the length of the sill from *a* to 2.

Fig. 6

7—To Stiffen Joist, nail a strip of 1x2 or 1x3 on each side in the form of a truss, as shown by the dotted lines in Fig. 7.

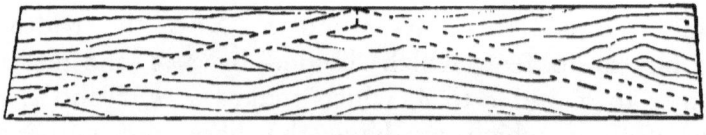

Fig. 7

8—To Find the Lengths and Bevels of Hip and Cripple Rafters.—Draw the plates as *a b* and *b c*, Fig. 8, then the seat of the hip, as *b d*, then the seats of the cripples, as 1 1, 2 2, 3 3, etc.; then draw the rise of the common rafter, as *d c*, then *c* to 1 is the length of the common rafters; then draw the rise of the hip, as *d f*, then *f b* is the length of the hip; then continue the seat of the common rafter until it equals the length of the rafter as 1 *g;* then draw *g b*, which is equal to the length of the hip, then continue the seats of the cripples until they strike the hip, *g b*, which gives the lengths of the cripples, also the top bevel, which is shown at *h;* then draw line from *g* parallel to *d c*, which gives the top bevel of the hip as shown

at g, but the bevel must not be used until after the hip
has been backed. The length of the cripples are shown

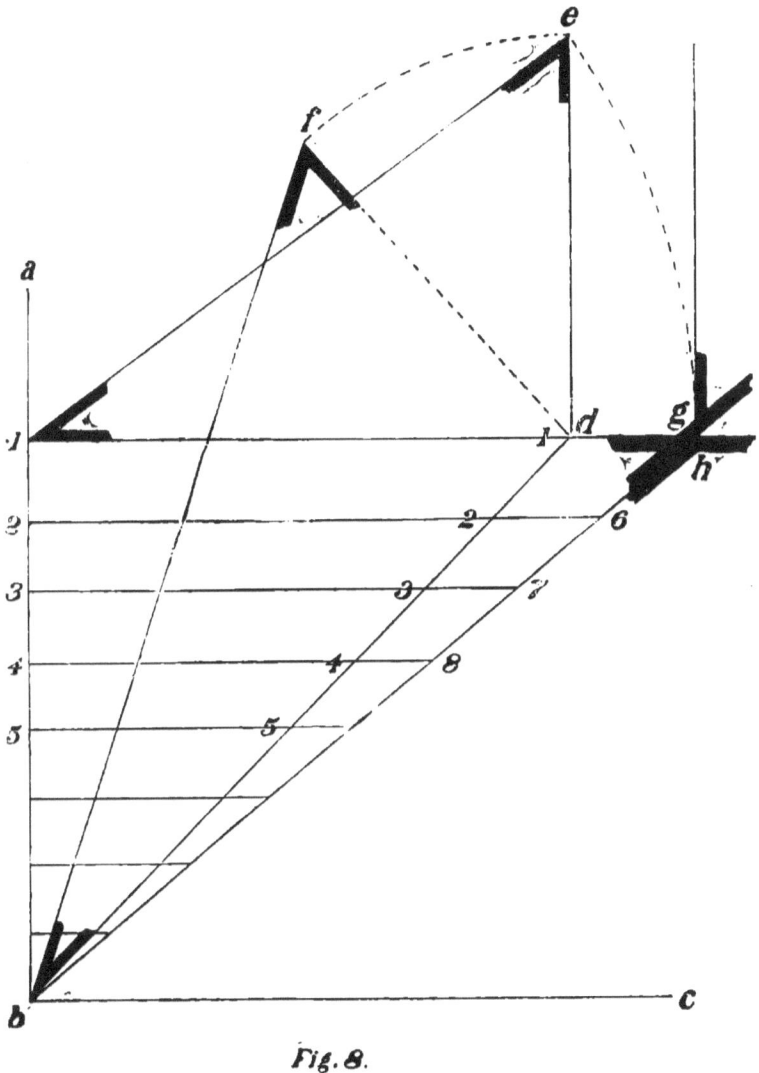

Fig. 8.

by the lines 2 6, 3 7, 4 8, etc. The bevel at b is the bevel
of the foot of the hip; the one at the top is shown at f.

The bevel of the foot of the common and cripple rafters is shown at c. The top bevel of the cripple is shown at h.

9—To get the Top Bevel of Hip Rafters.—With a, b, c, as plates, draw the seat of the hip as $b\,d$, and the

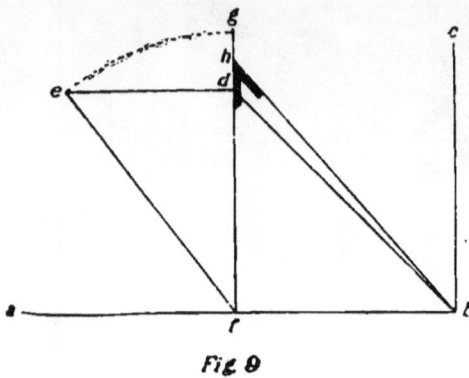

Fig 9

seat of the common rafter as $f\,d$. Now draw the rise of the common rafter as c d, and connect c and f. Make $f\,g$ equal to $f\,c$; divide $g\,d$ into two equal parts, as h; connect h and b, and the bevel at h is the bevel for the top of the hip when the hip is not backed.

10—To get the Cuts and Lengths of Hip, Valley and Cripple Rafters of Roofs of Different Pitches.—

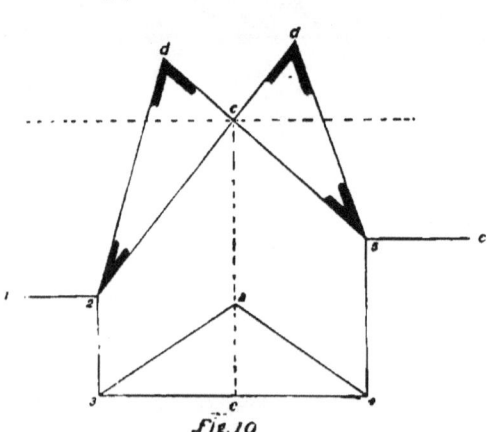

Fig. 10

In Fig. 10, 1, 2, 3, 4, etc., represent the plates of the building, 2 c and 5 c the seat of the valleys. Draw the rise of the common rafter as a c, then 3 a and a 4; show the lengths and cuts of the common rafter, then draw the rise from c at right angles to the seat of the valleys, making it equal to a c; then 2 d and 5 d. Show the lengths and cuts of the valleys. In Fig. 11 we divide the building into two parts, as shown by the lines representing the plates of the building, 1, 2, 3 and 4, 5, 6. The dotted lines show the seat of the valley rafters and the seat of the comb or ridge. Then draw lines 2 7, 2 8, 5 9 and 5 10, equal in length to the common rafters in their respective

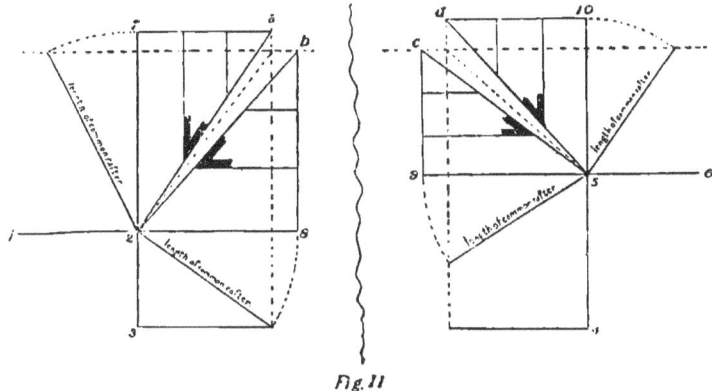

Fig. 11

positions; then draw the ridge line, as 7 *a*, *d* 10, 8 *b* and 9 *c*. Then draw the valley lines, as 2 *a*, 2 *b*, 5 *c* and 5 *d*, which show the position of the valleys if they were dropped down to a level. Then draw the cripples as shown, thus finding the length and cut of each one.

11—**To Get the Length of Rafters.**—We will take a span of 16 feet 10 inches and a rise 4 feet 2½ inches, or ¼ pitch; one-half the span equals 8 feet 5 inches, the run of

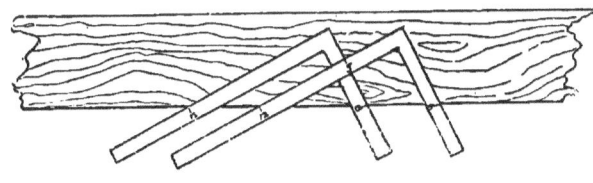

Fig. 12

the rafter, with a rise of 4 feet 2½ inches. In a quarter pitch roof the rise of the rafter to each foot is 6 inches, so we take 12 on the blade of the square and 6 on the tongue and place it on the rafter as shown in Fig. 12, taking the length

as many times as feet in the run, which is 8, which brings
us to the position in Fig. 13. We still have 5 inches in
the run, which we measure off at right angles to the tongue,

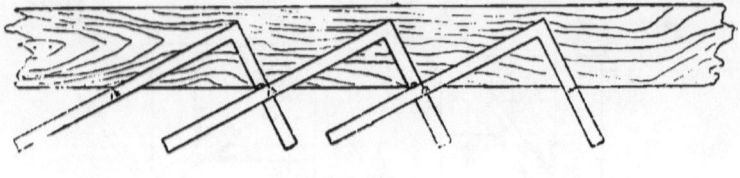

Fig. 13

as shown, thus giving the length and top cut of the rafter.
For hips and valleys for square roofs use 17 on the blade
instead of 12.

Hip rafters may be laid out in the same manner by
using 17 instead of 12 for the run. This rule applies only
to retangular roofs.

12—To Get the Lengths and Cuts of Hips and
Cripples of a Square Roof.—Draw the plates of the
building as 1, 2, 3, 4, Fig. 14 ; then draw the comb line,
as *a b;* then the seat of common rafters, as *d c* and *c c;*
then the seat of the hip and cripples, as *c* 3 and 5, 6, 7,
etc.; then draw the rise of the hip, as *c f;* then the line
f 3, which is the length of the hip, and *f* 3 the cuts. Then
with the compasses draw the arc from *f* around to *g;* then
connect *g* and *a*, which is the length of the common rafter,
and *g a* the cuts. Then draw line *h a* at right angles
to *g a;* then, with *a* as a centre, draw arcs from the
seats of the cripples around to *h a*, as 5 5, 6 6, 7 7, etc.;
then connect *h g*, which is the length of the hip ; then draw
lines from 5, 6, 7, etc., parallel to *g a*, connecting with *h g*.
These are the lengths of cripples ; the bevel at *g* 2 is the
top cut.

13—To Find the Back Cuts of Cripple Rafters
without a Diagram.—(Rule.) The length of the common rafter on the blade and the run of the common rafter

on the tongue of the square will give the cut on the back of the cripple rafters.

EXAMPLE.—Let the rise be 6 feet and the run 8 feet. the length of the common rafter is 10 feet. Now take 10

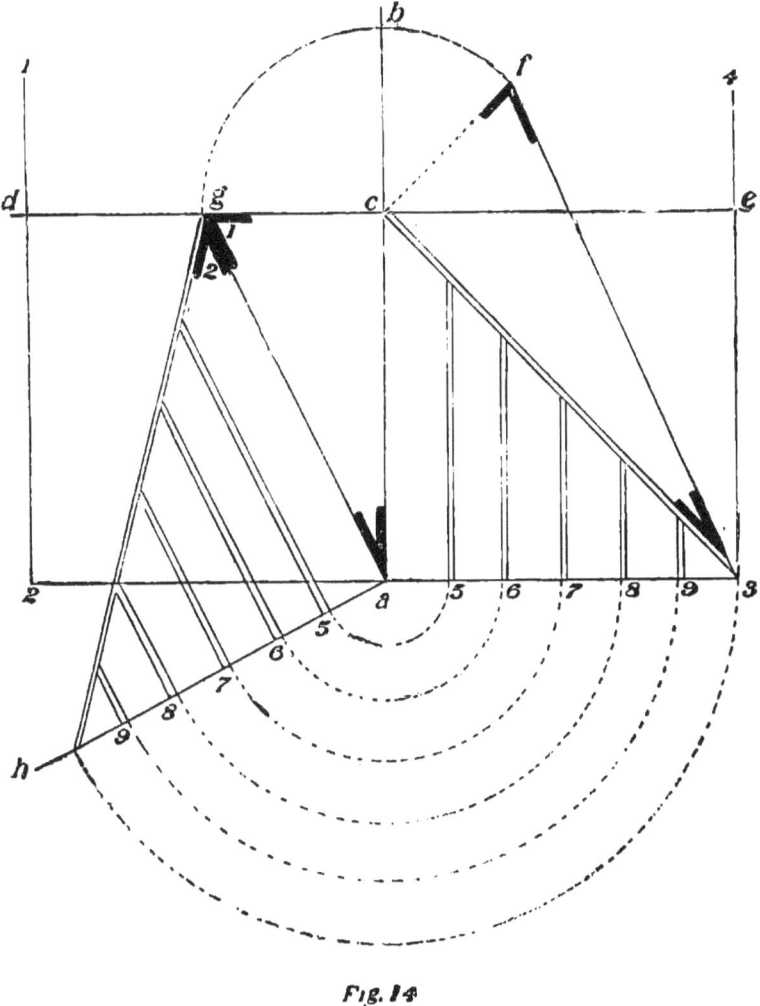

Fig. 14

on the blade and 8 on the tongue of the square and the blade will give the back cut of the cripples.

14—How much Shorter to Cut Cripple Rafters.—

One-quarter pitch roof:

They cut 13.5 inches shorter each time when spaced 12 inches.

They cut 18 inches shorter each time when spaced 16 inches.

They cut 27 inches shorter each time when spaced 24 inches.

One-third pitch roof :

They cut 14.4 inches shorter each time when spaced 12 inches.

They cut 19.2 inches shorter each time when spaced 16 inches.

They cut 28.8 inches shorter each time when spaced 24 inches.

One-half pitch roof :

They cut 17 inches shorter each time when spaced 12 inches.

They cut 22.6 inches shorter each time when spaced 16 inches.

They cut 34 inches shorter each time when spaced 24 inches.

15—To Approximate the Number of Squares in a Roof.—If $\frac{1}{4}$ pitch, find the floor surface and multiply by $1\frac{1}{2}$; if $\frac{1}{3}$ pitch, multiply by $1\frac{1}{3}$; if $\frac{1}{4}$ pitch, multiply by $1\frac{1}{4}$, etc.

EXAMPLE.—Find the number of squares in a roof 30x40 feet, $\frac{1}{3}$ pitch : 30x40 = 1,200; 1,200x1$\frac{1}{2}$ = 1,800, or 18 square.

16—The Length of Rafters for the Most Common Pitches may be found as follows :

One-quarter pitch, multiply the span by .559; $\frac{1}{3}$ pitch, multiply the span by .6; $\frac{3}{8}$ pitch, multiply the span by .625; $\frac{1}{2}$ pitch, multiply the span by .71; $\frac{5}{8}$ pitch, multiply the span by .8; Gothic or full pitch, multiply by 1.12.

17—To Find the Length and Bevel of Common Rafters with the Square and Rule.—In this example

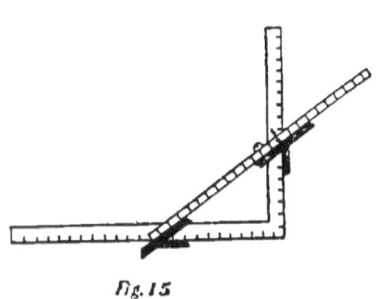

we have a rafter of 8 feet rise and 12 feet run. We measure from 12 on the blade of the square to 8 on the tongue, which is $14\frac{7}{16}$ inches, or in feet the length of the rafter is 14 feet 5$\frac{1}{4}$ inches ; the bevels are found by using the bevel as shown in the cut, Fig. 15.

Fig. 15

18—Backing of Hip Rafters.—Draw 1 2 and 2 3, Fig. 16, to represent the plates of the building, then the seat of the hip, as 2 4; then the hip, as 2 5. Take any point of the hip, as *c*, and draw a line at right angles to 2 5 until it strikes the seat, 2 4; then continue the line at

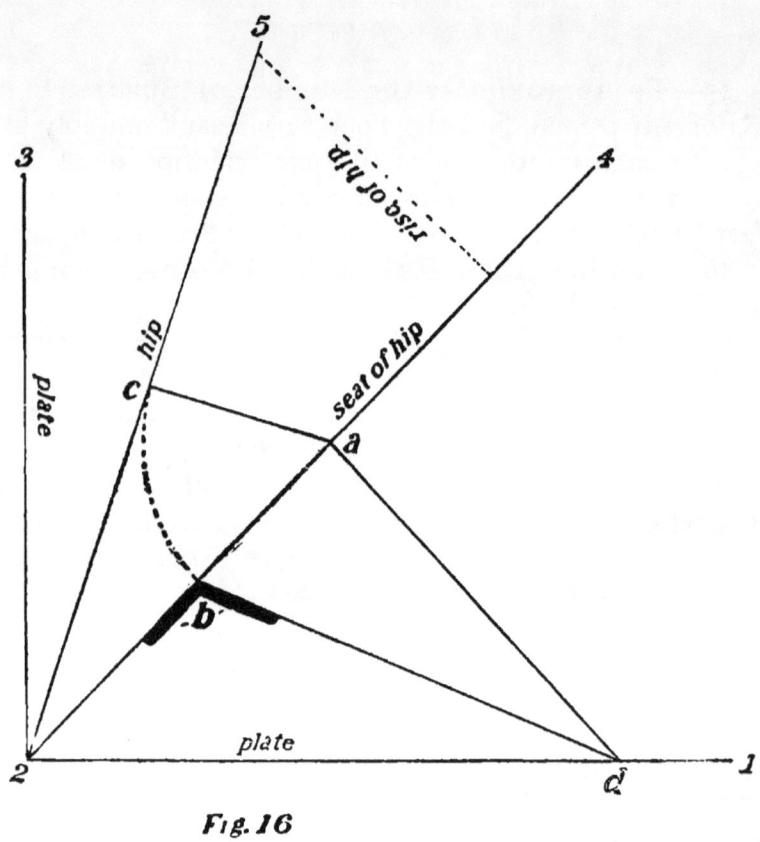

Fig. 16

right angles to the seat, or 2 4, until it strikes the plate, as point *d;* then, with *a* as centre and *a c* as radius, strike an arc bisecting 2 4 at *b;* then draw line from *b* to point *d* on the plate ; then the bevel at *b* is the bevel for backing the hip. Fig 17 shows application.

19—To Find the Bevel for Backing the Hip Rafters for an Octagon Roof.—Draw the plate as *a d e;*

then draw the common rafter, as *a b;* then the seat and full size of hip, as *d c;* then draw line from 5 to 6; then, with *d* as centre and *d* 1 as radius, describe arc 1 2 ; then

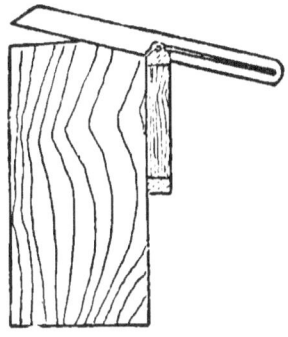

Fig. 17

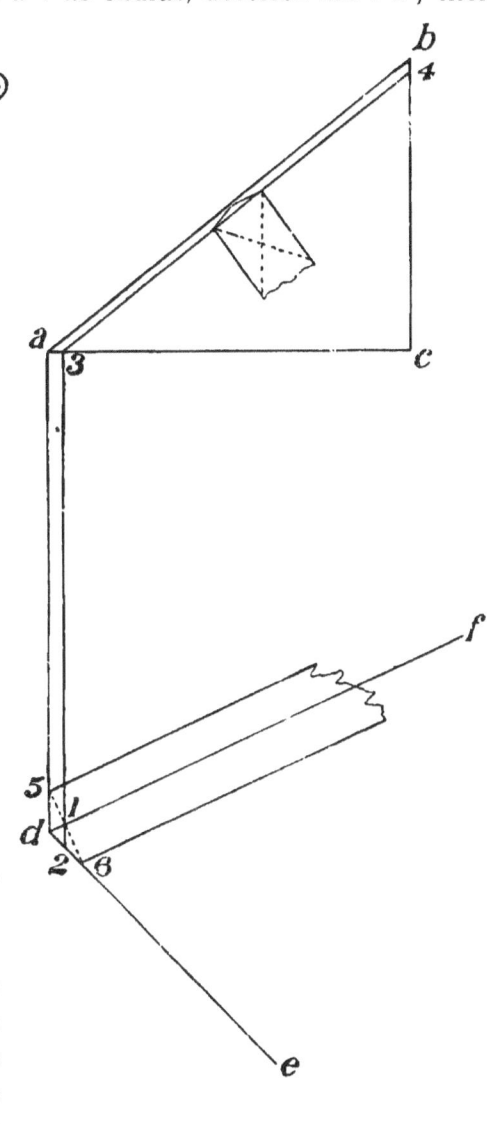

draw line from 2 parallel to *a d* to point 3, and continue parallel to *a b.* Then lay off the thickness of the rafter on 3 4, and draw the bevel lines as shown. This rule applies to any roof.

20—To Find the Bevel for Backing Hip Rafters.—Take the length of the hip on the blade of the square and the rise of the roof on the tongue and the tongue will give the desired bevel.

Fig. 18

21—To Get the Bevels to Mitre Purlins, when the Purlin Sets Square with the Rafters.—Draw *a c c*, representing the slope of the roof; then continue *c c*, making it equal in length to *a c*, as *d c;* connect *a* and *d*, thus finding the bevel for the top or face of purlins, as shown at *a*. Now drop the perpendicular from *c* indefinitely; then draw a line from *a* at right angles to *a c* until it strikes the perpendicular at *f*. Make *a g* on *a c* equal to *a e;* connect *g* and *f*, and the bevel at *g* will be the bevel for the side of the purlin.

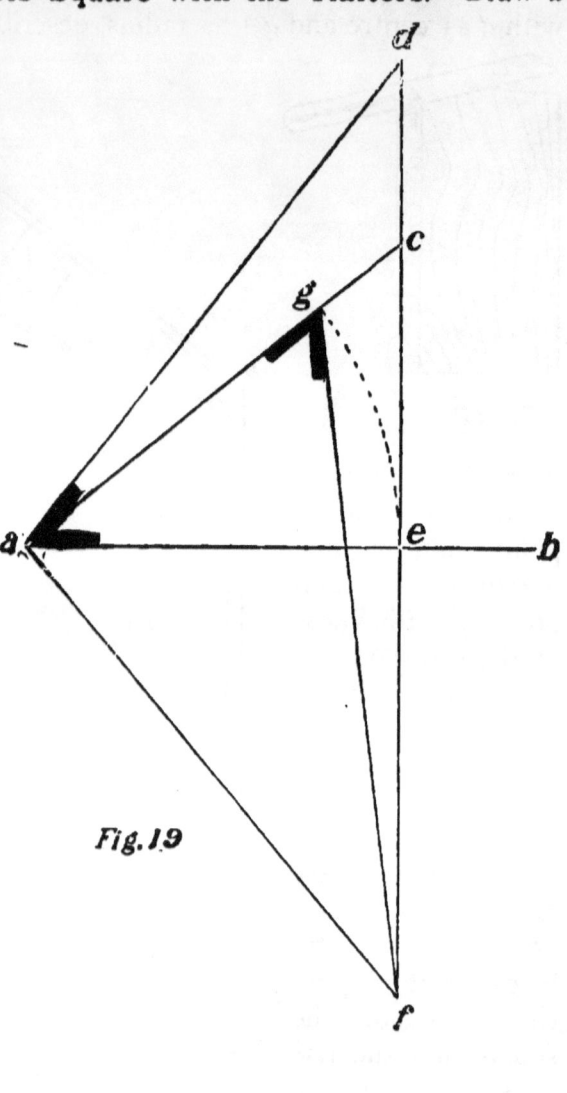

Fig. 19

22—To Find the Bevels to Cut Sheathing for a Roof.—Draw level line, as $a\,b$, Fig. 20, then draw $c\,b$, showing the pitch of the roof ; then from any point on this line let fall a perpendicular, as $d\,g$; then let fall a perpendicular from b, as $b\,f$. Now, with d as centre and $d\,b$ as radius, strike an arc intersecting $a\,b$ at c; now, from the intersection of the perpendicular line, $d\,g$, produced at j, draw line parallel to $a\,b$, intersecting perpendicular, $b\,f$; now from this point draw a line to d, thus giving the bevel for the face of the board. Then, with g as centre and $g\,h$ as radius, strike an arc at i; then draw a line from i to c, thus giving the bevel for the edge of the boards.

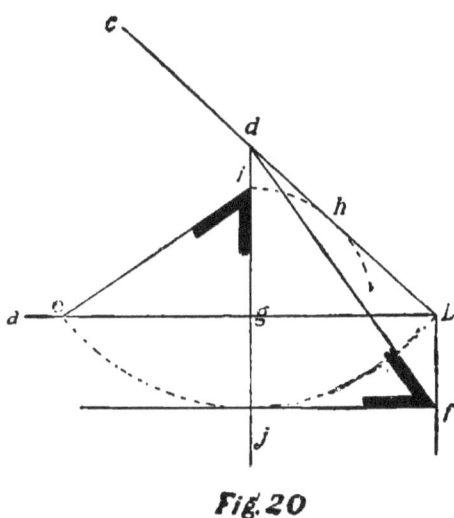

Fig. 20

23—To Get the Bevels of Chords or Purlins of a Square Steeple.

—Draw a section of one side of the steeple, as *a b c d*, Fig. 21, and draw the centre line, *e f*.

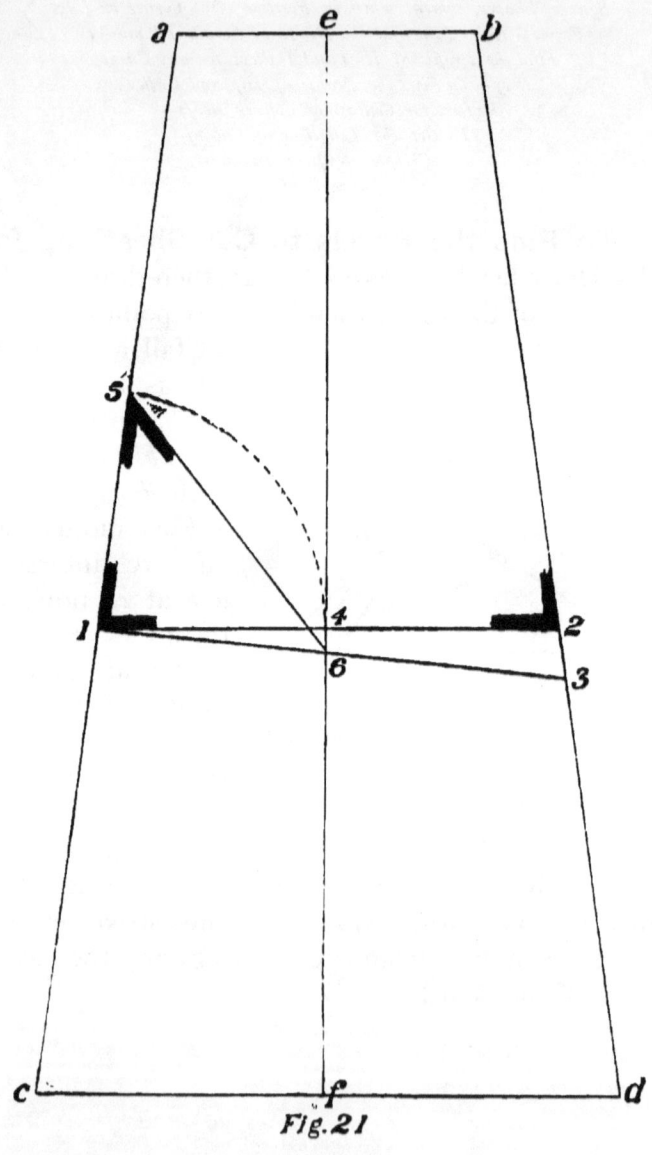

Fig.21

Now draw the line of purlin as 1 2. The bevel at 1 or 2 will be the bevel for the face of the purlin. Now draw a

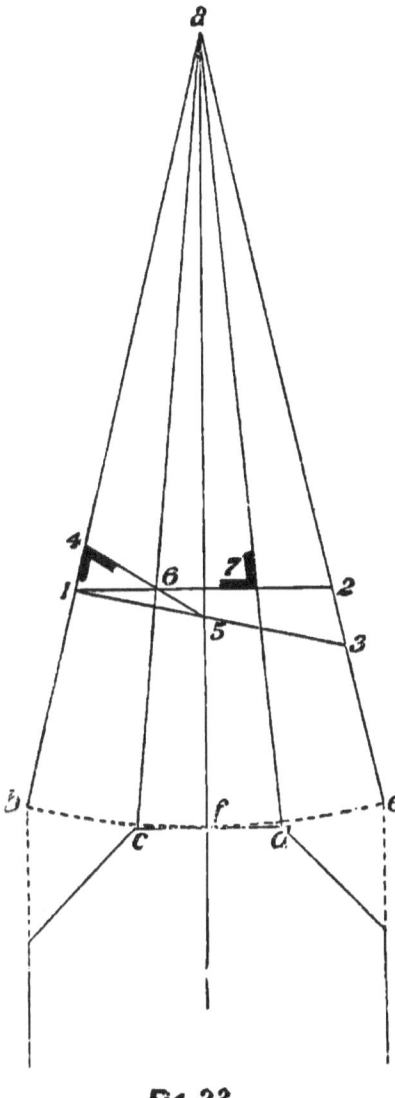

line from 1 at right angles to $a c$, as 1 3; make 1 5 equal to one-half of 1 2; connect 5 and 6, and the bevel at 5 will be the bevel for the top or edge of the purlin.

24—To Get the Bevels of the Chords or Purlins of an Octagon Steeple.—Draw an elevation as shown by a b c d and e, Fig. 22, making $a b$ and $a e$ equal to $a f$. Now draw the line of the purlin, as 1 2; then draw a line from 1 at right angles to $a b$ until it strikes $a c$; now make 1 4 equal to one-half of 6 7; connect 4 and 5. The bevel at 7 is the bevel for the face of the purlin and the one at 4 is for the top or edge of the purlin.

25—To Find the Bevels to Cut the Braces for a Square Steeple.—Draw a side of the steeple, as $a b c d$.

Fig. 22

Fig. 23; then the chords, as 1 4 and 3 2; then the line of the braces, as 1 2 and 3 4. The bevels at 1 and 2 being the bevels for the face of the

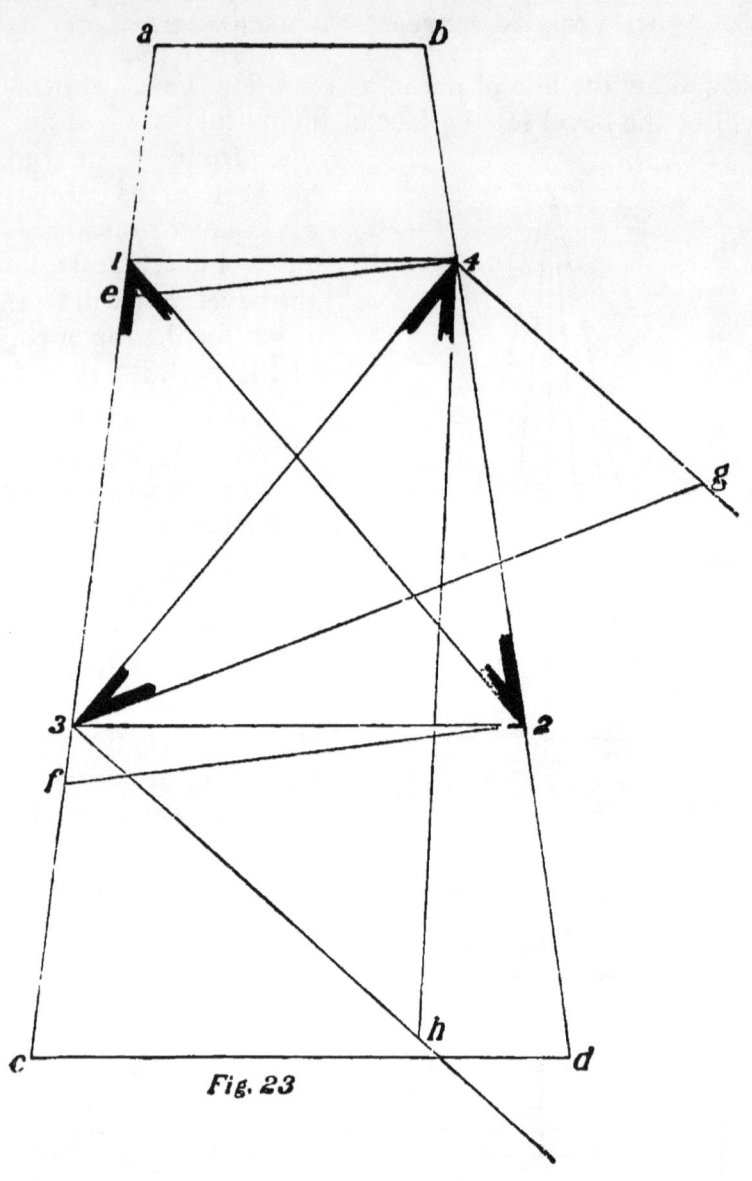

Fig. 23

brace. Now draw lines from 4 and 2 at right angles to
b d until they strike *a c*, as *c* 4 and *f* 2; now draw lines
from 3 and 4 at right
angles to 3 4, and
make 4 *g* equal to *c*
4, and 3 *h* equal to
f 2; connect 4 *h* and
3 *g*, thus finding the
bevels for the side
of the braces, as
shown at 3 and 4.
The bevels at 1 and
4 being for the top
end of the brace and
3 2 for the bottom.

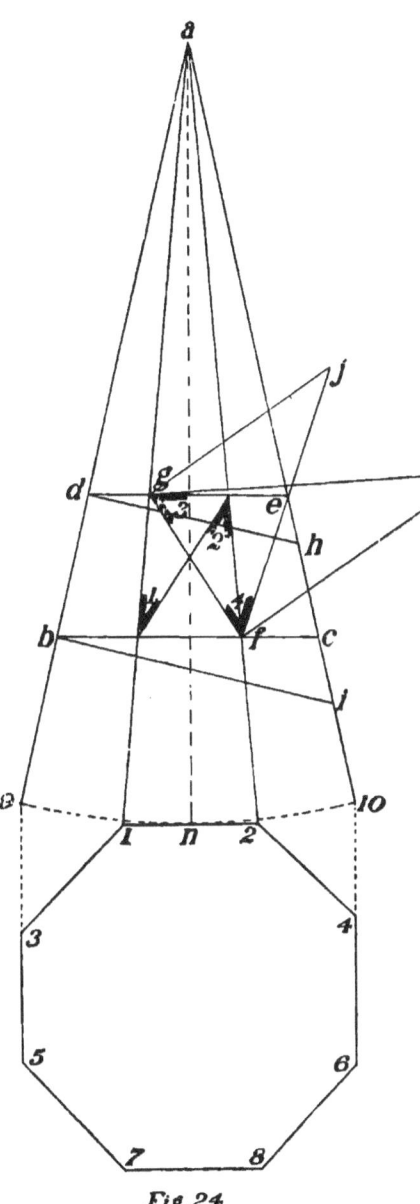

Fig. 24

26—To Find the Bevels to Cut the Braces for an Octagon Steeple.—

Draw an elevation
as *a* 9 1 2 10, Fig.
24; now draw the
line of the chords,
as *d c* and *b c*, also
the line of the braces,
as *g f* and 1 2, thus
finding the bevel for
the face of the brace,
as shown at 1 and 2.
Now draw lines
from *b* and *d* at right
angles to *a* 9 until
they strike *a* 10, as
d h and *b i*; now
draw a line from *g*
at right angles to *g f*.

making it equal to *d h;* then draw a line from *f* at right angles to *g f,* making it equal to *b i;* connect *g k* and *f j,* thus finding the bevels for the side of the braces, as shown at 3 and 4. The bevels 2 3 being for the top end of the brace, and 1 4 for the bottom.

27—To Get the Cut of Braces where Their Diagonal is Plumb when in Position, as shown in Fig. 25. Take the run of the brace, multiplied by .70711, on the blade of the square and the rise on the tongue, and the angle formed by a line drawn between these two points and the blade of the square is the bevel to cut the brace, applied on all four sides.

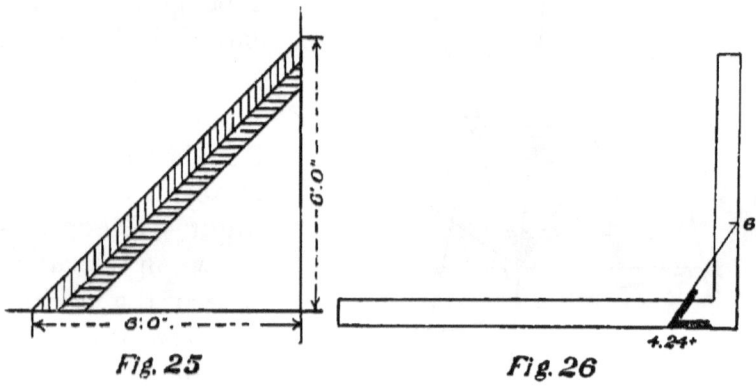

Fig. 25   *Fig. 26*

EXAMPLE.—Find the cut of a brace 6 feet run and 6 feet rise. The run, 6 feet, by .70711 = 4.24266. Now draw a line from 4.24' on the blade to 6 on the tongue, and the bevel on the blade is the bevel to cut the brace, as shown in Fig. 26. For the top multiply the rise by .70711 and proceed as above.

28—To Get the Cut of a Brace of Square Timber, which, when in Position, one Corner or Edge Forms a Ridge Line and the Diagonal Stands Plumb.—On the base *a b,* Fig. 27, draw the slant *a c.* From any point on *a b* draw the perpendicular *d e;* Now, with *a d* as base and perpendicular, draw the triangle *a b c,* Fig. 28; from *a* draw *a d* at right angles to *a c,* making it equal in length to *d e* Fig. 27; now connect *d* and *c,* and the bevel at *d* is the bevel to cut the top end of the brace applied on both sides. To get the bottom bevel use *c d,* Fig. 27, to draw the triangle, and make *a d,* Fig. 29, equal

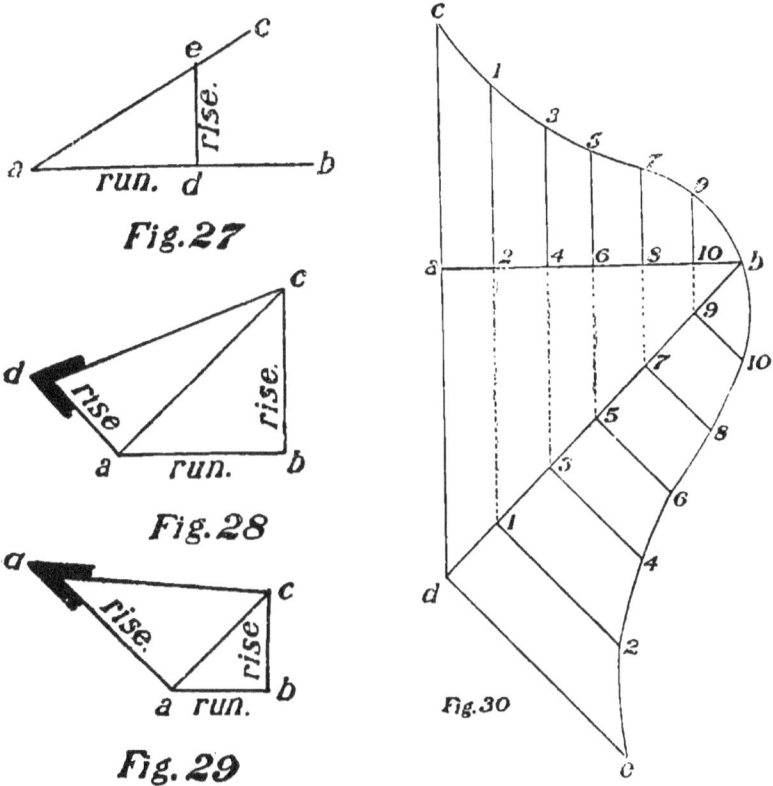

Fig.27

Fig.28

Fig.29

Fig.30

to *a d,* Fig. 27. The bevel at *d* is the bevel to cut the bottom. The same bevel is used on all four sides of the stick.

29—To Find the Profile of Hips and Valleys for any Curve Roof.—Let *a b,* Fig. 30, be the seat of the common rafter and *c b* the profile; now draw the seat of the hip or valley, as *b d;* then divide *a b* into any number of spaces, as 2, 4, 6, etc.; from these points draw lines at right angles to *a b* intersecting the profile of the common rafter and the seat of the hip, *b d;* then from these points on the seat of the hip continue these lines at right angles to seat of the hip, making 9 10 on the hip equal to 9 10 on the common rafter, and 7 8 on the hip equal to 7 8 on the common rafter; 5 6 on the hip equal to 5 6 on the common rafter, etc.; the points thus found are points on the profile of the hip rafter; then connect *b* 10, 10 8, etc., with the curved line, as shown, thus giving the profile of the hip rafter.

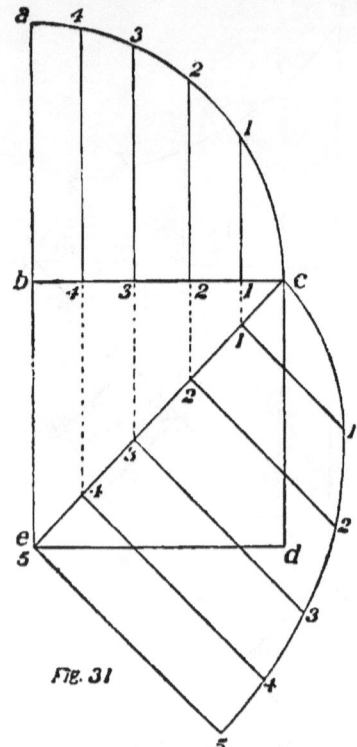

FIG. 31

30—To Find the Profile of Hip and Valley Rafters for Concave or Convex Roofs.—In Fig. 31, *b c d e* represents a quarter section of the floor plan; *b c* is the seat of the common rafter and *c c* is the seat of the hip. Now draw the profile of the common rafter, as *a c;* then divide the base, *b c,* into any number of spaces, 1, 2, 3, etc., and through these spaces draw lines at right angles to *b c,* continuing then to the profile of the common rafter, *a c,* and the seat of the hip, *e c;* then from these intersections on the seat of the hip continue the lines at right angles to the seat of the hip, making the line 1 1 on the hip equal to 1 1 on the common rafter, and 2 2 on the hip equal to 2 2 on the common

rafter, 3 3 equal to 3 3, etc. The points thus found by
these lines are points on the profile of the hip; connect
c 1, 1 2, etc., as shown, thus giving profile of hip.

**31—To Get the Length and Cut of Cripple Raf-
ters in a Curve Roof.**—Draw the plates, as *a b* and *b c*,
Fig. 32, and the seat of the hip, as *a c*. Now draw the
rise and profile of the common rafter, as *c e* and *e b;* lay

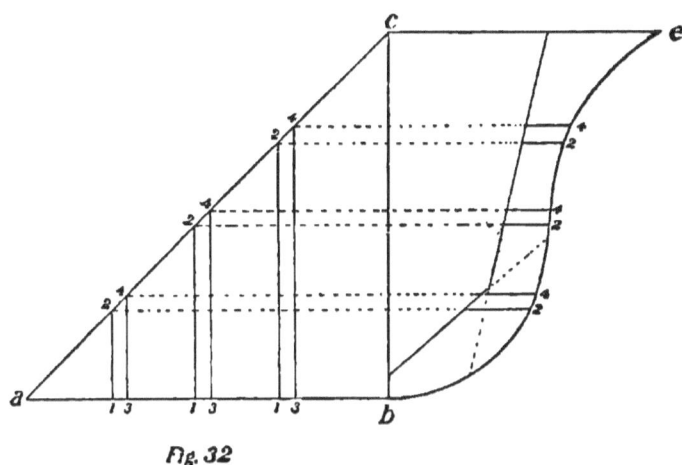

Fig. 32

off the seats of the cripples, as 1 2, 3 4, etc., making 1 3
the thickness of the cripple rafter. Now continue these
lines from where they strike the seat of the hip parallel to
a b until they strike the profile of the common rafter.
Then *b* 4 will be the length of the cripple, 4 will be the
long length and 2 the short length, or 4 will be the line of
the cut on one side and 2 the line of the cut on the other
side.

CHAPTER IV.

32—To Lay Out Horizontal Sheathing for a Dome Roof.—Draw the roof as shown by *a b c*, Fig. 33, and divide it in half by a perpendicular line, which continue up indefinitely; then divide *a b* into as many spaces as you desire boards, as 1, 2, 3, etc. Then draw a line from *a* striking point 1 and continue until it bisects the perpendicular, which is the centre, and this point and *a* and this point and 1 is the radius for the first board; then draw a line from 1 through 2 and continue to the perpendicular, thus giving the centre and radius for second board; then draw the line 2 6 and repeat the operation, etc.

This rule applies to any shape roof of a circular base.

33—To Lay Out Perpendicular Sheathing for a Dome Roof.—Draw the spring of the roof, as *a d b*, Fig. 34, and divide in half by *c d;* then divide *d b* into equal parts (as many as desired), and from these points let fall perpendiculars to the base line, *c b;* then, with *c* as centre, continue these lines as semi-circles, as shown by the dotted lines; then continue the line *d c* indefinitely; then on the outside circle lay off the width you want the boards at the base, as 5 5, and draw a line from this point to *c*, as *c* 5; this shows the ground plan and width of the board at the several different points. Then on the indefinite line make 5 11 equal to *d b* on the circle; this is the length of the board. Then divide this line into as many equal

parts as the circle of the roof and make 6 6 equal to 1 1,
7 7 equal to 2 2, 8 8 equal to 3 3, etc.; then connect 5 6,
6 7, etc., which gives the pattern of the sheathing boards.

The same rule applies to any shape of roof having a circular base.

34—To Construct an Elliptical Dome.—In Fig. 35
a b shows the ellipse and base, *c d, e f*, etc., show the
rafters, which are a semi-circle with *c d, e f* and *h g*, etc.,

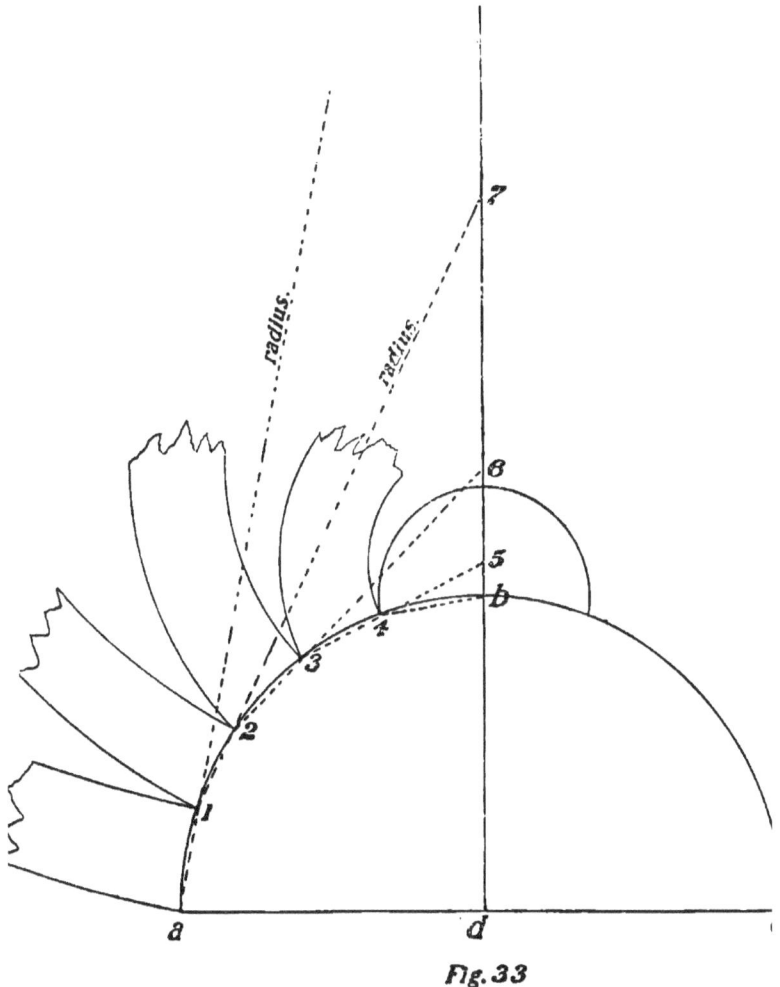

Fig. 33

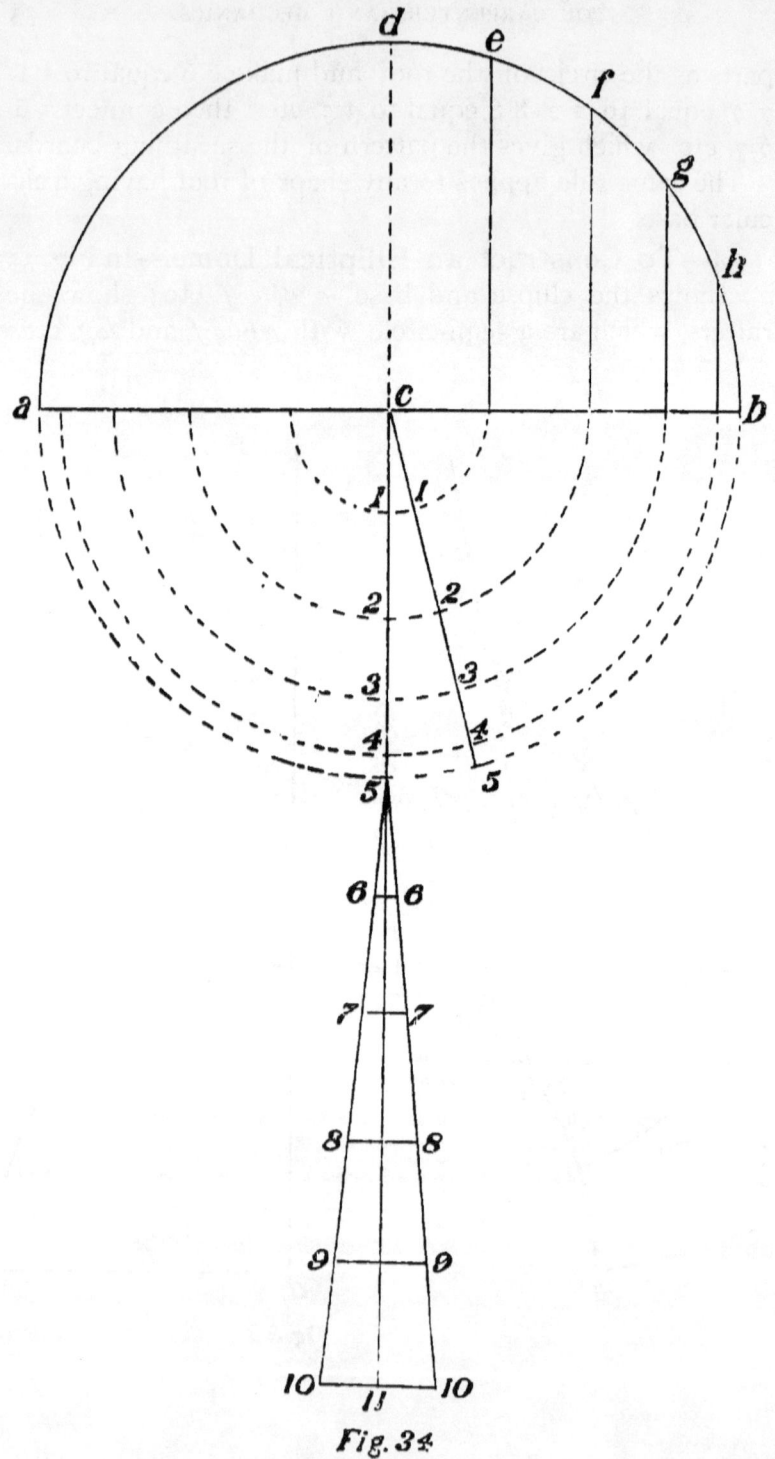

Fig. 34

are the radius; the other lines show the bridging cut between the rafters to receive the sheathing, which runs from
side to side. To cut the sheathing divide the semi-ellipse
into as many parts as you wish boards, or make the spaces
equal to the width of the board; then draw lines from these

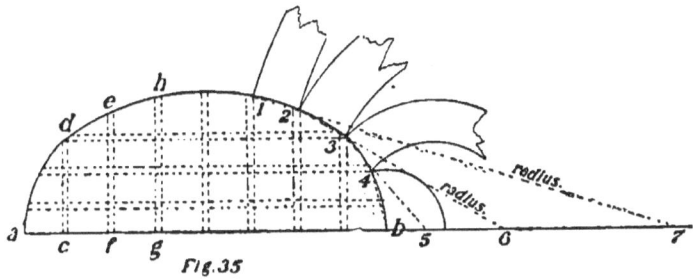

Fig. 35

points, as shown, from 1 through 2 to the base line, which
gives the radius of one board; from 2 through 3 gives the
radius of another; repeat the operation until you have the
radius of all the boards.

35—To Lay Out the Plancher for a Conical Roof.—
The following diagram, Fig. 36, will show how to lay out
the planceer for a conical roof: *A* and *b* is the radius for
the planceer, and *c d*, which
is drawn at right angles to the
rafter until it strikes the centre
line, *a d*, is the radius for the
facia, if it is put on square to
the rafter.

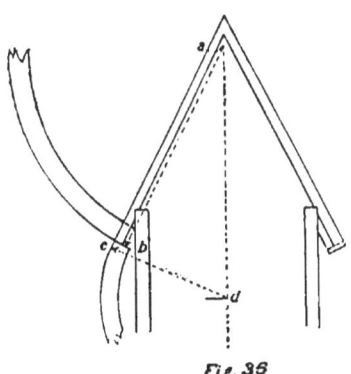

Fig. 36

**36—To Work Out the
Crown Moulding for a Con-
ical Roof when the Facia
is Set Square with the
Rafter.—**Draw a half section
of the roof, showing position
of the moulding, as Fig. 37; now take a plank of the required thickness and with radii *a b* and *a c* draw the arcs
a b and *c d*, Fig. 38; draw a line radiating from the centre

of the circle across one end of the plank, as *a c*, Fig. 38.
Cut the end of the plank off and with the bevel at *b*, Fig.
37, mark off the moulding as shown in Fig. 39. The
plank can then be cut on the band saw and the moulding
worked out by hand.

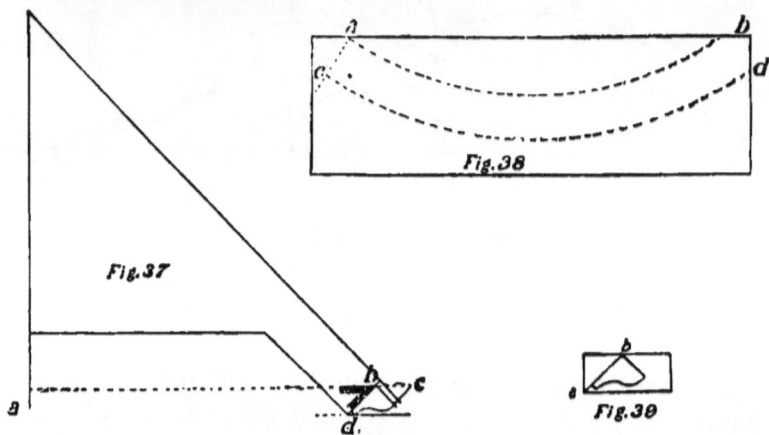

37—To Bisect a Given Angle.—In Fig. 40 *a b c*
represents the angle. With any radius and *a* as centre, describe the arc, 1 2; then, with same radius and 1 and 2 as
centres, describe the arcs intersecting at 3; draw a line
from *a* through intersection 3.

**38—To Draw a Line at
Right Angles to Another
without the Use of a
Square.**—With *a* as centre,
Fig. 41, and any radius, describe the arc *c d;* then,
with *d* as centre and same
radius, describe the arc *a c;*
then, with *c* as centre, de-
scribe the arc *c f;* then, with *c* as centre, describe the arc

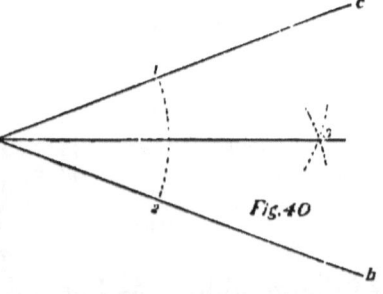

c f; draw line from *a* through intersection at *f*.

**39—To Draw Two Lines Forming Four Right
Angles without the Use of a Square.**—Draw line *a b;*

then, with a b as centres and any radius of more than
half the length of a b, describe arcs intersecting, as
shown at c d; then draw a line through these intersections.

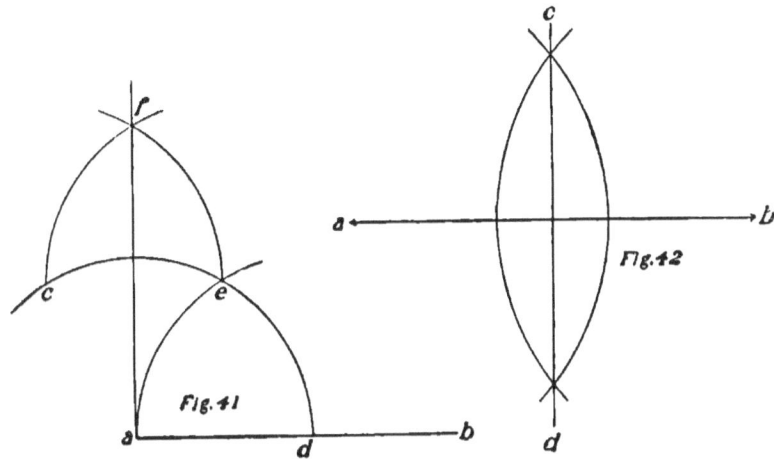

CHAPTER V.

40—To Bisect a Right Angle.—Take *a* as centre,
Fig. 43, and any radius, and draw the arc *b c*. Now,
with *b c* as centres and the same radius, draw the arcs bisecting *b c* in 1 and 2; draw lines from' *a* through 1
and 2.

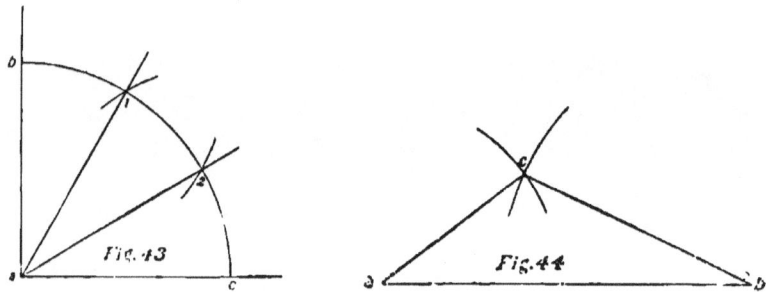

**41—To Draw a Triangle when the Lengths of
the Sides are Given.**—Draw the length of one side, as
a b, Fig. 44; then, with *a* as centre and the length of one
of the other sides, describe an arc, as shown; then, with *b*
as centre, describe an arc, as shown, using the length of
the third side as radius; then connect this intersection
and *a b*.

42—To Draw a Triangle when the Length of One Side is Given.

—Draw the side or base, as *a b*, Fig. 45; then, with *a b* as radius, strike the arc *a c;* then with the same radius and *a* as centre, find point *d;* connect *a d* and *d b*.

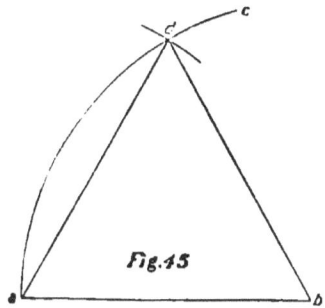

Fig.45

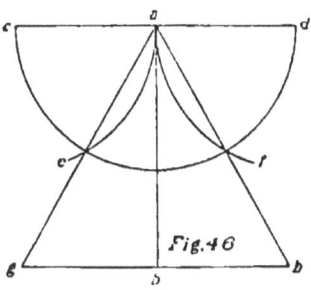

Fig.46

43—To Draw an Equilateral Triangle when the Perpendicular is Given.

—Draw *a b* for the perpendicular, Fig. 46; then draw *c d* and *g h* at right angles to *a b;* then, with any radius and *a* as centre, draw the semi-circle,

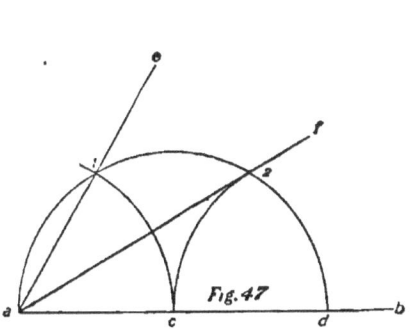

Fig.47

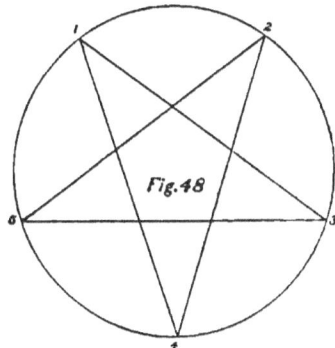

Fig.48

c e f d; then, with *c* as centre, find the point *e;* then, with *d* as centre, find the point *f;* then draw the line *a h* through the point *f;* then draw the line *a g* through *e*.

44—To Draw an Angle of 60° or 30°.

—Draw the line *a b*, Fig. 47, and with any point on *a b*, as *c*, for centre and *c a* as radius, draw the arc *a* 1 to 2 *d*. With *a* as centre and same radius find point 1; draw line from *a* through 1; 1 *a c* = 60°; with *d* as centre and same radius find point 2; 2 *a d* = 30°.

45—To Draw the Five Point Star.—Draw the circumference and divide it into 5 equal parts, 1, 2, 3, etc.; connect 1 and 3, 3 and 5, 5 and 2, 2 and 4, and 4 and 1.

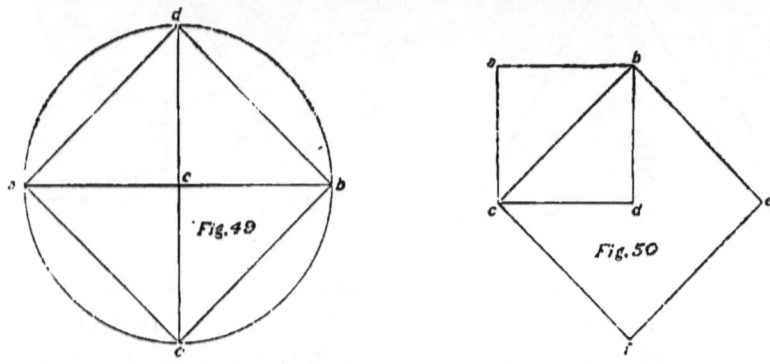

Fig. 49   Fig. 50

46—To Draw a Square when the Diagonal is Given.—Draw the diagonal, *a b*, Fig. 49; bisect it at *c* and draw the line *d e* at right angles to *a b;* then with *a c* as radius and *c* as centre strike a circle ; then connect *a d*, *d b*, *b e* and *e a*, which is the square required.

47—To Find a Square Twice the Area of a Given Square.—Draw the given square, as *a b c d*, Fig. 50; then, with the diagonal, *c b*, as one side, draw the square, *c b e f*, which will be twice the area of the first square.

48—To Draw a Square Having the Area of Two Given Squares.—Draw one side of each of the given squares so as to form a right angle, as *a b* and *b c*, Fig. 51; connect *a c*, and, with this line as one side, draw the square, 3, which is equal in area to 1 and 2.

The above rule applies to circles as well as squares; *a b* and *b c* represent the diameters of the smaller circles, and *a c* the diameter of a circle which is equal in area to the two small ones.

49—To Draw a Rhombus when the Diagonal and Length of Side are Given.—First draw the di-

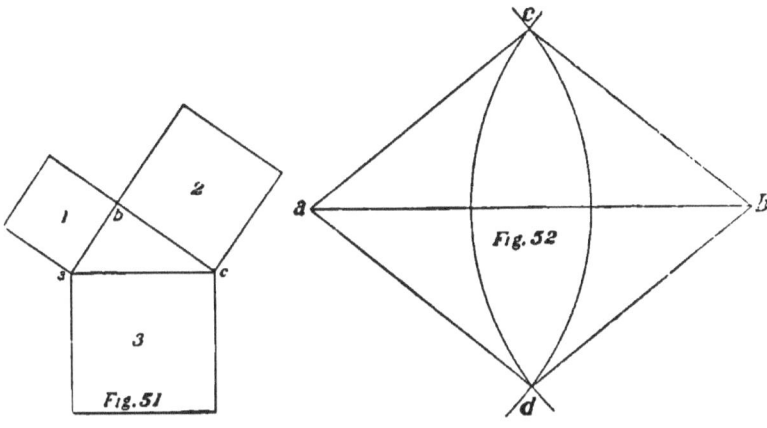

Fig.51

Fig.52

agonal, as *a b*, Fig. 52; then, with the length of the side as radius and *a b* as centres, strike the arcs intersecting at *c* and *d;* then connect *a c*, *c b*, *b d* and *d a*, which gives the desired rhombus.

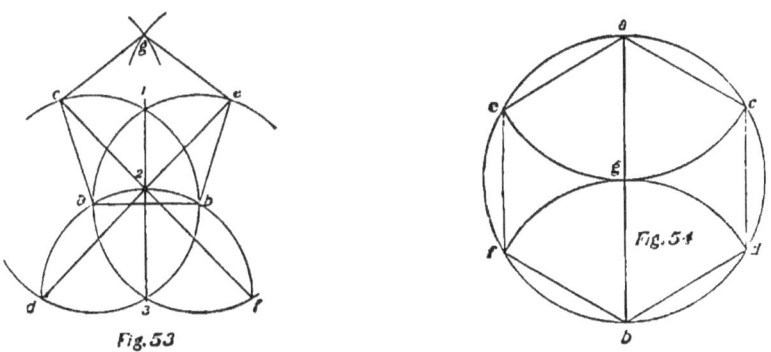

Fig.53

Fig.54

50—To Draw a Pentagon when One Side is Given.—With *a b* as base and radius and *a b* as centres, Fig. 53, strike the circles *c d* and *e f;* then draw the per-

pendicular connecting 1 and 3; then, with 3 as centre, strike the circle *d a* 2 *b f,* thus giving points *d* 2 and *f;* then draw the line *d c* from *d* through point 2, thus giving point *c;* then draw the line *f c,* from *f* through 2, giving point *c;* then, with *c* and *c* as centres, find point *g;* connect points *a c, c g, g c* and *c b.*

51—To Draw a Hexagon when the Long Diameter is Given.—Draw *a* and *b* as the diameter ; then, with half the diameter as radius, Fig. 54, and *a* as centre, strike the arc *c c;* then, with *b* as centre, strike the arc *f d;* then, with *g* as centre, strike a circle ; then connect *a c, c d, d b, b f, f c* and *c a.*

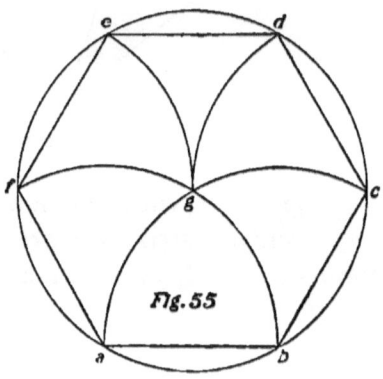

Fig. 55

52—To Draw a Hexagon when the Length of One Side is Given.—With *a b* as one side, *a* as centre and *a b* as radius, Fig. 55, strike the arc *f b;* then, with same radius and *b* as centre, strike the arc *a c;* then, with *g* as centre, strike a circle ; then, with *c* as centre, find point *d;* then, with *f* as centre, find point *c;* connect *a f, f c, c d, d c* and *c b.*

53—Several Ways of Drawing an Octagon.— When you have the distance from one side to the other given, to draw the octagon: First draw a square, Fig. 56, of that size;

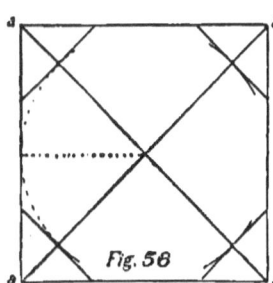

Fig. 56

then draw diagonal lines from each corner, as *a a, a a;* then take the distance from the centre to the outside, as shown by the dotted line, and measure the same distance from the centre on the lines, *a a;* then draw lines from this point at right angles to *a a*, and you have the octagon.

54—To Draw an Octagon within a Square.— First Method: Draw the square, as *a b c d*, Fig. 57; then continue *a b* and *c d*, as shown, and draw the diagonal, *c c*, at an angle of 45°; then make *c g* and *f c* equal to *a c;* then from *f g* draw the dotted lines parallel to *c a b;* then, with *c 2* as radius and *a b c d* as centres, draw the arcs, as shown ; then draw the diagonals, as shown, completing the octagon.

Second Method: First, draw the square, Fig. 58; then,

with the four corners as centres and half the diagonal as a radius, find points c, f, g, h, i, j, k and l. Then connect $f l$, $h j$, $k e$ and $i g$.

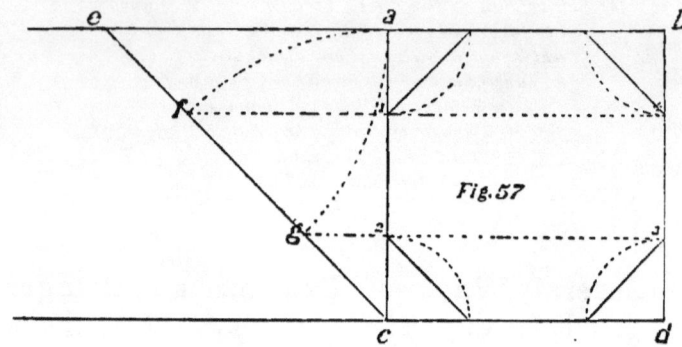

Fig.57

55—To Draw a Parallelogram within a Trapezium.—In Figs. 59 and 60 $a \, b \, c \, d$ represent the trapezium. Bisect each of its sides at the centre, as 1, 2, 3, 4; connect 1, 2, 3, 4 and you have a parallelogram.

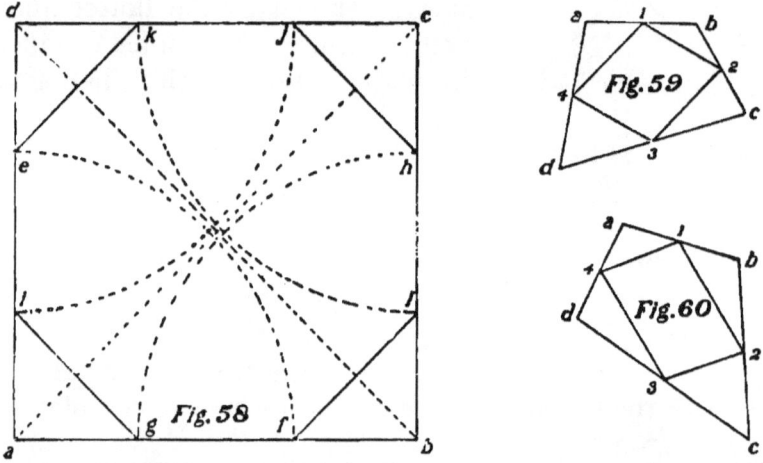

Fig.58

Fig.59

Fig.60

56—To Reduce a Square Stick to an Octagon.—
Place the blade of the square on the stick in the position shown in Fig. 61, and 7 and 17 on the blade will give the chamfer lines, as shown.

57—To Draw a Regular Polygon of any Number of Sides, when the Length of One Side is Given.

—Take the length of the side for a base, as *a b*, Fig. 62; then, with *a b* as radius and *a* as centre, draw the semi-circle, *d b;* then divide the semi-circle into as many

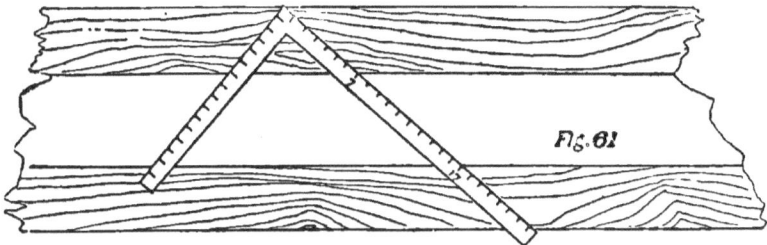

Fig.61

equal parts as there are sides to the polygon, in this case 7; then, as we have one side, *a b*, we skip the first division and connect *a* and 2; then from the centre of *a 2* and *a b* draw lines at right angles until they meet at *c*, which is

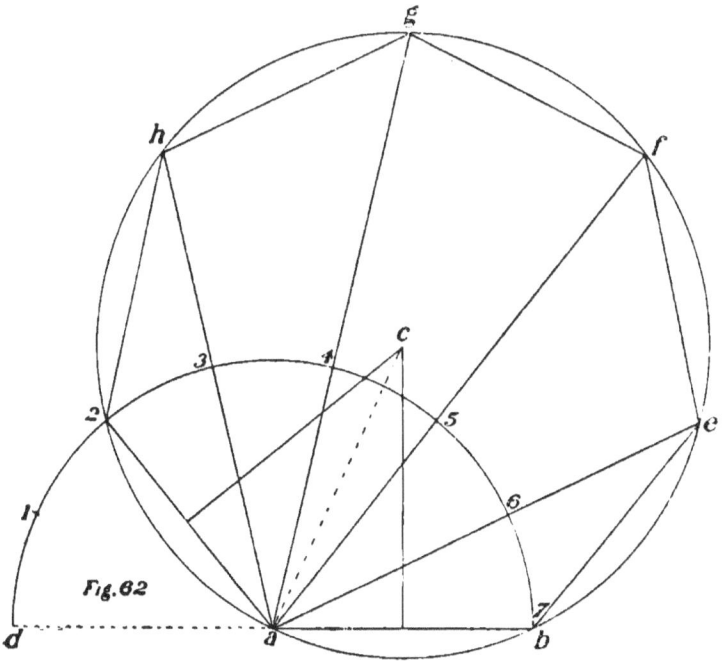

Fig.62

the centre of the polygon. Then, with *c* as centre and *c a*
as radius, draw the circle ; then draw lines from *a* through
points 3, 4, 5 and 6, striking the circle at *h, g, f* and *e;*
connect 2 *h, h g, g f, f e* and *c b.*

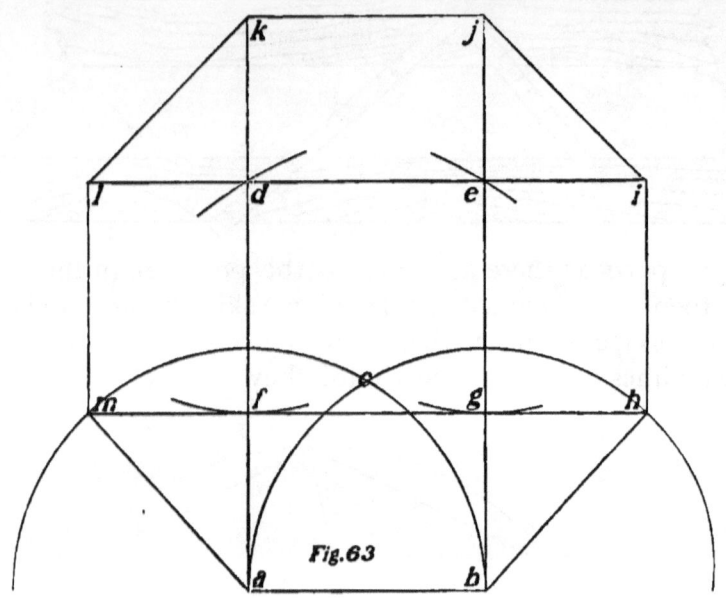

Fig. 63

**58—To Draw an Octagon when the Side or Base
is Given.**—Draw the line, *a b*, for the base, Fig. 63, and
from *a* and *b* draw two indefinite perpendicular lines ; then
take the distance from *a* to *b* and describe the two half-
circles ; then, using the same radius, from point *c* find
point *d* on the perpendicular, from which draw a horizontal
line connecting at *e* ; then, with the same radius, find point
f, from which draw a horizontal line connecting at *g*, thus
forming the square, *d, e, f, g*. Then from *g* draw the line
g h, equal in length to *g b;* then the line *e i*, then *c j, d k,
d l* and *f m*—all equal to *g b;* then connect *b h, h i, i j, j k,
k l, l m* and *m c*.

59—To Find the Greatest Square that can be Inscribed in a Given Circle.—Draw the diameter, *a b;* bisect it at *c* and draw the perpendicular, *d c,* at right angles to *a b;* connect *a d, d b, b c* and *e a.*

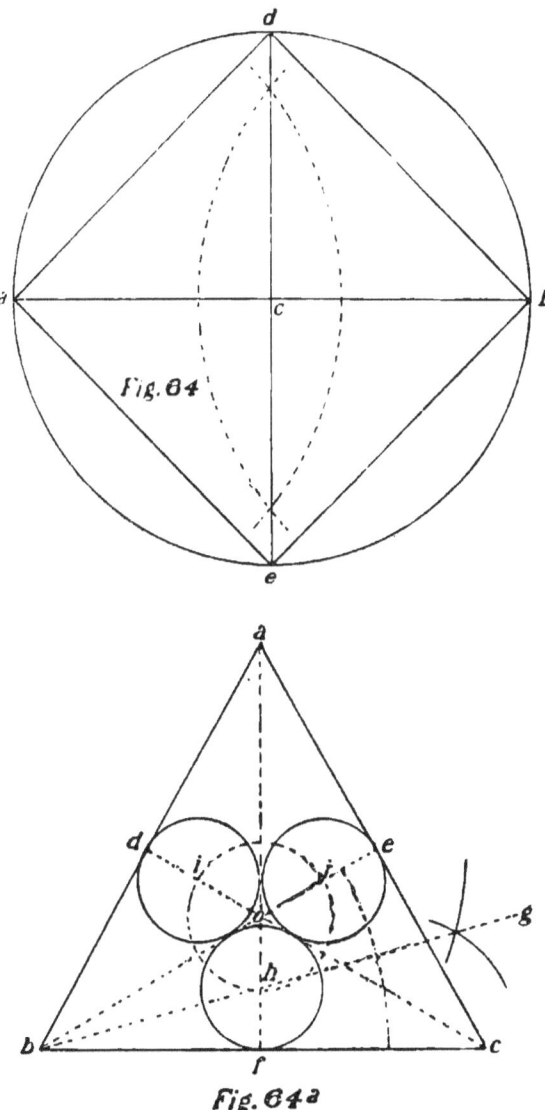

Fig. 64

Fig. 64ª

60—Within an Equilateral Triangle to Draw Three Equal Circles, Each Tangent to Two Others and to One Side of the Triangle.—Bisect the angles, *a, b, c,* Fig. 64*a,* as shown by *b c, d c* and *a f;* bisect the angle, *c b c,* by *b g,* cutting *o f* in *h.* With *o* as centre and *o h* as radius draw a circle, thus finding points *i* and *j,* which are centres and *h f* the radius of the desired circles.

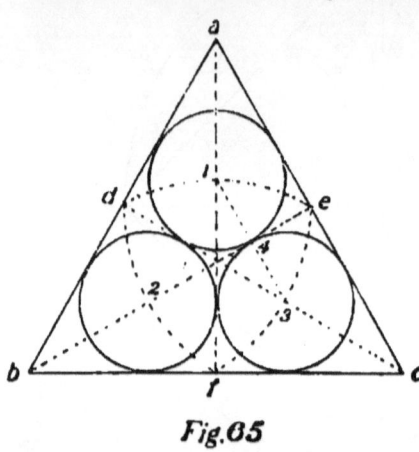

Fig. 65

61—Within an Equilateral Triangle to Draw Three Equal Circles, Each Tangent to Two Others and to Two Sides of the Triangle.—Bisect the angles, *a, b, c,* Fig. 65, as shown by *b c, d c* and *a f.* With *d c f* as centres and *d e* as radius draw the arcs *e f, f d* and *d e,* finding the points 1, 2, 3. Join 1 3, cutting *b e* in 4; then 1 2 3 are centres and 3 4 the radius of the desired circles.

61—Within a Given Square to Draw Four Equal Semi-Circles, Each Tangent to One Side of the Square and their Diameters Forming a Square.—

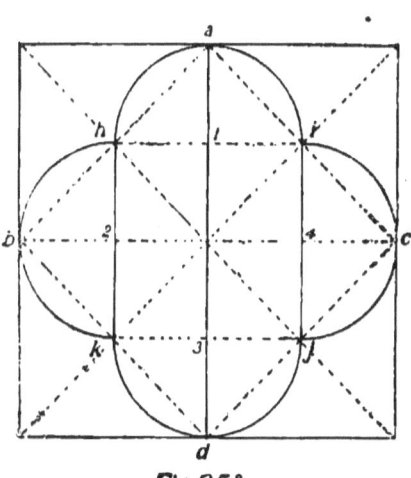

Fig.65ª

Draw the diagonals and diameters, as shown in Fig. 65a. Connect *a c*, *c d, d b* and *b a*, cutting the diagonals in *h, i, j* and *k;* then connect *h i*, *i j, j k* and *k h*, thus finding points 1, 2, 3, 4, which are the centres, and 1 *a* the radius of the desired semi-circles.

62—Within a Given Square to Draw Four

Equal Semi-Circles, Each Tangent to Two Sides of the Square and their Diameters Forming a Square.—

Draw the diagonals and diameters, as shown in Fig. 66.

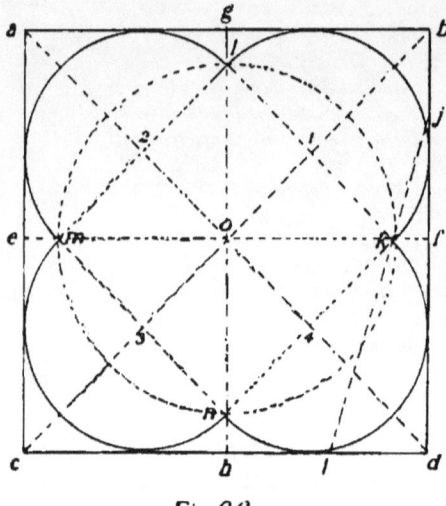

Bisect *b f* in *j;* bisect *h d* in *i;* connect *i* and *j*, thus finding point *k*. With *o* as centre and *o k* as radius draw a circle finding points *l*, *m* and *n;* connect *l m*, *m n*, *n k* and *k l*, thus finding points 1, 2, 3, 4, which are the centres, and 1 *l* the radius of the desired semi-circles.

Fig. 66

63—Within a Given Square to Draw Four Equal Circles, Each Tangent to Two Others and One Side of the Square.—

Draw the diagonals and diameters, as shown

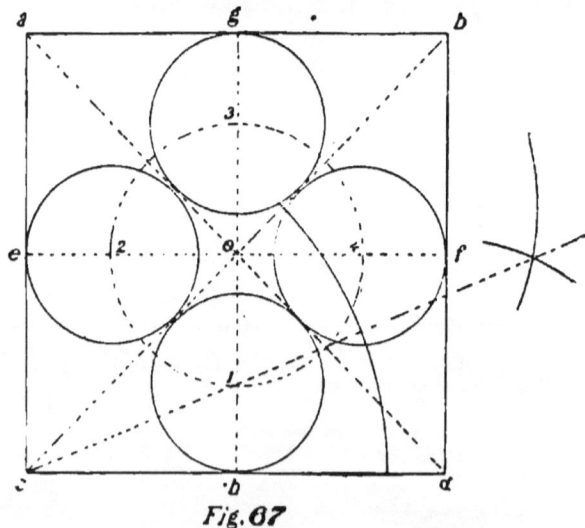

Fig. 67

in Fig. 67. Bisect the angle *o c d* by the line *c i*, cutting *o h* in 1; with *o* as centre and *o* 1 as radius draw a circle, thus finding points 2, 3, 4, which are the centres and 1 *h* the radius of the desired circles.

64—Within a Given Square to Draw Four Equal Circles, Each Tangent to Two Others and to Two Sides of the Square.— Draw the diagonals and diameters, as shown in Fig. 68. Connect *g f*, *f h*, *h c* and *c g*, thus finding points *i, j, k* and *l*, which are the centres, and *i m* the radius of the desired circles.

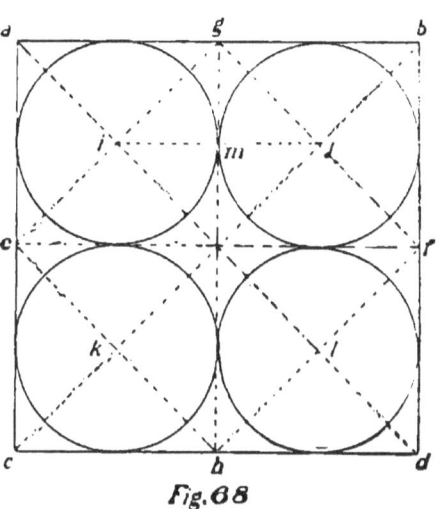

Fig. 68

65—Within a Given Circle to Draw Three Equal Circles Tangent to Each Other and the Given Circle.—Divide the given circle, Fig. 69, into six equal parts by the diameters *a b*, *c d* and *e f;* continue the line *c d* to

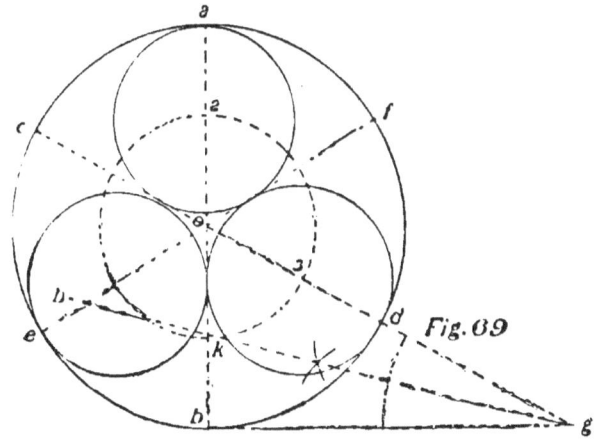

Fig. 69

strike the base line at *g;* bisect the angle *o b g* with the
line *h g,* thus finding point *k;* with *o* as centre and *o k* as
radius draw a circle, thus finding points 1, 2, 3. which are
the centres of the desired circles, of which 2 *a* is the radius.

**66—Within a Given Circle to Draw Four Equal
Circles Tangent to Each Other and the Given
Circle.**—Divide the circle, Fig. 70, into eight equal parts
with the diameters *a b, c d,* etc.   Continue the line *e f* to
meet the base line at *i;* bisect the angle *o b i* with the line

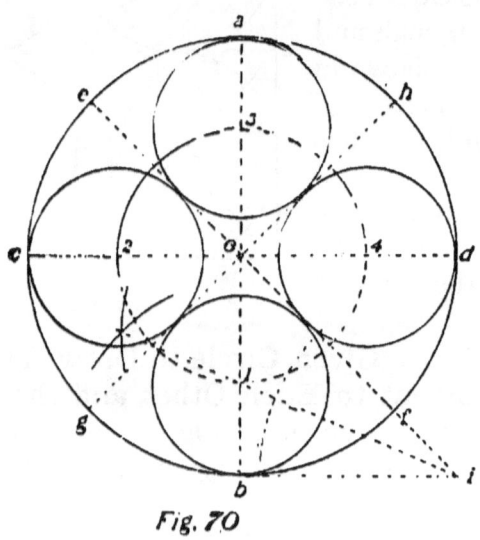

Fig. 70

j i, thus finding point 1; with *o* as centre and *o* 1 as radius
draw a circle finding points 2, 3, 4, which are the centres
of the desired circles, and 3 *a* the radius.

To draw any number of circles, divide the circle into
twice as many equal parts as circles desired and proceed
as above.

**67—Within a Given Circle to Draw any Number
of Semi-Circles Tangent to the Given Circle and
their Diameters Forming a Regular Polygon.**—
Draw the two diameters *a b* and *c d* at right angles to each

other, Fig. 71; then divide the circle into twice as many parts as there are semi-circles required, commencing to space from *a;* then draw diameters from each of these points; then connect *a* and *d,* finding point *f;* then, with *e f* as radius and *c* as centre, strike a circle, thus finding points 1, 2, 3; then connect *f* 3, 3 2, 2 1 and 1 *f,* thus giv-

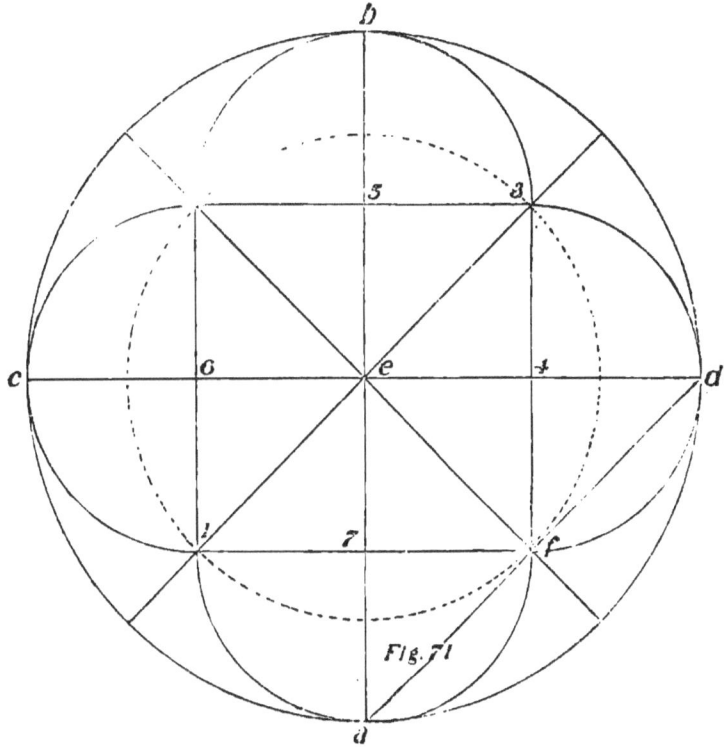

Fig. 71

ing points 4, 5, 6, 7, which are the centres for the semi-circles, and from any of these points to the given circle is the radius, as 4 *d.*

68—To Divide a Circle into Concentric Rings Having Equal Areas.—Divide the radius, *a c.* Fig. 72, into as many parts as areas required, as 1, 2, 3, etc. With *a c* as a diameter draw the semi-circle *a* 4 5 6 *c;* draw lines

from points 1, 2, 3 at right angles to *a c*, meeting the
semi-circle at 4, 5, 6; with *c* as centre and *c* 4, *c* 5 and *c* 6
as radii draw the concentric circles.

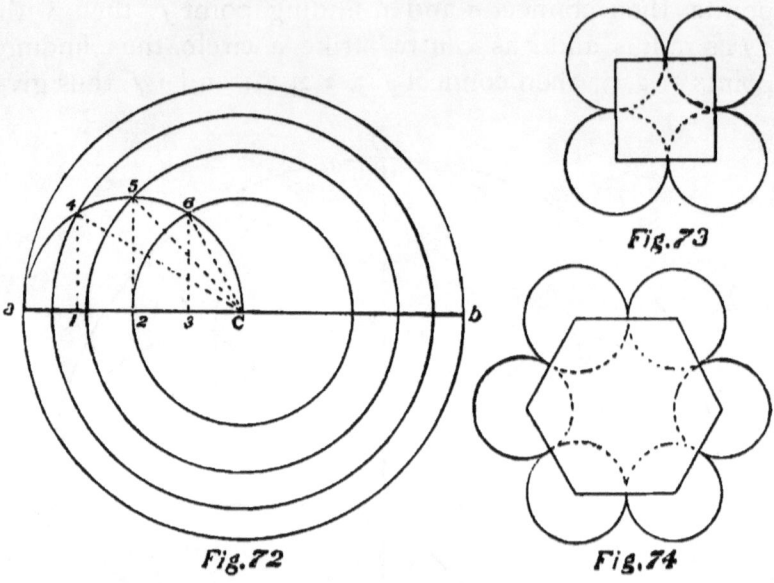

Fig.73

Fig.72

Fig.74

**69—To Draw any Number of Tangential Arcs of
Circles Having a Given Diameter.**—Draw a polygon
of as many sides as arcs required (four and six). With
each angle as centre and half of one side as radius draw
the arcs, as shown in Figs. 73 and 74.

**70—To Divide the Circumference of a Circle into
any Number of Equal Parts.**—Draw the circle, Fig.
75. and establish the diameter *a b;* divide the diameter
into as many equal parts as is desired in the circumference.
With *a b* as centres and *a b* as radius draw arcs intersecting at *c;* draw a line from *c* through the second division on the diameter and 1 *b* will be one of the desired
parts on the circumference. In this example the number
of parts are 8.

RULE II.—To find the length of any division of a circumference, multiply the diameter by 3.1416 and divide

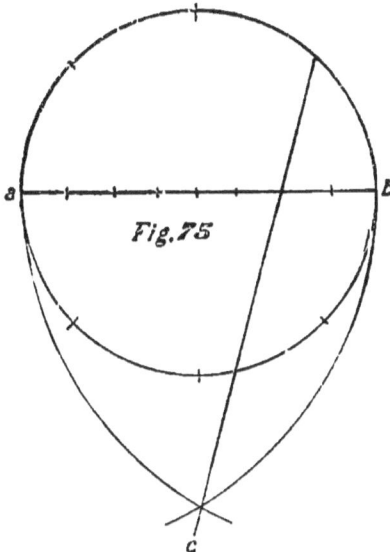

the answer by the number of parts in the circumference; this will give the length of one of the parts.

CHAPTER VIII.

71—At Point c on the Line a b to Draw Two Arcs of Circles Tangent to a b and the Two Parallels a h and b e Forming an Arch.

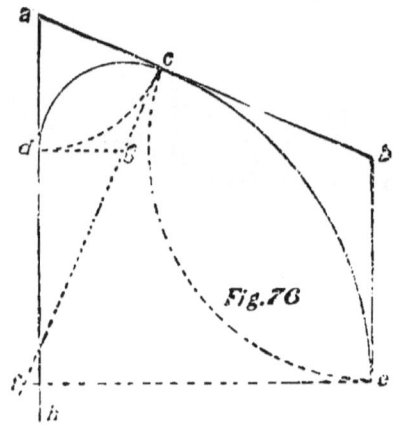

—Make a d, Fig. 76, equal to a c and b e equal to b c; draw c f at right angles to a b and d g at right angles to a h; with g as centre and radius g d draw the arc d c; draw e f at right angles to b c; with f as centre and f c as radius draw the arc c e, completing the arch.

72—To Draw an Ellipse.—Draw the rectangle a b c d, Fig. 77. A b represents the long diameter and a c half the short diameter; divide a b into two equal parts, as a c and

c b; then divide *a c* and *a c* into the same number of equal parts, as 1, 2, 3, etc.; then draw lines from *c* to 5, 6, 7, etc.; then draw lines from *c* to 1, 2, 3, etc.; then draw the curved line through the intersections, as shown.

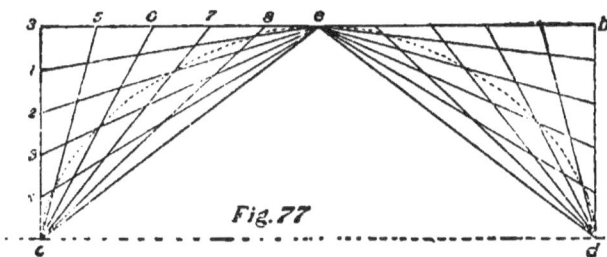

Fig. 77

73—To Draw an Ellipse with a String.—Draw the long diameter, Fig. 78, as *a b;* then half the short diameter, as *c d;* then, with *c* as centre and *a d* as radius, describe arcs bisecting *a b* at 1 and 2, at which points drive a nail to fasten the string; then fasten the string at 1 and stretch to *c*, at which point place a pencil inside the string and carry the string to 2 and make fast; then keep the string tight and run the pencil along on the inside of the string and the mark will be the ellipse; 3 and 4 shows position of pencil and string on the curve.

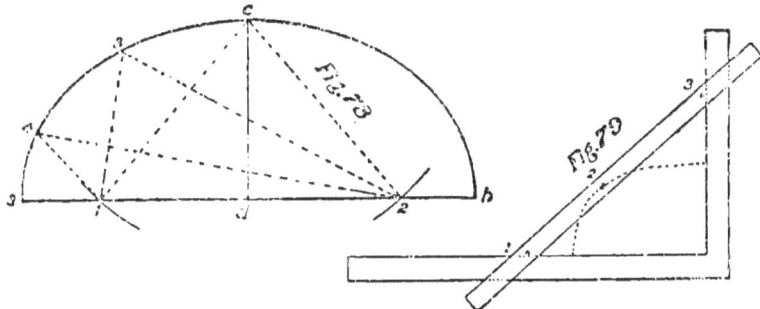

74—To Draw an Ellipse with the Square.—Take a strip of wood, as shown in Fig. 79, say ½"x1", to use as a rule; then drive a nail through the stick about an inch from one end, as 1; then make the distance between 1 2

equal one-half the short diameter of the ellipse and 2 3 equal to one-half the long diameter; drive another nail at 3 and at 2 make a hole for a pencil, place the pencil in the hole and slide the stick from a perpendicular position to a horizontal one, keeping the nails against the inside of the square, and the pencil will describe an ellipse.

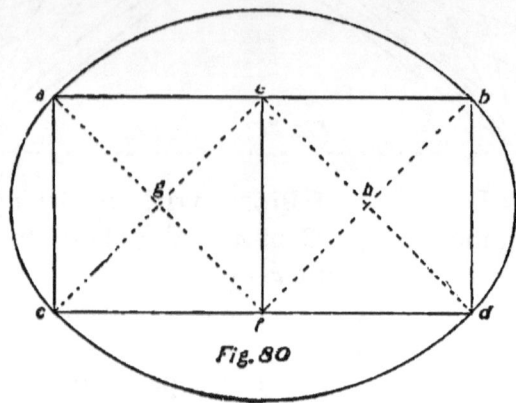

Fig. 80

75—To Draw a Curve Approximating to an Ellipse.—Draw the squares *a c f c* and *e d b f*, Fig. 80; then draw the diagonals intersecting at *g* and *h;* then, with *f*

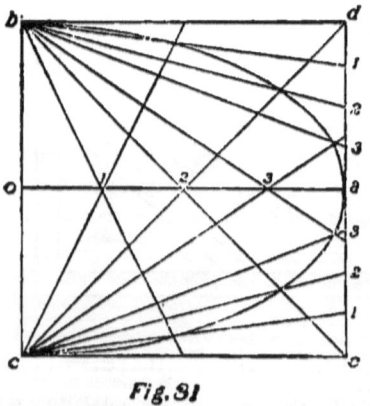

Fig. 81

as centre and *f a* as radius, draw arc *a b;* then, with *e* as centre and same radius, draw arc *c d;* then, with *h* as centre and *h b* as radius, draw arc *b d;* then, with *g* as centre and same radius, draw arc *a c*, completing the curve.

76—To Draw an Ellipse when the Axes are Given.—Place the axes at right angles at their centres, Fig. 81, and on them draw a rectangle *b d e c*, representing half; divide *o a* and *d a* into the same number of equal

parts, as 1, 2, 3, etc.; draw lines from c and b through
1, 2, 3, etc., and the intersections, as shown, are the points
of the curve.

**77—With the Axes, as a c and d e, of an Ellipse
Given, to Draw the Curve.**—Place the axes at right
angles to each other, as in Fig. 82, bisecting at centre b.
Then, with a as centre and d b as radius, draw arc 1 2;

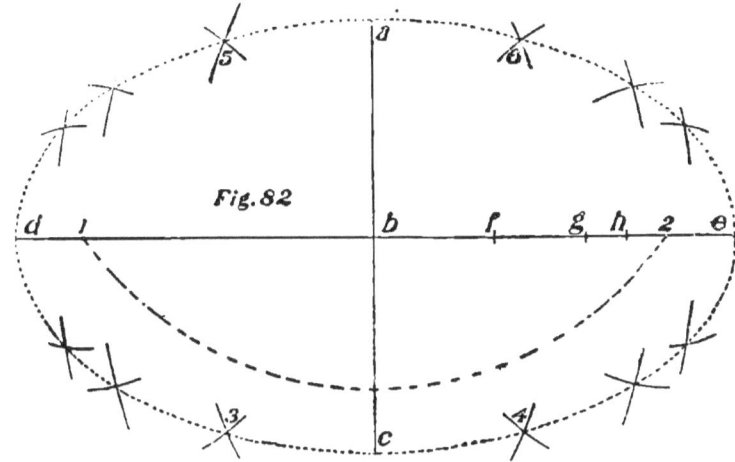

Fig.82

between b and 2 take any point, as f, with centres 1 and
2 and radius f d, draw arcs on each side of d e; with same
centre and radius f e draw arcs intersecting those drawn.
Then take any point between b and 2 and repeat the above
operation; then take any
other point between b and 2
and repeat until you have
as many points as desired;
then through these points
draw the curve.

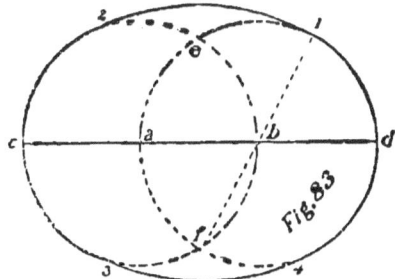

Fig.83

**78—To Draw a Curve
Approximating an El-
lipse.**—Draw an indefinite line, as c d, Fig. 83; then, with
a as centre and a b as radius, draw a circle; then, with b as
centre, draw another circle; then with intersecting points

f and *c* as centres and *f* 1 as radius draw arcs 1 2 and 3 4, thus completing the curve.

79—When the Two Axes are Given, to Draw a Curve Approximating an Ellipse.—With *c d* as the major axis and *a g* the minor axis, Fig 84, draw lines connecting *a d* and *a c;* then, with *b* as centre and *b a* as radius, draw the semi-circle, finding points *e* and *f,* from which points draw lines at right angles to *a d* and *a c,* intersecting at *g;* then, with *g a* as radius and *g* as centre, strike arc 1 2; then, with *i* as centre and *i* 2 as radius, strike arc 2 *d,* and repeat same for other side.

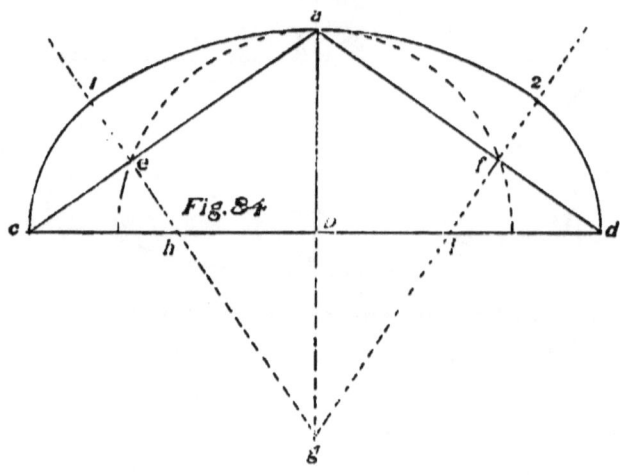

Fig. 84

80—To Draw an Ellipse with the Trammel.— Take and tack a frame to the floor or drawing board, as shown by 1, 2, 3, Fig. 85, leaving a space between the strips of three-eighths of an inch; then, on the trammel, make *d e* equal to the semi-minor axis and *d f* equal to the semi-major axis; then put a three-eighth-inch pin in the trammel at *e* and *f* and place the same on the frame with the pins in the slot; then draw the trammel around and *d* will describe the ellipse.

81—To Draw an Oval.—With *a b* as the short diam·
eter and *a g* as radius, Fig. 86, draw a circle; then draw
the line *c d* at right angles to *a b* through the centre *g;*
then draw the lines *a f* and *b e* through *d;* then, with *b* as

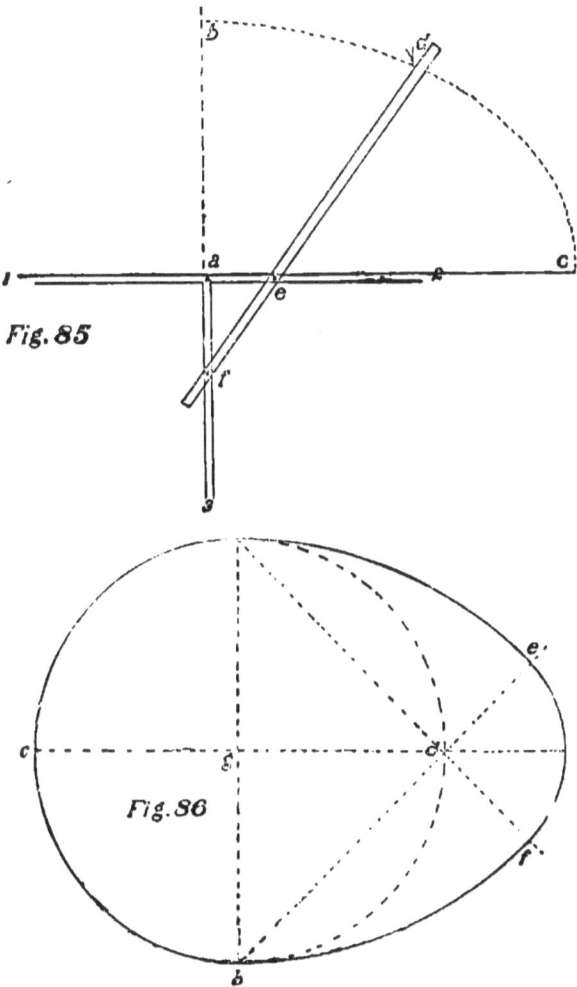

Fig. 85

Fig. 86

centre and *b a* as radius, draw the arc *a e;* then, with *a* as
centre and same radius, draw the arc *b f;* then, with *d* as
centre and *d e* as radius, draw the arc *e f.*

82—Upon a Given Line, *a b*, to Draw an Oval.—
Bisect *a b* at *c*, Fig. 87, and draw at right angles *c d;* with
b as centre and *b a* as radius draw the arc *a d*. Bisect the
quarter circle *a e* in *f* and through *f* draw *b g*, which gives

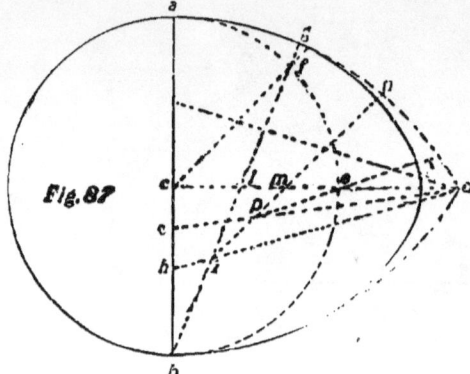

Fig. 87

a g as the first part of
the curve. Now, bi-
sect *c b* in *h* and draw
h d; then the intersec-
tion *i* is the centre and
i g the radius for the
second part of the
curve. Bisect *e l* in *m*
and through *m* draw
i n, which gives *g n* as
the second part of the
curve. Bisect *c h* in *o* and draw *o d;* the intersection *p*
is the centre and *p n* the radius for the third part of the
curve. From *p* draw *p e t* through *e* and *n t* is the third
part of the curve; with *e* as centre and radius *e t* draw the
curve to the line *c d*. Repeat the operation for the other
half of the curve. On the diameter *a b* draw a semi-circle,
thus completing the oval.

83—To Draw an Involute of a Square.—With the
square as 1, 2, 3, 4, first continue the sides, as shown by
the dotted lines, Fig. 89; then, with 1 as centre and 1 4 as
radius, draw arc 4 5; then, with 2 as centre and 2 5 as
radius, draw arc 5 6; then, with 3 as centre and 3 6 as radius, draw arc 6 7; then, with 4 as centre and 4 7 as radius,
draw arc 7 8, etc.

**84—To Draw a Spiral Composed of Semi-Circles
whose Radii Shall be in Geometrical Progression.—**
Draw an indefinite line, as *a b*, Fig. 90. With 1 as centre
and 1 2 as radius, draw first semi-circle 2 3; then, with 2
as centre and 2 3 as radius, draw semi-circle 3 4; then,
with 3 as centre and 3 4 as radius, draw semi-circle 4 5, etc.

85—To Draw a Spiral Composed of Semi-Circles, the Radii Being in Arithmetical Progression.—Draw

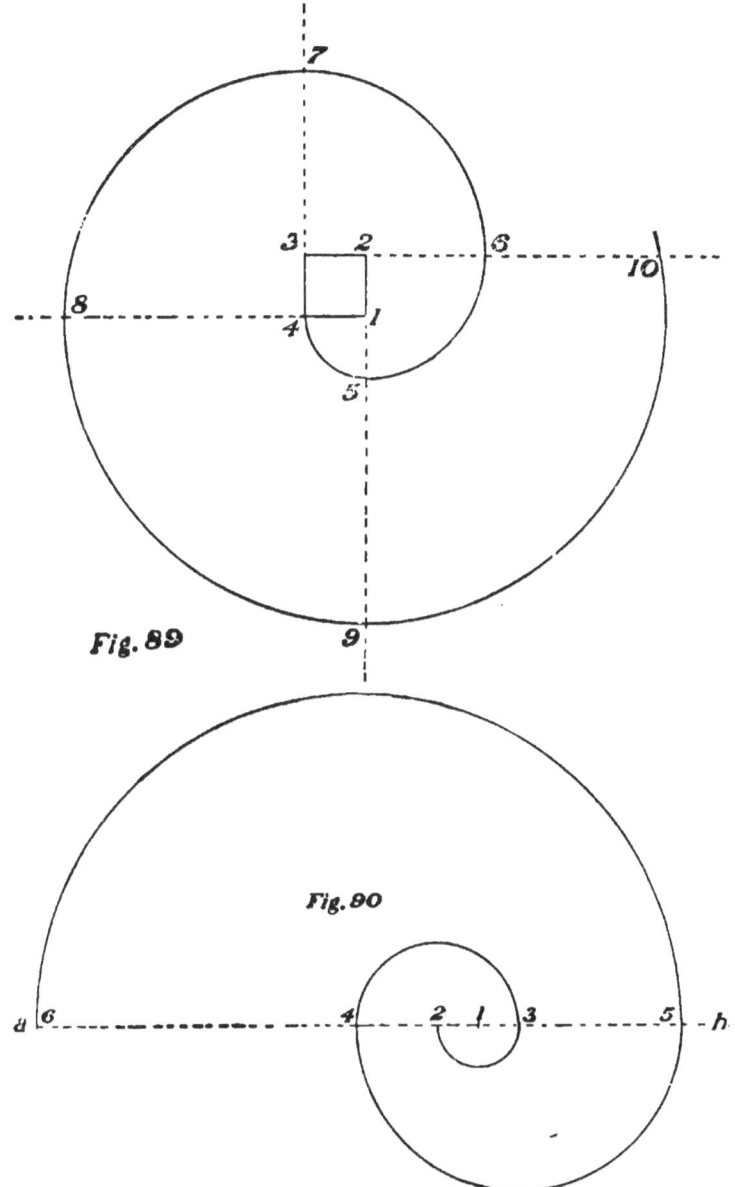

Fig. 89

Fig. 90

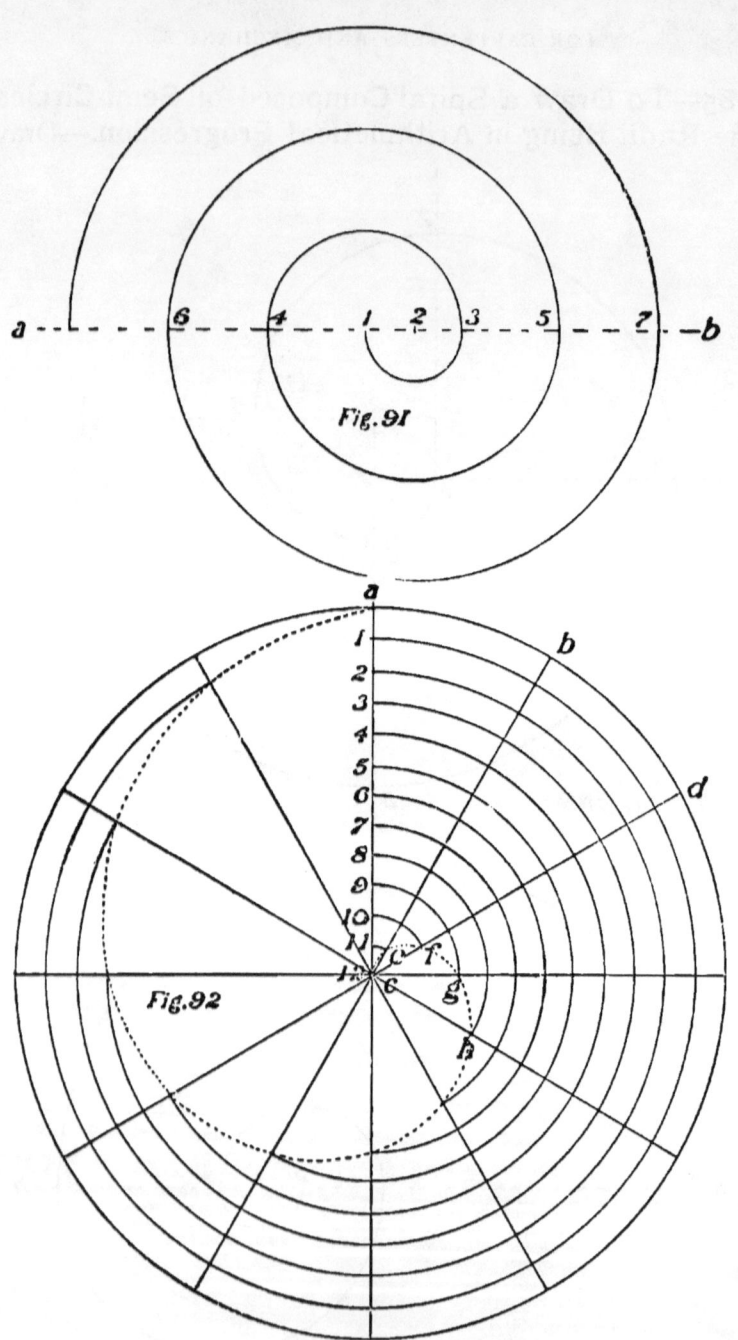

Fig. 91

Fig. 92

an indefinite line, as *a b*, Fig. 91; then take any point as centre and the radius of the small semi-circle, as 1 2; with 2 as centre draw the semi-circle, 1 3; then, with 1 as centre and 1 3 as radius, draw the semi-circle 3 4; then, with 2 as centre and 4 2 as radius, draw semi-circle 4 5, etc.

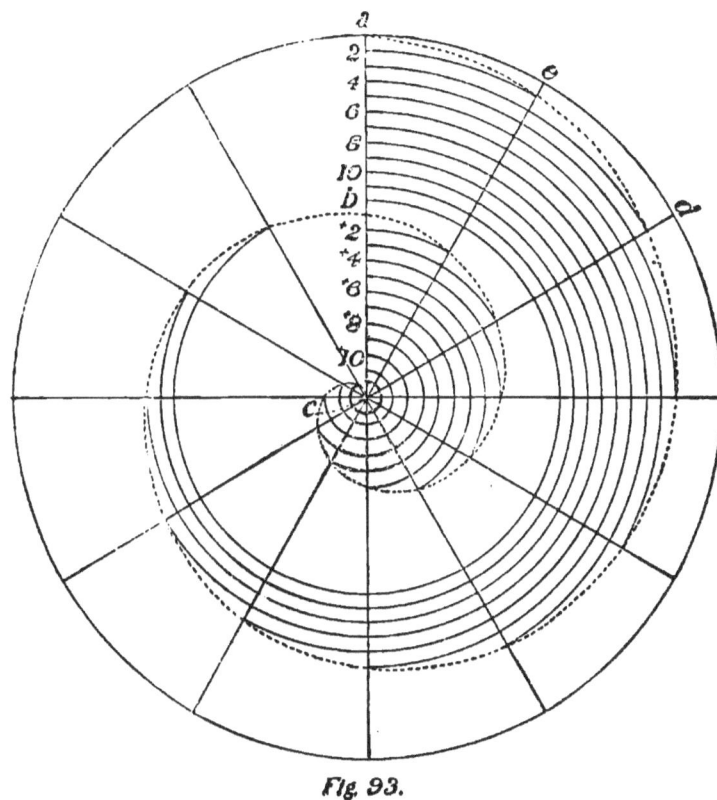

Fig. 93.

86—To Draw a Spiral of One Turn.—First draw a circle, Fig. 92, as large as the spiral is to be; then divide it into any number of equal parts (in this case twelve), as lines *a b c*, etc.; then divide any one of these lines into as many equal parts as the circle is divided; then with centre *c* and radius *c* 11 draw arc 11 *c;* then, with same centre and radius *c* 10, draw arc 10 *f;* then, with same centre and radius c 9. draw arc 9 g and continue until all the points are found; through these intersections draw the curves.

87—To Draw a Spiral of any Number of Turns (in this case two).—Draw a circle the size of the spiral, Fig. 93; then divide it off into any number of equal spaces, say 12, as a, c, d, etc.; then divide any radius, as a c, into as many equal parts as there are turns to the spiral; then divide these spaces into as many equal parts as the circle, as 1, 2, 3, 4, etc.; then, with c as centre and c 2 as radius, draw arc intersecting c c; then, with c as centre and c 3 as radius, draw arc intersecting d c, etc.; continue up to 12; then commence with c as centre and c $^+$2 as radius and draw arc to e c; then through these points draw the curve.

88—To Draw a Scroll for a Stair Railing.—Draw
the eye of the scroll, as the circle *a b c d*, Fig. 94; draw
the diameters *a b* and *c d;* connect *c* and *b;* bisect *c o* at *e*
and draw *e l* parallel to *a b;* draw a line from 6 parallel to *c d,* as 6 *k;* bisect *c o* at 3 and draw 3 2; make *o* 4
equal to *o* 3 and draw *j* 5 parallel to *a b;* bisect *o* 7 and
draw 1 2; with 1 as centre and 1 *f* as radius draw arc *f g;*
with 2 as centre and 2 *g* as radius draw arc *g h;* with 3
as centre draw arc *h i*, etc. To draw the inner curve take
7 as centre and 7 *f* as radius and draw arc *f m;* with 6
as centre and 6 *m* as radius draw arc *m n.*

**89—To Draw a Spiral when its Greatest Diam-
is Given, in this Case One of Three Turns.**—Divide
the diameter *o p*, Fig. 95, into 8 equal parts, as 1, 2, 3, etc.;
with 4 5 as diameter draw the circle *a c b d* for the eye of
the spiral. Draw the two diameters *a b* and *c d* and divide them into twice as many equal parts as there are
turns to the spiral, as 1, 2, 3, 4, 5, 6, etc., in the enlarged
eye. Now, with 1 as centre and 1 *b* as radius draw the
arc *b f* to strike a horizontal line from 2 through 1; with 2
as centre and 2 *f* as radius draw arc *f g* to strike a perpendicular line from 3 through 2; with 3 as centre and 3 *g* as
radius draw arc *g h* to strike a line from 4 through 3 and
so continue until the spiral is completed.

In a spiral of one turn the diameter of the eye is about

three-tenths of the length of the greatest diameter; in one of two turns, about one-sixth ; in one of three turns, about one-eighth; in one of four turns, about one-tenth.

90—To Draw an Ionic Volute.—Let *a b* be the vertical measure of the volute, Fig. 96; divide *a b* into seven equal

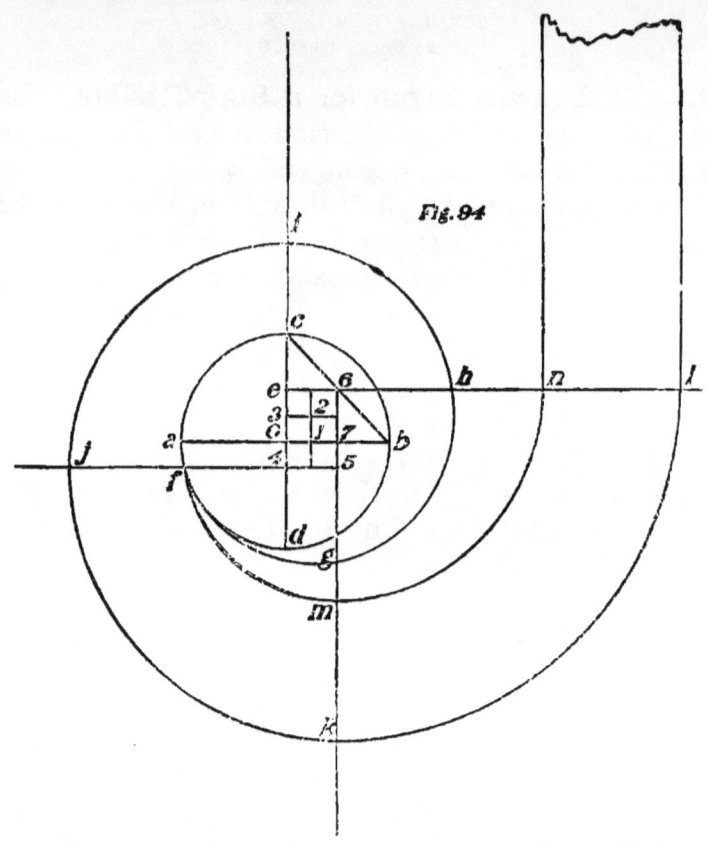

Fig. 94

parts and from point 4 draw a line at right angles to *a b;* at any point on this line draw a circle whose diameter is equal to one of the divisions on *a b*. Draw the square *a b c d;* bisect each of its sides and draw the square *e* 12 11 *f;* draw the diagonals *e* 11, *f* 12; divide the diagonal 12 *l* into three equal parts and draw 8 7 and 4 3 and continue the

lines as shown, making *h g* equal to one-half *i j;* with 1 as
centre and 1 *a* as radius draw arc *a b* to meet a line through
1 and 2; with 2 as centre and 2 *b* as radius draw arc *b c* to
meet a line through 2 3; with 3 as centre and 3 *c* as radius

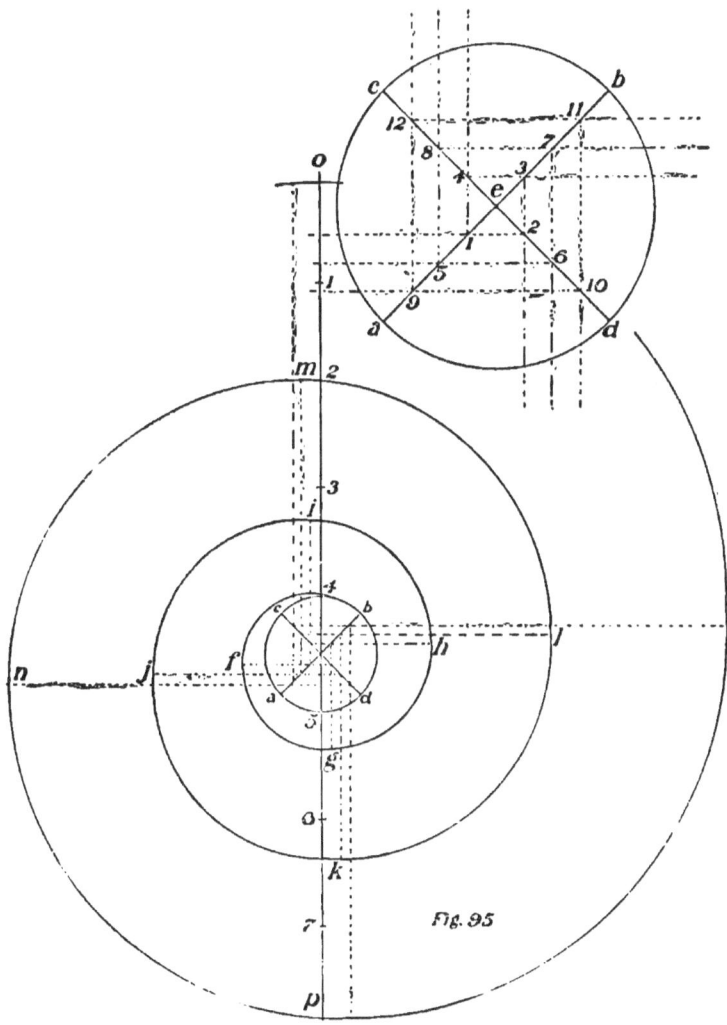

Fig. 95

draw arc *c d* to meet a line through 4 3, etc. The centres
to draw the inner curve are shown by the dots on the diagonals, which is the centre of the space between the
angles of the squares.

91—To Draw a Parabola when the Abscissa *a b*
and the Ordinate *a c* **are Given.**—Draw the rectangle
a b c d, Fig. 97, and divide *c d* and *d b* into the same number of equal parts; draw lines from *b* to meet points 1, 2,
3, etc., on *c d;* then draw lines from points on *d b* parallel

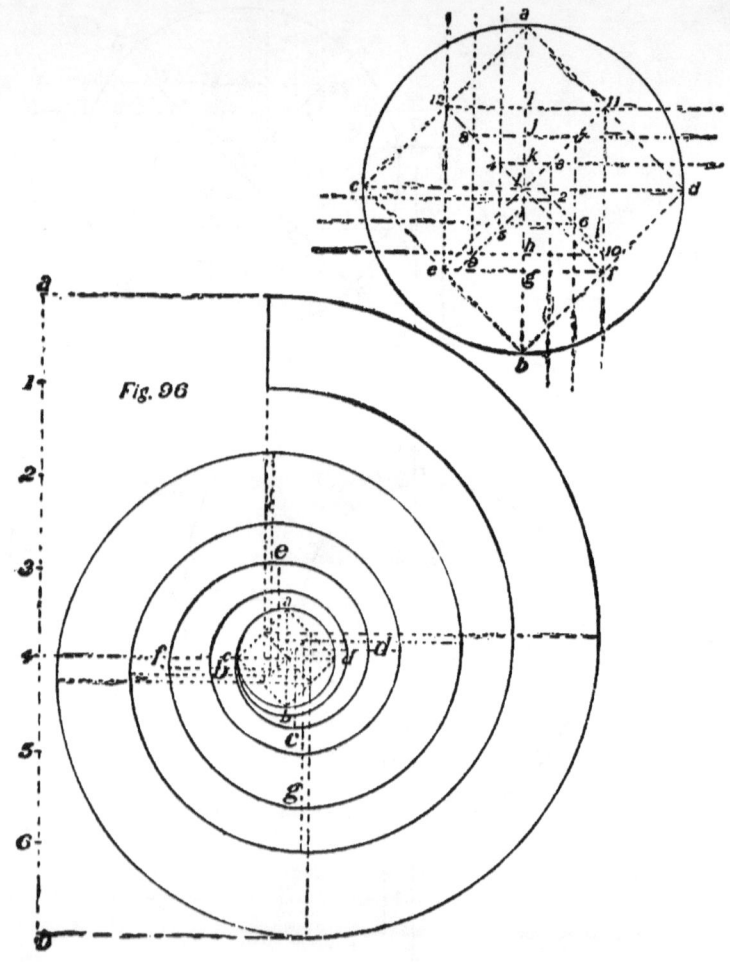

Fig. 96

to *a b;* draw line 1 until it intersects 1 *b;* draw line 2 until it
intersects 2 *b*, etc.; these intersections are points on the
line of the curve.

92—To Draw an Hyperbola when the Diameter
a b, **the Abscissa** *b c* **and the Double Ordinate** *d e*

are Given.—Complete the rectangle *b c d f*, Fig. 98, and divide *f d* and *d c* into the same number of equal spaces, as 1, 2, 3, etc.; from *b* draw *b* 1, *b* 2, etc., and from *a* draw the intersecting lines *a* 1, *a* 2, etc.; through the intersections

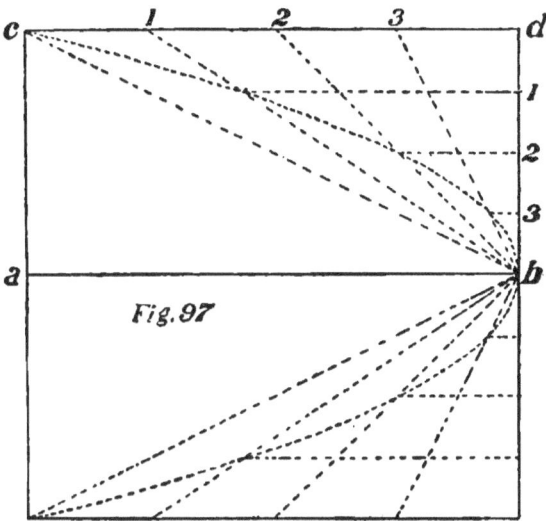

Fig.97

of these lines draw the curve *b d*. Repeat for the other half of the curve.

93—To Draw a Cycloid.—Draw the rolling circle, as *b*, 1, 2, 3, etc., Fig. 99, and divide the semi-circle into any

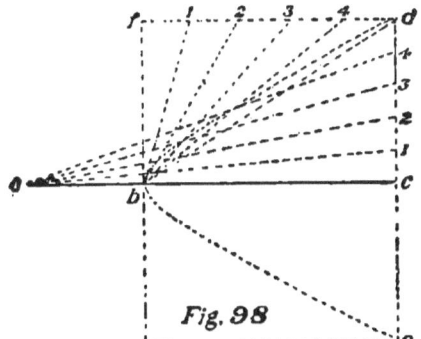

Fig. 98

number of equal parts, as 1, 2, 3, etc.; make the spaces on *a b* equal to those on the semi-circle; draw a line from *d* parallel to *a b*; draw lines from the points on *a b* perpendicular to meet the line *c d* at *o o o*, which are the centres of the rolling circle in its several positions; with these points as centres and the radius of the rolling circle draw the arcs 12 *c*, 11 *c*, 10*c*.

From 1, 2, etc., the points on the semi-circle, draw
lines parallel to *a b* to meet the arcs 12 *c*, 11 *c*, etc.,
at *c c*, etc.; draw the curve through points *c, c, c*, etc.   For
the other half of the curve reverse and proceed as above.

**94—To ·Draw an Epicycloid; also to Draw a
Hypocycloid.**—Draw the curve of the directing circle, as
a b, Fig. 100, and the curve of the rolling circle, as *b*, 1, 2,
etc.; divide the semi-circle *b d* into any number of equal
parts, as 1, 2, 3, etc.; make the spaces on *a b* equal to those on

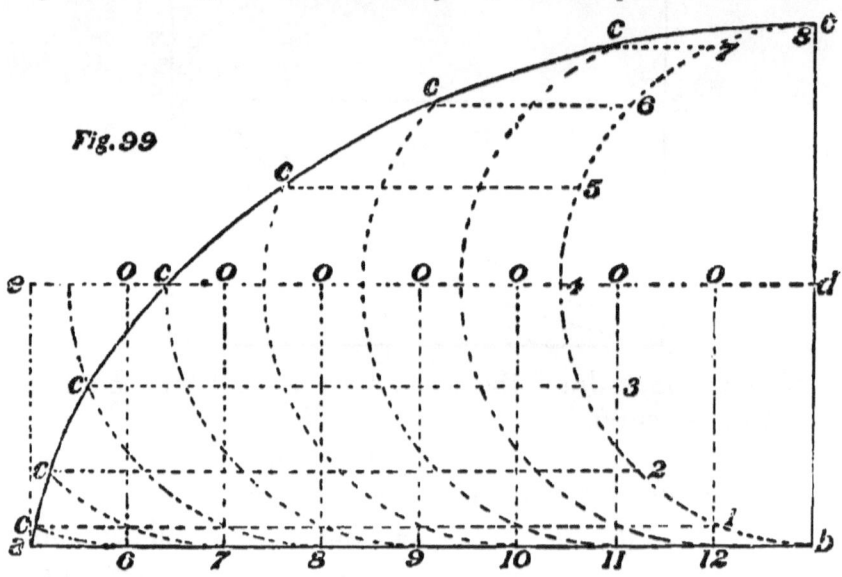

Fig.99

the semi-circle *b d*, spacing from *b;* with the centre of the
directing circle as a centre, draw an arc from *c*, giving the
line of centres of the rolling circle.   Draw lines from the
centre of the directing circle radiating through the points
k, j, i, etc., thus finding the centres of the rolling circle in
its several different positions, as *o o o*, etc.; with these
points as centres and radius of the rolling circle draw the
arcs, *k c, j c*, etc.; with the centre of the directing circle as
centre draw arcs from 1, 2, 3, etc., to meet the arcs from
c, f, g, etc.; the intersections of these arcs are points on
the curve, as shown; draw the curve through the points

c, c, c, etc. When the diameter of the rolling circle is equal to the radius of the directing circle the hypocycloid be-comes a straight line, Fig. 101.

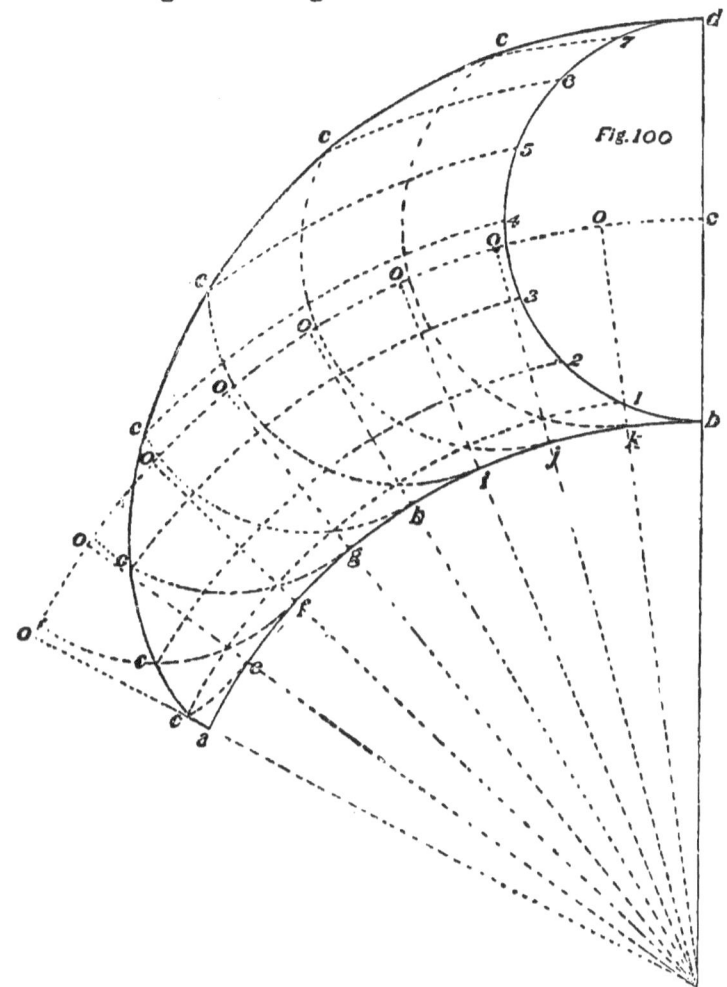

Fig.100

95—To Describe the Involute of a Circle.—Divide the given circle, Fig. 102, into any number of equal spaces, as 1, 2, 3, etc.; draw a line from 2 tangent to the circle and equal in length to the arc 1 2; draw line from 3 tangent to the circle and equal in length to the arc 3 1. Repeat at each of the points and draw the curve through the points *a*, *b*, *c*, *d*, etc.

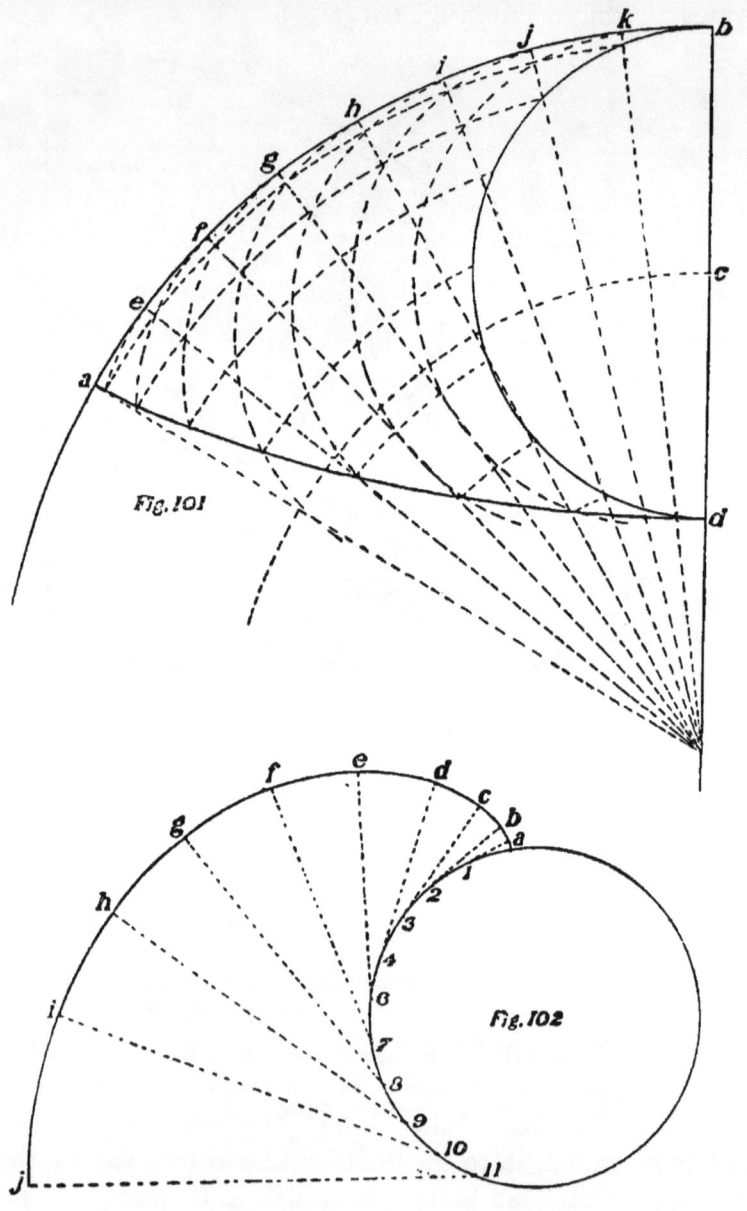

Fig. 101

Fig. 102

96—Lancet Gothic Arch.—A lancet Gothic arch is one whose radius is greater than its width, as shown in Fig. 103.

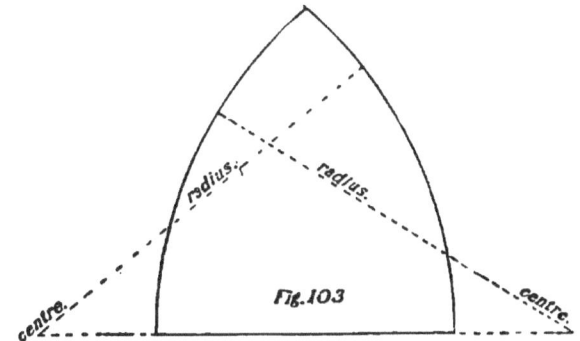

Fig. 103

97—To Draw the Gothic Elliptical Arch.—Divide the span *a b* into three equal parts at *c* and *d*, Fig. 104;

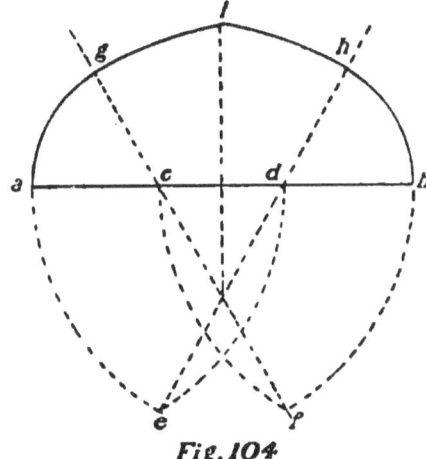

Fig. 104

with *b c* as radius and *a*, *c, d, b* as centres draw the arcs, as shown, finding points *e* and *f;* now. from *e* and *f* draw lines through *c* and *d*, as shown; with *c* and *d* as centres and *a c* as radius draw arcs *a g* and *h b*, and with *e* and *f* as centres and *e h* as radius draw arcs *g i* and *i h*, completing the curve of the arch.

98—To Draw the Lancet Gothic Arch when the Span and Rise are Given.—On the base line, Fig. 105, mark the span *a b* and from the centre draw the rise *c d;* now connect *a d* and *d b*, and from the centre of these lines draw a line at right angles to strike the base line, as *g f* and *e h;* now *g* is the centre and *g b* the radius to draw the arc *d b*, and *h* the centre and same radius to draw the arc *a d*.

99—Gothic Arch.—The most common Gothic arch is one whose radius is equal to its width, as shown in Fig.

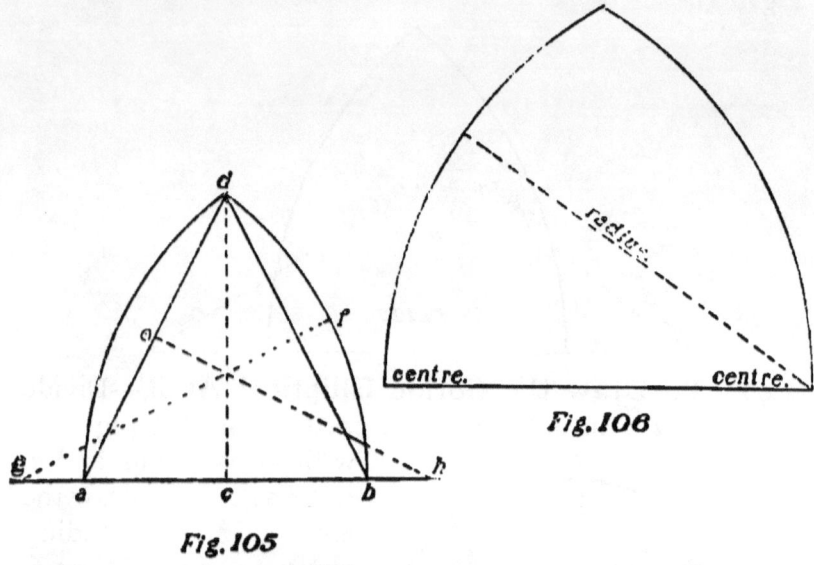

Fig. 105

Fig. 106

106.   All Gothic arches are easily struck from the centre, as shown on the plans and drawings.

100—Drop Arch.—A drop arch is one whose radius is less than its width, as shown in Fig. 108.

Another form of drop arch is shown in Fig. 109.

101—Three-centre Arch.—With *a b* as width of arch and *c* as centre, Fig. 110. take *c a* as radius and strike semi-circle *a b;* then, with *a* as centre and *a b* as radius, strike arc *b c;* then, with *b* as centre and same radius, strike arc *a d;* then, with *c* as centre and *c f* as radius, strike arc *g f;* then, with *d* as centre and same radius, strike arc *g h*, thus completing the arch.

102—Four-centre Arch.—To strike a four-centre arch divide the width into four equal spaces, as 1 2 3. Fig. 111 ; then, with 1 as centre and 1 *a* as radius, strike semi-circle *a* 2 ; then, with 3 as centre and same radius, strike semi-circle 2 *b;* then, with *a b* as radius and *a* as centre, strike arc *b c;* then, with same radius and *b* as centre, strike arc *a d;* then, with *c* as centre and *c e* as radius, strike arc *g c ;* then, with same radius and *d* as centre, strike arc *f g*, completing the arch.

103—To Draw the Tudor or Gothic Arch.—Let *a b* be the span and *c d* the rise, Fig. 112; with *a b* as radius and *c* as centre, draw an arc through the perpendicular at *e*, connect *c* and *c*, make *a g* and *b h* equal to *c f;* now, with *a b* as radius and *g* and *h* as centres, find points 1 1 and 2 2 on the base line ; drive a nail in each of these points to attach a string ; fasten the string at 2 and carry it around the pencil at *c* and make fast at point 1 on the opposite side ; now draw the pencil from *c* to *a*, keeping the string tight, and it will describe the arch ; then reverse the string for other side.

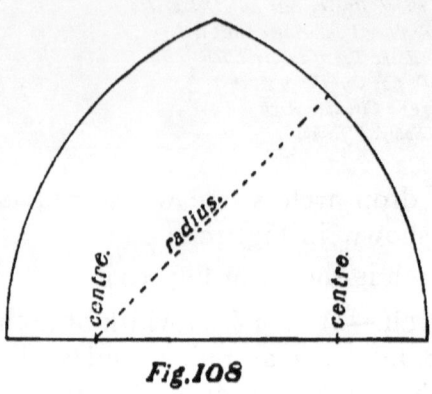

Fig.108

104—To Draw the Soffit or Veneering of a Drop or Gothic Arch with Splayed Jambs.

—Draw a section of the arch, showing the position of the jambs, Fig. 113. From one of the centres, as *c*, draw a perpendicular line indefinite, as *c d;* continue the face line of jamb *a* to bisect *c d* at *d;* then *d* is the centre and *d c* and *d f* the radii to draw the soffit or veneering. For the length, make *e g* equal in length to the curve *c h;* make 1 2 equal to 3 4 and draw 1 *g*, showing the slope of the veneering at the top of arch.

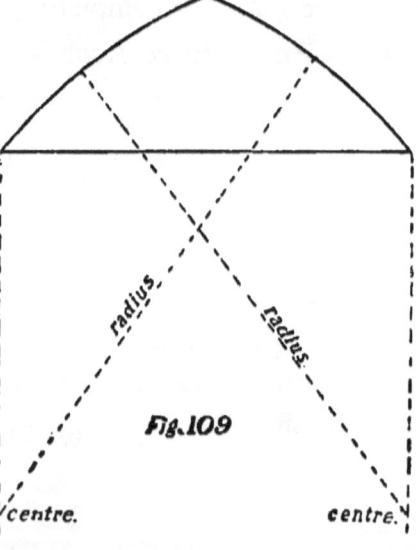

Fig.109

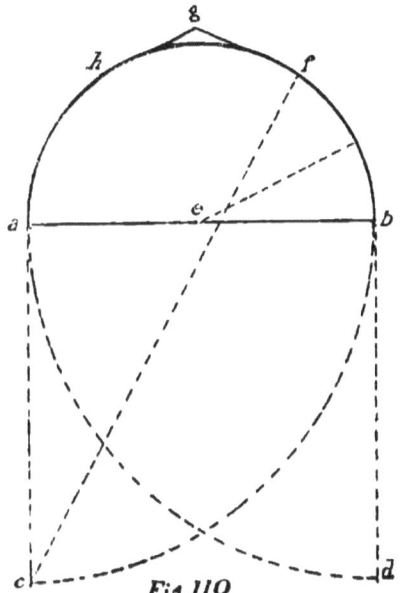

Fig.110

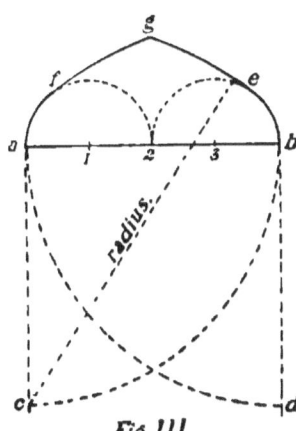

Fig.111

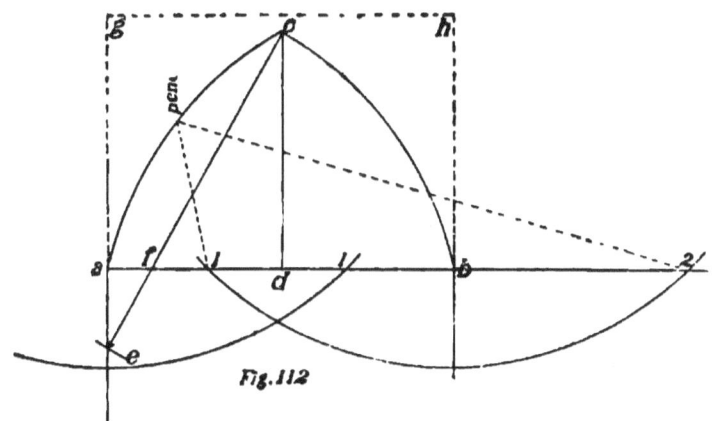

Fig.112

105—To Lay Out the Soffit or Veneering of an Arch which Cuts Through a Wall at an Angle.—

Draw the lines of the wall, as *a b* and *c d*, and the jambs

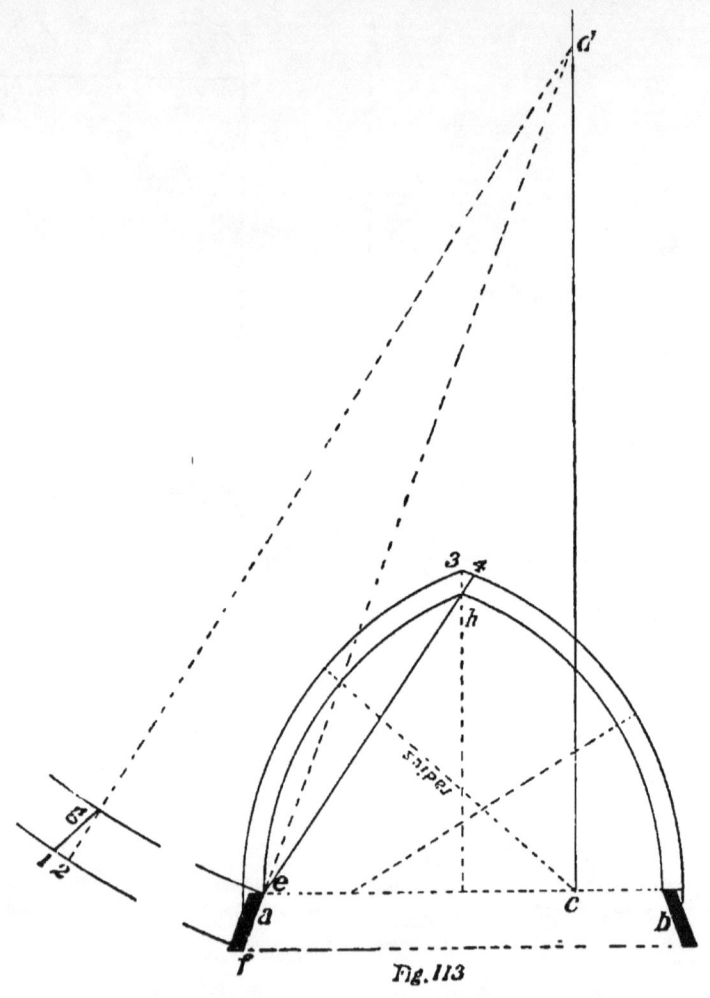

Fig. 113

of the arch, as *a c* and *b d;* draw the diameter of the arch, as *a c*, and on this diameter draw the arch *a* 1 2 3, etc.;

divide the arch into any number of equal spaces, as 1 2 3, etc., and from these points let fall perpendicular lines to strike the wall line c d; now draw a c, Fig. 115, making it equal in length to a 1 2 3, etc., Fig. 114, and divide it into the same number of equal spaces as 11, 12, 13, etc.; from

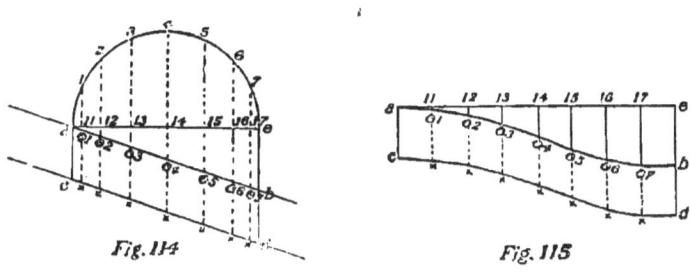

Fig. 114   Fig. 115

these points let fall perpendiculars, as shown, making 11 01 equal to 11 01, Fig. 114, and 12 02 equal to 12 02, Fig. 114, etc.; draw the curve a b through these points, 01, 02, etc.; from points 01, 02, etc., continue the lines, making 01 x equal to 01 x, Fig. 114, and 02 x equal to 02 x, Fig. 114, etc.; make a c and b d equal to a c and b d, Fig. 114, and draw the curve c d through the points x x x, etc.; a b c d is the plan of the soffit or veneering.

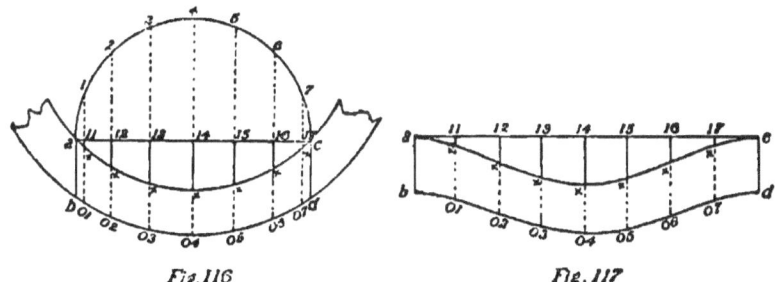

Fig. 116   Fig. 117

106—To Lay Out the Soffit or Veneering of an Arch Through a Circular Wall.

—Draw the curve of the wall, as a c and b d, then the jambs of the arch as a b and c d; with a c as diameter, draw the arch a 1, 2, 3, etc.; divide the arch into any number of equal spaces, as 1, 2,

3, etc., and drop perpendicular lines from these points to the curve *b d*, as shown; now draw the line *a c*, Fig. 117, making it equal in length to *a* 1, 2, 3, etc., Fig. 116, and divide it into the same number of equal spaces ; from these points drop perpendicular lines, making 11 *x* equal to 11 *x*, Fig. 116, 12 *x* equal to 12 *x*, Fig. 116, etc.; draw the curve through points *x*, *x*, *x*, etc., continue the lines from *x*, *x*, etc., making *x* 01 equal to *x* 01 in Fig. 117, and *x* 02 equal to *x* 02 in Fig. 117, etc.; draw the curve through these points ; *a b c d* is the plan of the soffit or veneering.

107—To Draw the Soffit or Veneering of an Arch which Breaks into an Arch Ceiling.—Draw

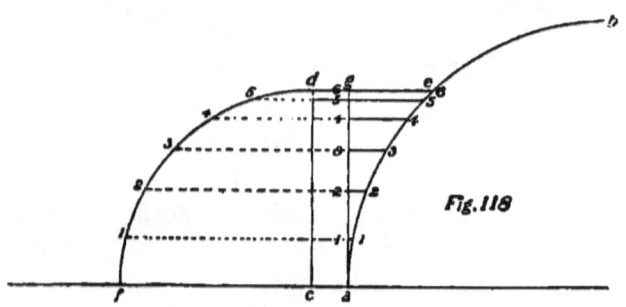

Fig.118

the curve of the ceiling, as *a b*, Fig. 118, and the position of the arch, as *c d c;* with *c* as centre and the height of the arch as radius, draw the quarter-circle *f d;* from *a* draw *a g*, parallel to *c d;* now divide the quarter circle *f d* into any number of equal parts, as 1 2 3, etc., and from these points draw horizontal lines to strike the curve *a b;* now draw *a b*, Fig. 119, making it equal to twice the length of the quarter-circle *f d* in Fig. 118, and divide it into twice as many spaces as the quarter-circle, as 1 2 3, etc., and from these points draw perpendiculars, making 1 1 equal to 1 1 and 2 2 equal to 2 2, etc., Fig. 118; through the points thus found draw the curve *a b;* make *a c* and *b d* equal to *c a*, Fig. 118, and draw *c d* parallel to *a b;* then *a* 1 2 3, etc., *b d c*, is the plan of the soffit or veneering.

108—To Draw the Soffit or Veneering of an Arch in a Circular Wall, the Top of the Arch being Level.—Draw the curve of the wall, as shown in Fig. 120, also the line or seat of the arch, as *a b*, and the

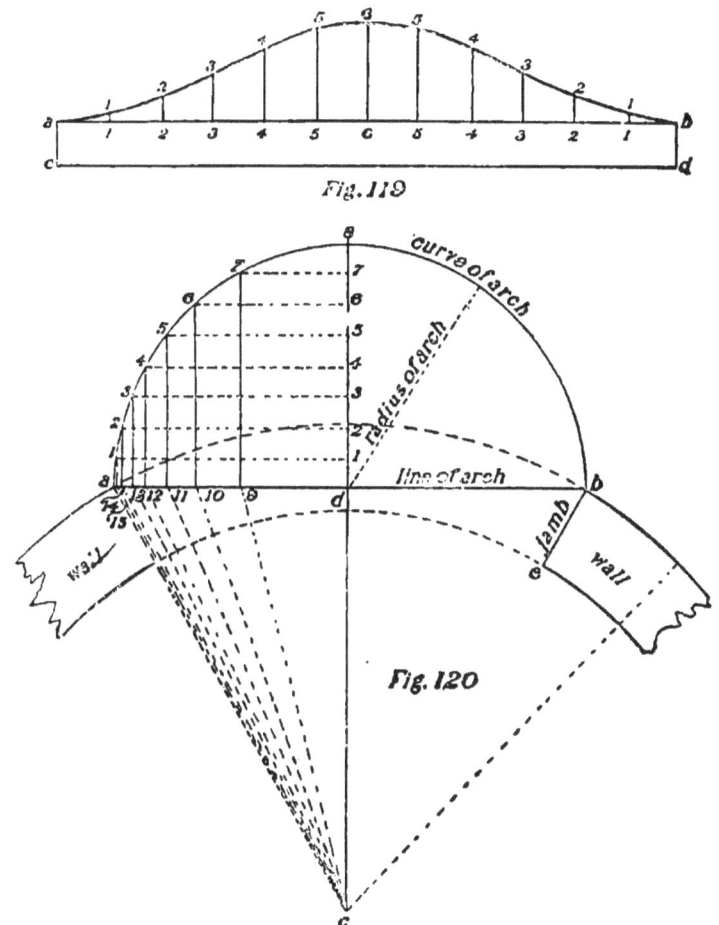

Fig. 119

Fig. 120

curve of the arch, as *a* 1 2, etc. ; now draw the centre line *c* 8 and divide *d* 8 into any number of equal parts, as 1 2 3, etc. ; from these points draw lines parallel to *a d*, to intersect the curve, as 1 1, 2 2, 3 3, etc. ; now from these points on the curve draw lines parallel to d 8, to strike the line a d, as 1 15, 2 14, 3 13, etc.; now draw lines radiating from c to the points 9, 10, 11, etc., as c 9, c 10, etc.; now draw the base line in Fig. 121, making it equal in length to d 8, Fig. 120, as a b, and divide it into the same number of equal parts as d 8, as 1, 2, 3, etc.; draw a c at right angles to a b, making it equal in length to c a, Fig. 120; with 1 as centre and c 15, Fig. 120, as radius, strike an arc at 8, and with c as centre and a 1, Fig. 120, as radius, draw an arc intersecting the first at 8; now, with 2 as centre and c 14 as radius, draw an arc at 9, and with 8 as centre and 1 2 as radius, strike an arc intersecting the first, and continue in this manner until all the intersections are found, making 3 10 equal to c 13, 4 11 equal to c 12, etc., and 9 10 equal to 2 3, 10 11 equal to 3 4, etc.; now draw lines from 1, 2, 3, etc., through the intersections thus found, making each one equal in

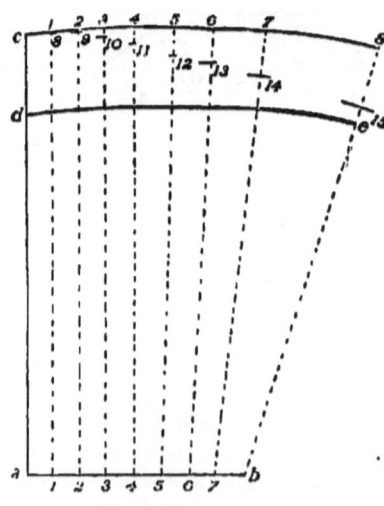

Fig. 121

length to a c, as 1 1, 2 2, 3 3, etc., and draw the curve through these points, as c 1, 2, 3, etc. This represents the outside curve of the soffit or veneering. Now make c d, Fig. 121, equal to the width of the jamb or c b, Fig. 120, and draw the curve d c parallel to c 8, thus completing the plan of one-half of the soffit, of which the other half is a duplicate.

109—To Lay Out the Soffit or Veneering of a Circular Arch with Splayed Jambs.—Draw a section of the Arch, Fig. 122, showing the position of the jambs, as *a* and *b;* continue the face lines of the jambs until they meet at *c*; then *c e* and *c d* is the radii to draw the soffit

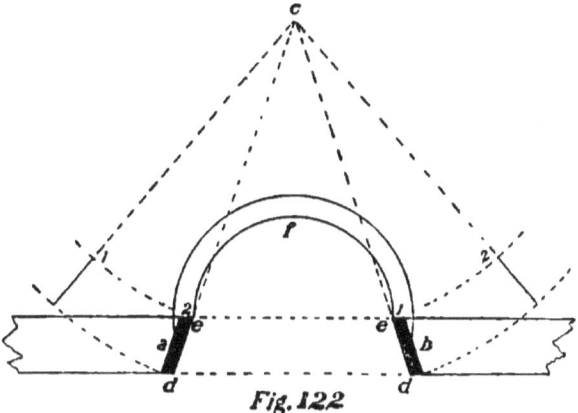

Fig. 122

or veneering for the arch. For the length make 1 2 equal in length to the arch *e f c*.

CHAPTER XI.

*To Lay Out the Joints in an Elliptic Arch—When any Three Points are Given, to Draw
a Circle Whose Circumference Shall Strike Each of the Three Points—To Find the
Centre of a Circle—To Find the Diameter or Radius of a Circle when the Chord
and Rise of an Arc are Given—To Draw an Arc by Intersecting—To Draw
an Arc by Intersecting Lines when the Chord and Rise are Given—To
Draw an Arc by Bending a Lath or Strip—When the Span and
Rise of an Arc are Given, to Draw the Curve—When the Chord
and Rise of an Arc are Given, to Draw the Arc—When
the Chord and Rise of an Arc are Given, to Find the
Radius—When the Chord and any Point on
an Arc are Given, to Draw the Curve.*

110—To Lay Out the Joints in an Elliptic Arch.—
Draw the arch *a b c*. Fig. 123, and divide the curve into
equal spaces, as 1, 2, 3, etc., making as many spaces as

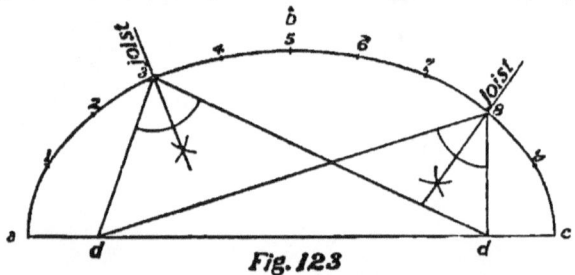

Fig. 123

joints required in the arch; draw lines from the foci *d d*
to the points on the curve and bisect the angle thus
formed, as shown. The lines bisecting this angle are the
lines of the joints. Repeat the operation for each joint.

**111—When any Three Points are Given, to Draw
a Circle Whose Circumference Shall Strike Each
of the Three Points.—**With *a, b* and *c* as the points,
Fig. 124, join *a* and *b* and *a* and *c* together, and draw lines
at right angles from the centre of *a b* and *a c*, bisecting at
d, which is the centre of the circle, and *d a* the radius.

112—To Find the Centre of a Circle.—Take any
three points on the circumference and join them, as *a, b, c,*

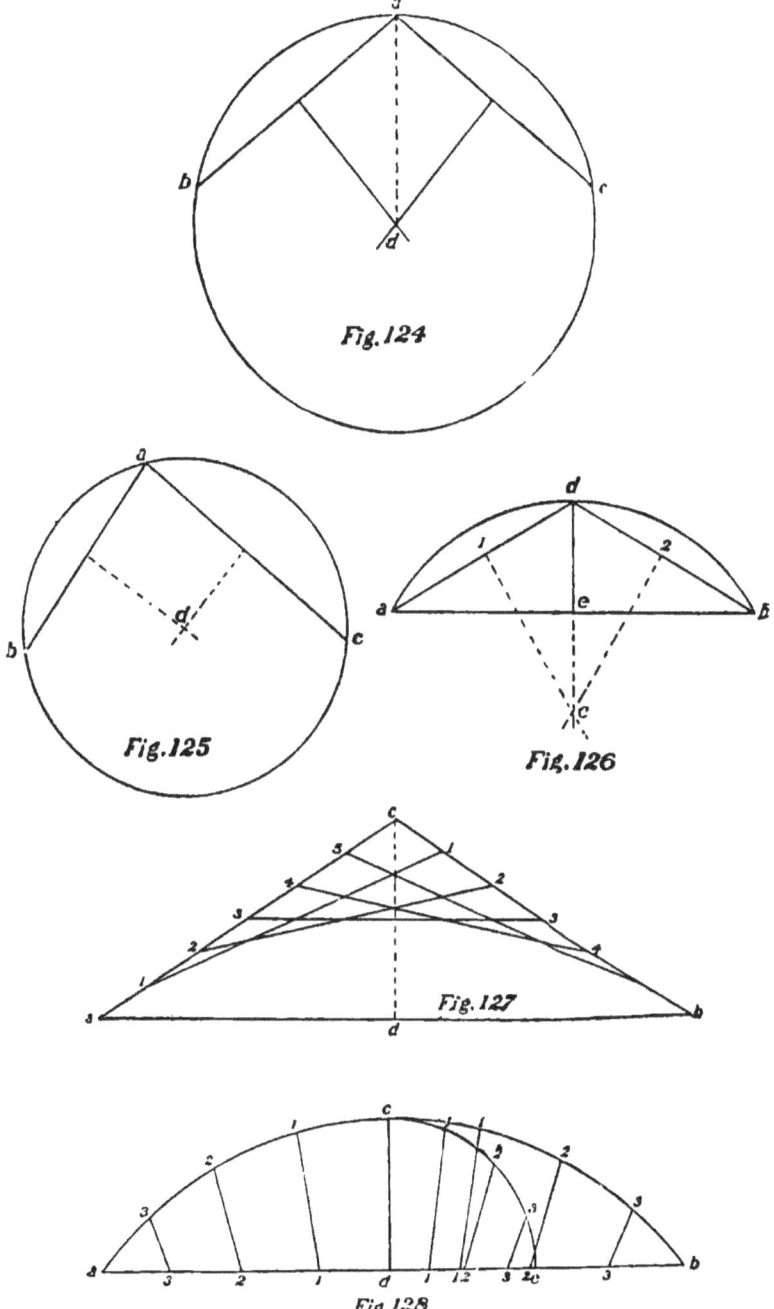

Fig.124

Fig.125

Fig.126

Fig.127

Fig.128

Fig. 125; then draw lines at right angles from the centre of *a b* and *a c* and the bisecting point *d* is the centre.

113—To Find the Diameter or Radius of a Circle when the Chord and Rise of an Arc are Given.— Draw the chord as *a b*, then the rise *d c*, Fig. 126; then connect *a d* and *d b*, then draw lines 1 *c* and 2 *c* at right angles, and from the centre of *a d* and *d b*, until they intersect at *c*, which is the centre and *c d* the radius.

114—To Draw an Arc by Intersecting Lines when the Chord and Rise are Given.—Draw the chord as *a b*, Fig. 127, then draw *c d* equal to twice the the rise, divide *a c* and *c b* into the same number of equal spaces and draw the lines as shown.

115—To Draw an Arc by Bending a Lath or Strip.—Let *a b* be the span and *c d* the rise, Fig. 128; with *c d* as radius and *d* as centre, draw the quarter circle *c c;* now divide *c c* and *c d* into the same number of equal parts, as 1, 2, 3, etc.; now divide *d b* and *d a* into as many equal parts as *d c;* now connect 1, 2, 3 on the quarter-circle and 1, 2, 3 on *d c*, as shown; now draw lines from the points on *a d* and *d b*, at the same angle and equal in length to the ones on the quarter-circle, as 1 1, 2 2, etc.; drive nails in these points and bend the strip around.

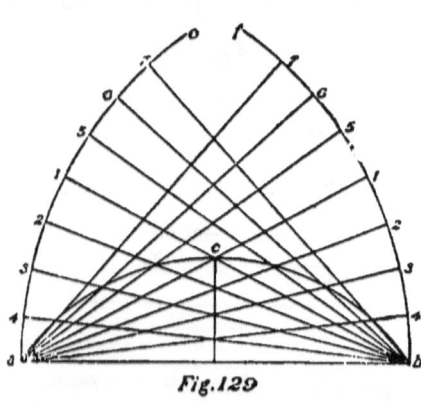

Fig.129

116—When the Span and Rise of an Arc are Given, to Draw the Curve.—Draw the span *a b* and rise *c*, Fig. 129; then, with *a* and *b* as centres and *a b* as radius, draw arcs *a c* and *b f;* now draw lines from *a* and *b* through *c* until they strike *a c* and *b f*, as *a* 1 and *b* 1; divide *a* 1 on *a e* and *b* 1 on *b f* into any number of equal spaces, as 1, 2, 3, etc.; make 5, 6, 7 equally distant, and draw the lines as shown; draw the curve through the intersections, as shown.

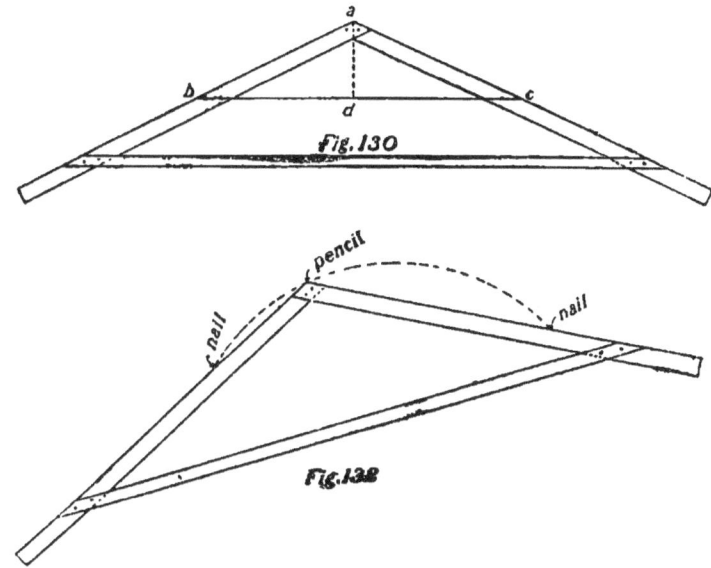

Fig. 130

Fig. 132

117—When the Chord and Rise of an Arc are Given, to Draw the Arc.

—Take two strips and joint the edges straight and make a frame, as shown; *b c* is the chord and *a d* the rise of the arc. Drive a nail in the floor or drawing-board on the outside edge of the frame at *b* and another one at *c;* then place the pencil at the point of the frame, *a*, and slide the frame around, keeping it tight against the nails, when the pencil will describe the curve, as shown in the Figures 130 and 132.

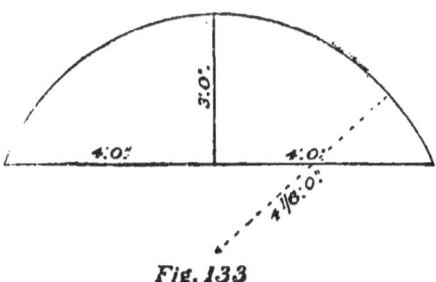

Fig. 133

118—When the Chord and Rise of an Arc are Given, to Find the Radius.—Square one-half the chord, divide this product by the rise, and to this answer add

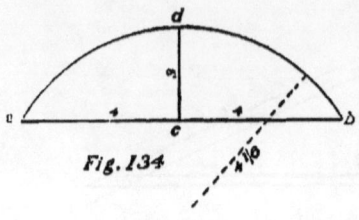

Fig. 134

the rise, and divide by 2; the answer is the radius. In Fig. 133, one-half the chord is 4, which squared equals 16, which divided by the rise equals 5⅓, to which add the rise equals 8⅓, which divided by 2 equals 4⅙, the radius.

RULE II.—Add together the square of half the chord and the square of the rise of the arc and divide this an-

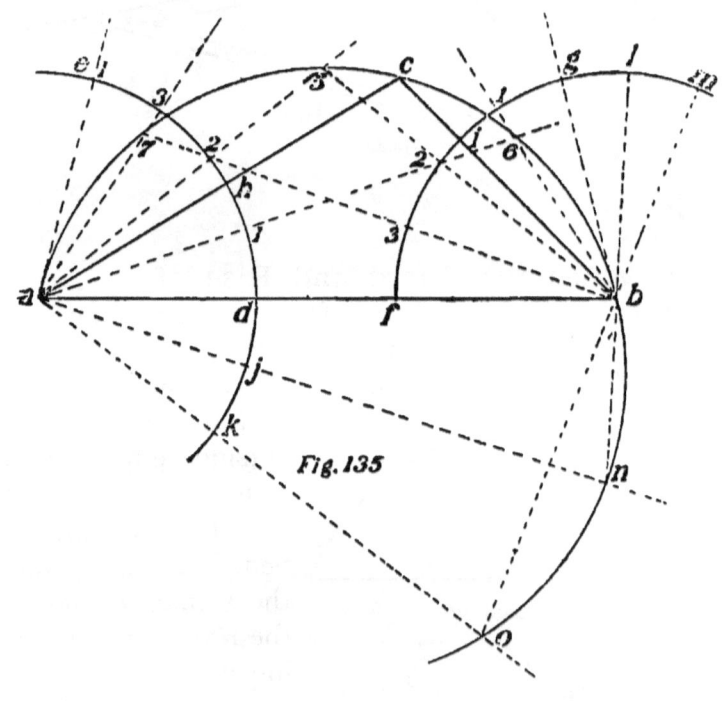

Fig. 135

which divided by 6, or twice the rise, equals 4⅙, the radius in Fig. 134.

119—When the Chord and any Point on the Arc are Given, to Draw the Curve.—Draw the chord *a b* and the given point *c*, Fig. 135 ; with any radius and *a* and *b* as centres, draw the arcs *c d* and *f g;* with *h* as centre and *f i* as radius, find point *c;* with *i* as centre and *h d* as radius, find point *g;* divide *c d* and *g f* into any number of equal spaces, as 1, 2, etc. (the more spaces, the easier to draw the curve); draw the lines as shown, and the intersections 4, 5, 6 show points through which to draw the curve. To find points on the curve below the chord, make the spaces *d j* and *j k* equal to the spaces on *c d* and draw the lines *a m* and *a o;* make spaces *g l* and *l m* equal to the spaces on *f g*, and draw lines *l n* and *m o;* *n* and *o* are the desired points.

CHAPTER XII.

120—Geometrical Definitions.

A point is a position without dimensions.

A line has one dimension—length.

A surface has two dimensions—length and breadth.

A solid has three dimensions—length, breadth and thickness.

A right angle is one whose two sides make an angle of 90° with each other; an acute angle is less than a right angle; an obtuse angle is more than a right angle.

A plane figure is a plane bounded on all sides by lines. If the lines are straight the space which they contain is called a polygon.

Polygons are named according to the number of their sides, as: A triangle is a plane figure of three sides; a quadrilateral is a plane figure of four sides: a pentagon is a plane figure of five sides; a hexagon is a plane figure of six sides; a heptagon is a plane figure of seven sides; an octagon is a plane figure of eight sides; a nonagon is a plane figure of nine sides; a decagon is a plane figure of ten sides: an undecagon is a plane figure of eleven sides: a dodecagon is a plane figure of twelve sides.

A circle is a plane bounded by a curved line all points of which are equally distant from the centre.

An equilateral triangle has all its sides and angles equal ; an isosceles triangle has two of its sides and two of its angles equal ; a scalene triangle has all its sides and angles unequal.

A quadrilateral is a plane figure bounded by four straight lines. A trapezium is a quadrilateral having no two sides parallel. A trapezoid is a quadrilateral having two of its sides parallel. A parallelogram is a quadrilateral having its opposite sides parallel. A square is a parallelogram having all of its sides equal and its angles right angles. A rectangle is a parallelogram having its opposite sides equal and its angles right angles. A rhombus is a parallelogram having all its sides equal, but its angles are not right angles. A rhomboid is a parallelogram having its opposite sides equal, but its angles are not right angles.

A diameter is any line drawn through the centre of a figure and terminated by the opposite boundaries.

A parabola is one of the conic sections. A hyperbola is a curve formed by the section of a cone when the cutting plane makes a greater angle with the base than the side of the cone makes.

121—Solids.—A tetrahedron is a solid bounded by four equilateral triangles. A hexhedron or cube is a solid bounded by six squares. An octahedron is a solid bounded by eight equilateral triangles. A dodecahedron is a solid bounded by twelve pentagons. An icosahedron is a solid bounded by twenty equilateral triangles.

122—Circumference, etc., of Circles.—To find the circumference when the diameter is known, multiply the diameter by 3.1416. To find the diameter when the circumference is known, divide the circumference by 3.1416. To find the area of a circle, multiply one-half the diameter by one-half the circumference. To find the circumference of an ellipse, multiply half the sum of the two diameters by 3.1416. To find the area of an ellipse, multiply

the long diameter by the short diameter and this product
by .7854. To find a square of equal area to a circle, multiply the diameter of the circle by .8862269, which amount
is one side of the square. The diameter of a circle multiplied by .707106 will give the side of an inscribed square.
To find a circle of equal area to a square, multiply one
side of the square by 1.128379; the answer will be the
diameter of the circle. When the length of the perimeter
and one axis of an ellipse are given, to find the length of
the other axis, divide the length of the perimeter by 1.6,
and from this quotient subtract the length of the given
axis; the answer will be the length of the other axis.

123—Cycloid and Epicycloid.—The cycloid is the
curve described by any point in the circumference of a
circle when the circle rolls along a straight line. An epicycloid is the curve described by any point in the circumference of a circle when the circle rolls along the outside
of another circle. A hypocycloid is the path described by
any point in the circumference of a circle when the circle
rolls along the inside of another circle.

An involute is the curve described by the end of a string
when unwinding the string from a cylinder.

124—To Find Areas.—To find the area of a triangle,
multiply the base by one-half the perpendicular; equilateral triangle, multiply the square of one side by .433;
trapezoid, multiply the sum of the two parallel sides by
the perpendicular difference between them and divide by
two; parallellogram, multiply the base by the perpendicular; trapezium, divide the figure into two triangles and
find the area of each; circle, multiply one-half the circumference by the radius, or multiply the square of the diameter by .7854; ellipse, multiply the long diameter by the
short diameter and by .7854; cylinder, multiply the length
by the circumference; globe, multiply the diameter by
the circumference, or multiply the square of the diameter

by 3.1416; cone, multiply the circumference of the base by one-half the slant height.

To find the arc of various polygons, see Page 47.

The areas of all circles are to one another as the squares of their like dimensions.

All solid bodies are to each other as the cubes of their like diameters or similar sides.

To find the solid contents of a globe, multiply the area by one-sixth of the diameter.

125—To Find the Area of a Circular Ring Formed by Two Concentric Circles.—Multiply the sum of the two diameters by their difference and the product by .7854.

To find the contents of a barrel or cask, multiply the square of the mean diameter by the length (both in inches) and this product by .0034; the answer will be the contents in gallons. To find the mean diameter of a barrel or cask, add to the head diameter two-thirds, or if the staves are but little curved, six-tenths of the difference between the head and bung diameters.

To find the side of a cube inscribed in a sphere or globe, multiply the diameter by .5774.

126—To Find the Patterns of a Circular Window Sill which is Set with a Bevel.—*A b c d* of the plan, Fig. 136, represents the plan of the sill and *e* the centre. The first thing is to find the size of lumber necessary to make the sill, which is done as follows: From the centre line *e f* draw the perpendicular *g h*, making it any desired length, and from *h* draw a line giving the slope of the sill as *h i;* now draw perpendicular lines from points *e, a* and *b* to strike the line *i h*, as *j k* and *b l;* now space down from *h* on *h g* the thickness of the desired sill and draw the horizontal line *m n* to strike *l b;* draw the line *o p* through *n* and parallel to *k h*, and *k h o p* shows the size of lumber that will be required to make the sill. The next thing is to find the patterns to be used after the stick is dressed to this shape. To find the pattern for the front edge: First continue the line *c b* until it strikes *g h*, as at

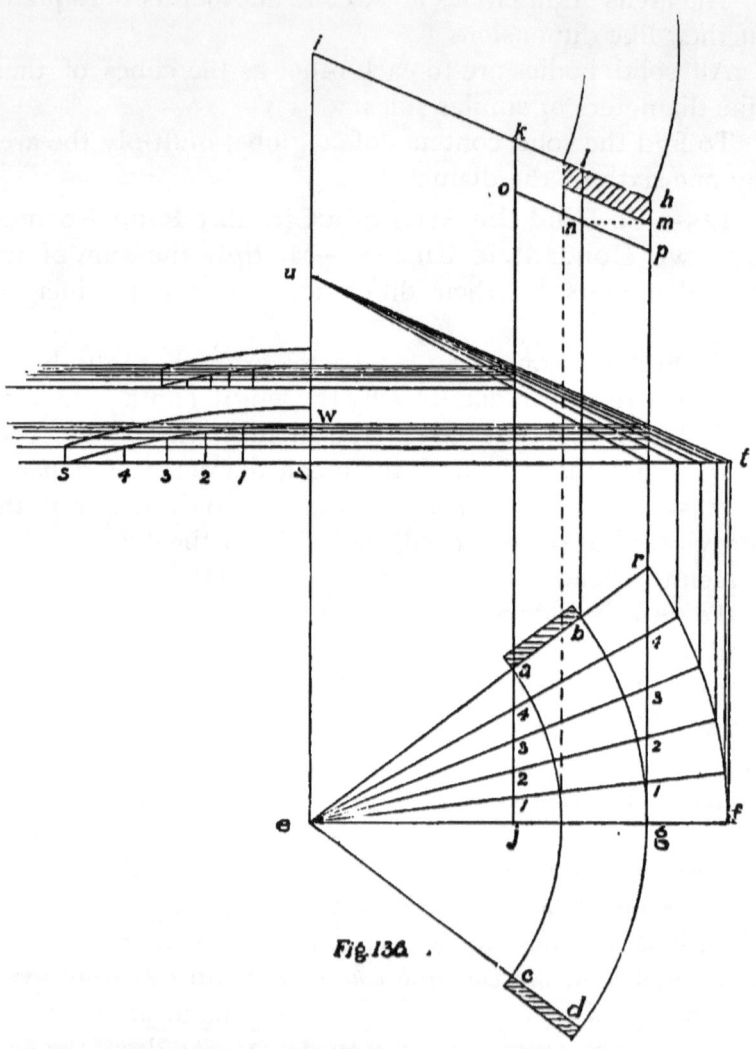

Fig. 136.

r; also continue the centre line *e g* and draw the arc *r f;* now divide the arc *r f* into any number of equal spaces and from these points draw lines to the centre *e;* now from these same points draw perpendicular lines to meet a horizontal line, as *s l*, and from *l* draw a line parallel to *i h*, as *u l*, and from the intersections of the perpendicular lines and *s l* draw lines to *u;* now from where these lines cross *p r* draw lines parallel to *s l;* now make *s v* equal to *r g* and space it into spaces of equal sizes to *r g*, commencing at *g* and spacing from it, as 1, 2, 3, etc.; draw perpendicular lines from these points to strike the horizontal lines, as shown—from 4 to strike the first horizontal line, 3 to strike the second, etc.; now draw a line through these intersections, which will give the curve of the pattern; draw the perpendicular at *s*, making it equal in length to the thickness of the sill and draw the upper curve parallel to *s w*, which gives one-half of the pattern for the face edge of the sill. The pattern of the inside edge is found in the same way, working from the line *k j*, as shown. The patterns are applied to the edge of the stick after it has been beveled, as shown at *k h o p*. It should then be worked out to these patterns, and the top pattern, which is found by using *i h* as radius, should then be bent down on the sill, when it will give the desired lines.

127—The Steel Square.—The standard steel square has a blade twenty-four inches long and two inches wide, and a tongue from fourteen to eighteen inches long and one and one-half inches wide. The blade is at right angles to the tongue.

In the centre of the tongue will be found two parallel lines divided into spaces, Fig. 137; this is the octagon scale. The spaces will be found numbered 10, 20, 30, 40, 50 and 60. To draw an octagon, say twelve inches square, draw a square twelve inches each way and draw a perpendicular and horizontal line through the centre. To find the length of the octagon side, place the point of the compasses on any one of the main divisions of the scale

and the other point of the compasses on the twelfth sub-
division ; then step this length off on each side of the cen-

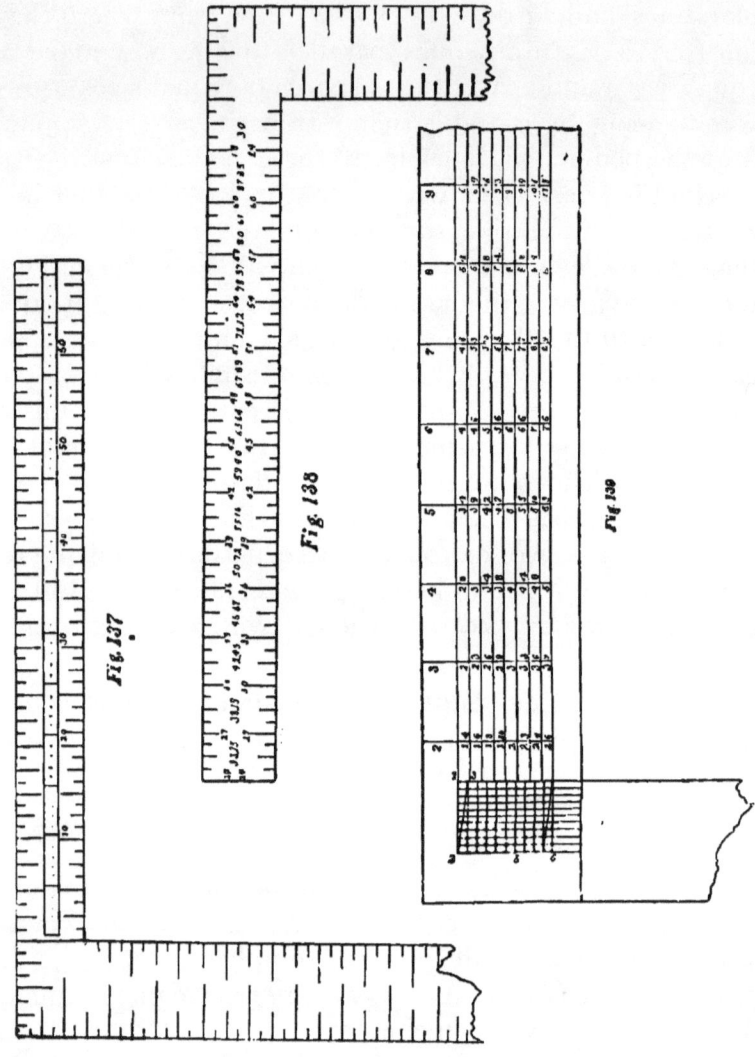

tre lines on the side of the square, which will give the points
from which to draw the octagon lines; the diameter of

the octagon must equal in inches the number of spaces taken from the square.

On the opposite side of the tongue will be found the brace rule, Fig. 138. At the end of the tongue will be found the figures $\frac{24}{24}33.95$; the $\frac{24}{24}$ indicates the rise and run of a brace and 33.95 is the length. The rest of the figures are used in the same way.

On one side of the blade will be found nine lines running parallel with the length of the blade and divided at every inch by cross lines, Fig. 139; this is the board measure. Under 12 on the outer edge of the blade will be found the various lengths of boards, as 8, 9, 10, 11, 12, etc. For example, we will take a board ten inches wide and eight feet long; to find the contents we look under 12 and find 8 between the first and second lines; we then follow this space along until we come to the cross line under 10, the width of the board, and here we find 6, 8, or six feet, eight inches, the contents of the board.

At the angle of the blade and tongue will be found the diagonal scale, by which an inch can be divided into one hundred equal parts and any number of these parts can be taken from the scale. For instance, if we want to find $\frac{7}{100}$ of an inch, place one point of the compasses on the diagonal line 2 3 at the intersection of the seventh line from 2 and the other point on line 1 2, which will give $\frac{7}{100}$ of an inch. To find $\frac{53}{100}$ of an inch, place the point of the compasses on line 3 2 at the intersection of the third line from 3 and the other point on this third line at the intersection of line 5 5, which gives $\frac{53}{100}$ of an inch. The line 2 6 is one inch in length and divided into ten equal parts, then each part contains $\frac{10}{100}$ of an inch, and as the diagonal will give any number from $\frac{1}{100}$ to $\frac{10}{100}$ the scale is easily understood.

To divide a board into equal spaces or strips, place the square on the board in the position shown, and if twelve

strips are wanted the line will be at 2, 4, 6, 8, etc.   If eight
strips are wanted, they will be at 3, 6, 9, 12, etc., Fig. 140;
six strips, 4, 8, 12, etc.

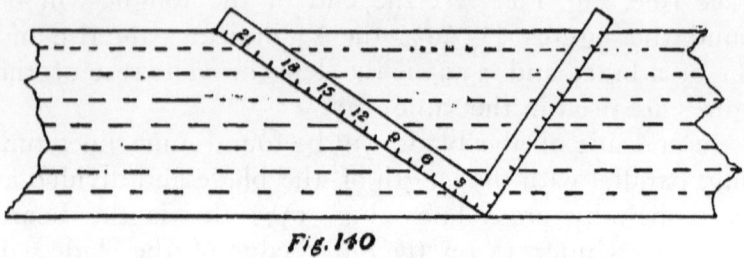

Fig. 140

128—To Prove a Square.

—Take a board with a per-
fectly straight edge, as in Fig. 141, and place the square
on as shown by the dotted lines and draw a line across

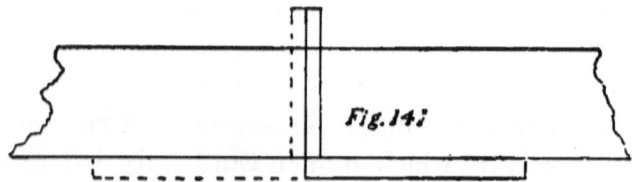

Fig. 141

the board along the tongue of the square; now turn the
square over, and if it is true the tongue will come right
up to the line, as shown.

129—To Prove or True a Straight-edge.

—Place
the straight-edge on a board and draw a pencil line, Fig.
142, the full length; now turn it over, and if it is true or

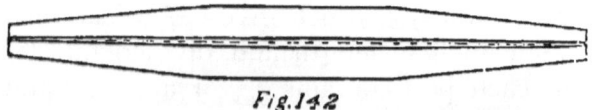

Fig. 142

straight the edge will come up to the line; but if hollow
it will be open in the centre, as shown, and if round or
full in the centre the ends will be open.

130—To Adjust a Level.—Place the level against a wall or some solid place, and place it so the "bead" in the glass is at the centre, and mark on the wall the position of the level ; now reverse the level, as shown, and mark the

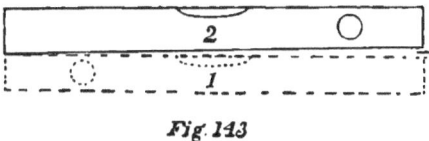

Fig. 143

second position ; now divide the space between the two positions at *b* and place that end of the level to that mark and turn the adjusting screw until the "bead" is in the centre, when the level will be true.

131—A Handy Improvement on the Ordinary Thumb Gauge is made as follows : In the end of the

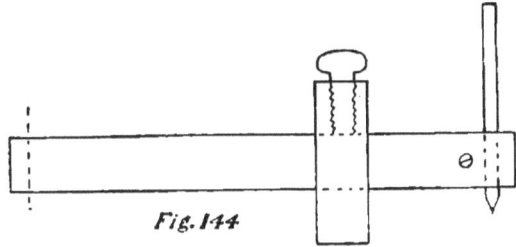

Fig. 144

gauge, Fig. 144, opposite the "scratch" or "tooth," bore a quarter-inch hole, and then with a fine saw rip the arm of the gauge back about an inch past the hole ; now put a small screw in, as shown, countersinking the head so as to come flush ; now insert a lead pencil and tighten the screw and you have a very convenient pencil gauge.

132—To Lay Out an Octagon Shingle.—Take the width of the shingle, Fig. 145, and measure up from the butt and draw a square line across the shingle, thus form- ing a square; then draw the two diagonal lines $a\,c$ and

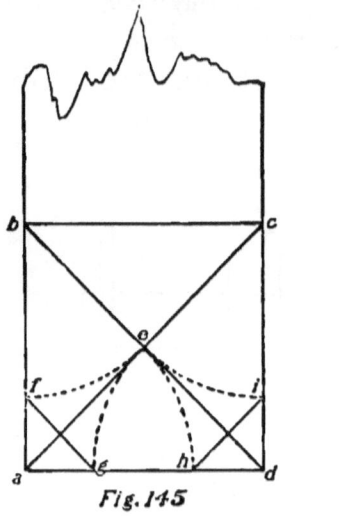

Fig. 145

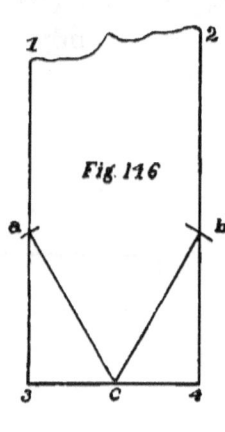

Fig. 146

$b\,d$, cutting in c; then, with $a\,c$ as radius and $a\,b\,c\,d$ as centres, find points f, g, h and i; then connect $f\,g$ and $h\,i$.

133—To Lay Out Diamond-Pointed Shingles.— Let 1, 2, 3, 4, Fig. 146, represent the shingles; then, with 3 and 4 as centres and 3 4 as radius, find points a and b;

then find centre of 3 4, as *c;* then connect *a c* and *b c.*
Take 3 4 as radius and *c* as centre and find points *a b;* then
connect *a c* and *b c.*

Fig. 147

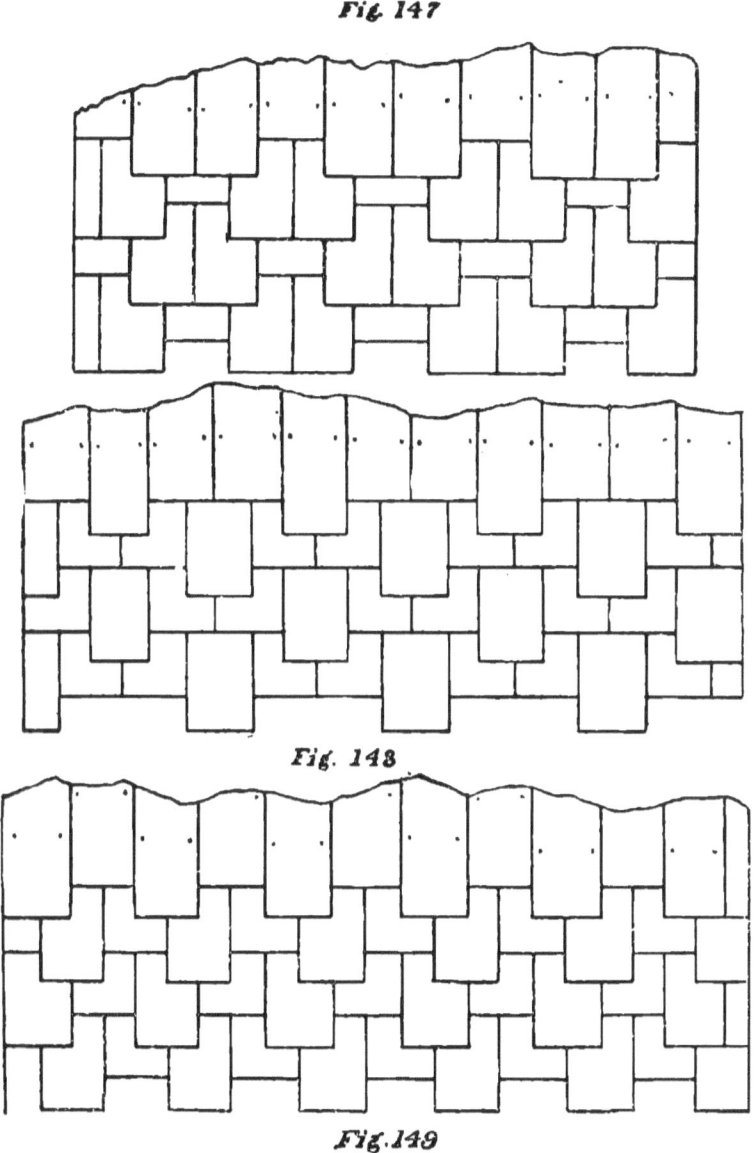

Fig. 148

Fig. 149

PATTERNS FOR LAYING GAUGED SHINGLES.

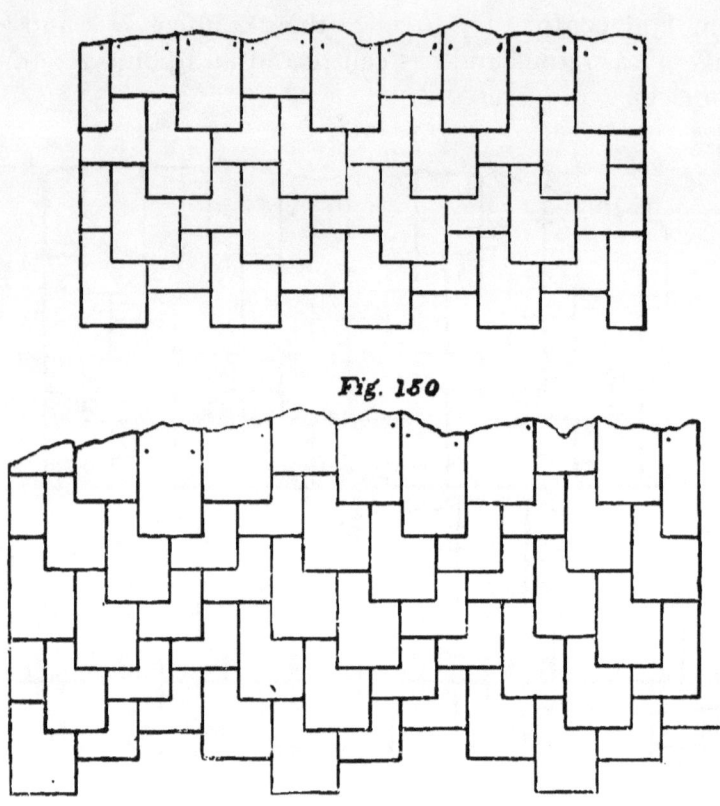

Fig. 150

Fig. 151

PATTERNS FOR LAYING GAUGED SHINGLES.

134—To Lay Out an Arch Lintel.—The rule is to use the width of the frame as radius. Example: *a b c d*, Fig. 152, represent the frame; now, with *a* as centre and *a b* as radius, draw the arc *b c;* with *b* as centre and same radius, draw arc *a c*, and with the intersection *c* as centre and same radius, draw the desired arc *a b*.

135—To Find the Pattern of Veneers for Circle Splayed Window or Door Jambs.—Draw a section of the frame, as *a* and *b*, Fig. 153; then continue the lines 1 *d* and 2 *c* until they meet at *c;* *c c* and *c d* is the radius to lay out the veneer.

136—To Find the Mitre Bevels for a Hopper of any Number of Sides.—Draw a "floor plan" of one of the angles, as *a b;* then the joint line *c d;* now draw *c f*

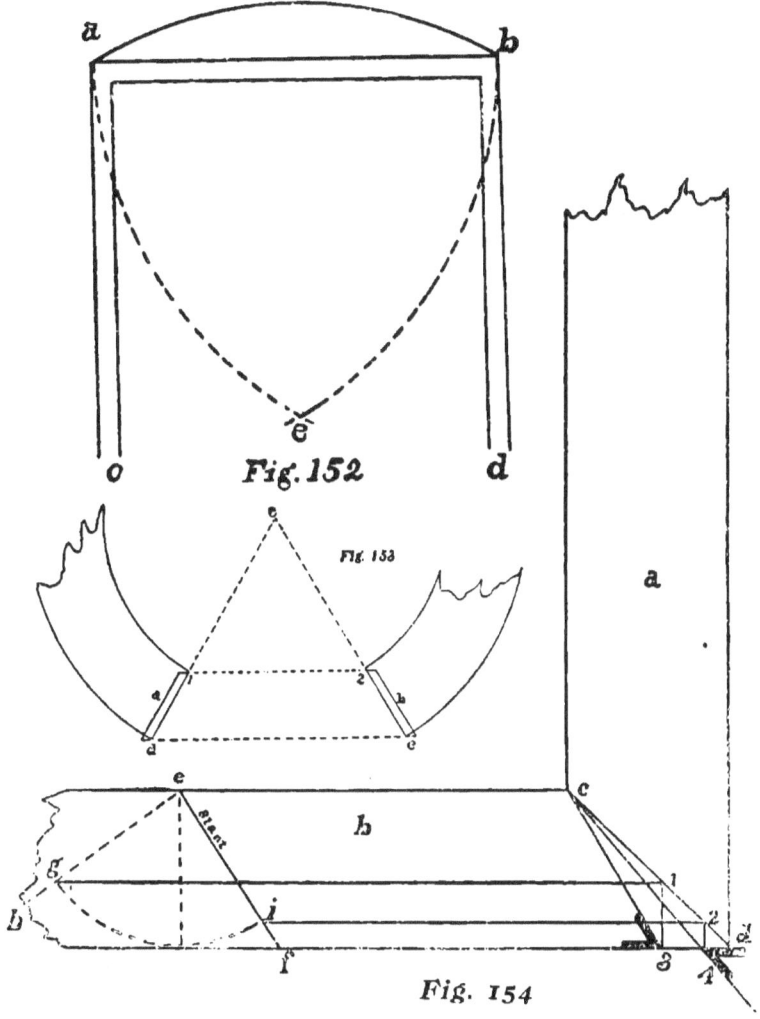

Fig. 152

Fig. 153

Fig. 154

equal to the slant of the sides of the hopper and draw *h c* at right angles to *c f;* with *c* as centre draw an arc touching the base line, thus finding points *g* and *i;* from these points

draw lines parallel to the base line, touching *c d* at 1 and
2; let fall perpendiculars to the base line, finding points 3

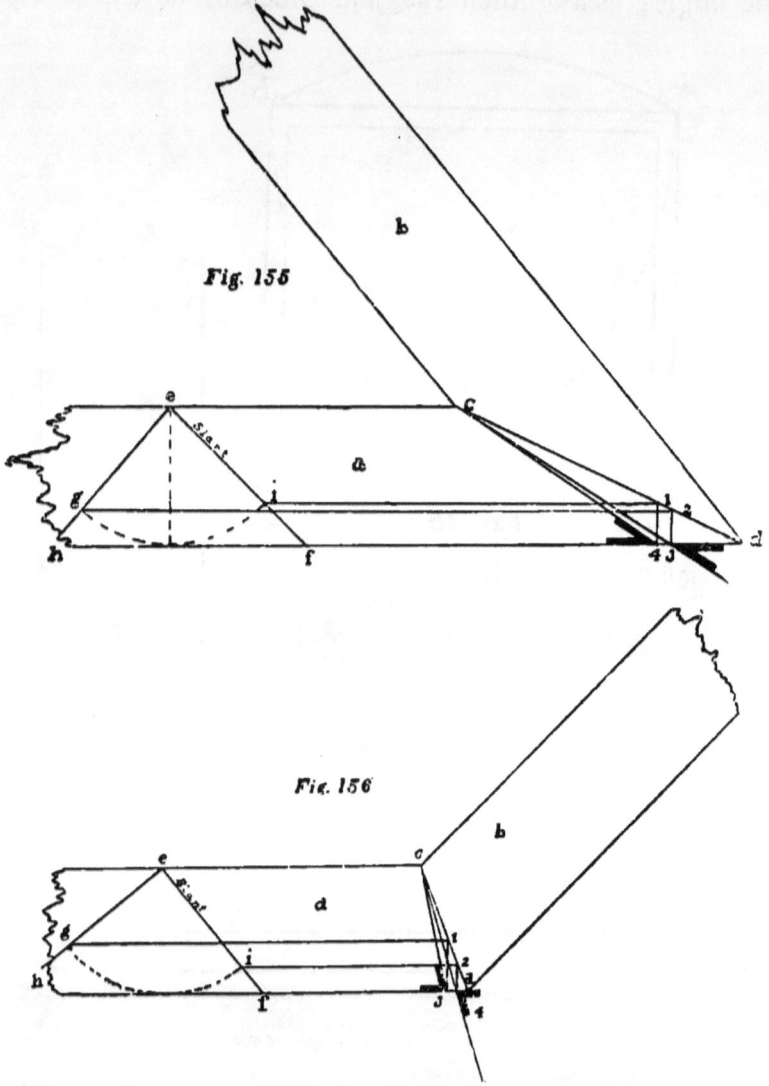

Fig. 155

Fig. 156

and 4; connect *c* and 3, thus giving the bevel for the face
of the work; then connect *c* and 4, thus finding the bevel
for the edge of the work, as shown in Figs. 154, 155, 156.

137—To Find the Bevels of a Hopper of any Number of Sides Having Butt Joints.—Draw a section of the floor plan as *a b*, Figs. 157, 158, 159. *c d* representing the angle; draw *e f* equal to the slant of the sides and *e g* at right angles to *c f*; then draw an arc striking

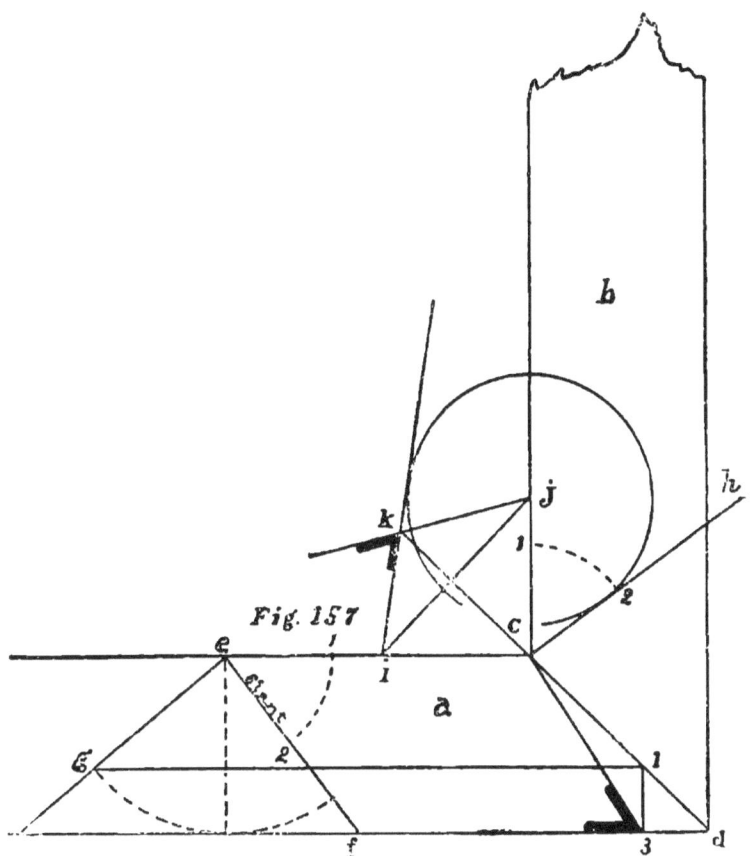

Fig. 157

the base line, as shown, using *c* as centre, thus finding point *g*; from *g* draw a line parallel to the base line until it strikes *c d* at 1; then drop a perpendicular from 1, as 1 3; connect *c* 3, thus finding the bevel for the face of the work; now make the angle 1 2 *c* equal to 1 2 *c* and draw *c h* through 2; now take any points on *c l* and *c e* of equal

distance from *c*, as *i j;* now, with *j* as centre, draw an
arc touching *c h;* then draw a line from *i* touching this
arc, as *i k;* then continue the angle line *c d* until it strikes
i k; now draw a line from *j* through this intersection,

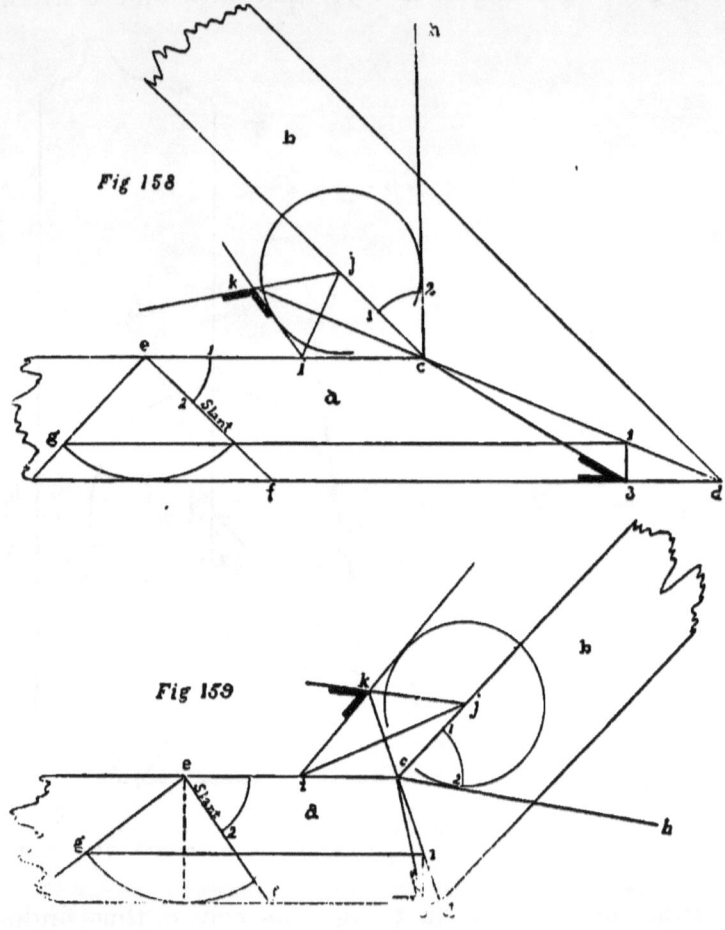

thus giving the bevel for the edge of the work. It will be
well to remember that the mitre for the face of the work
is always taken from the line at right angles to the slant.

**138—To Get the Bevels for a Hopper of any
Number of Sides** (in this case 8).—Draw a section of

the floor plan of the hopper, as *a b c d* and *e*, Fig. 160; *b c*, *c e*, etc., represent the seat of the angles; from *e* and at right angles to *c e* draw the depth of the hopper, as *e f;* then connect *c* and *f;* now bisect *c d* at *g* and draw a line perpendicular to *c d*, as *g h;* now, with *c* as centre and *c f* as radius, find *i* on *g h;* then connect *i c* and *i d*, thus giving the bevels for the face of the work, as shown at *c;* now draw a line at right angles to *g h* through *c;* then, with *c*

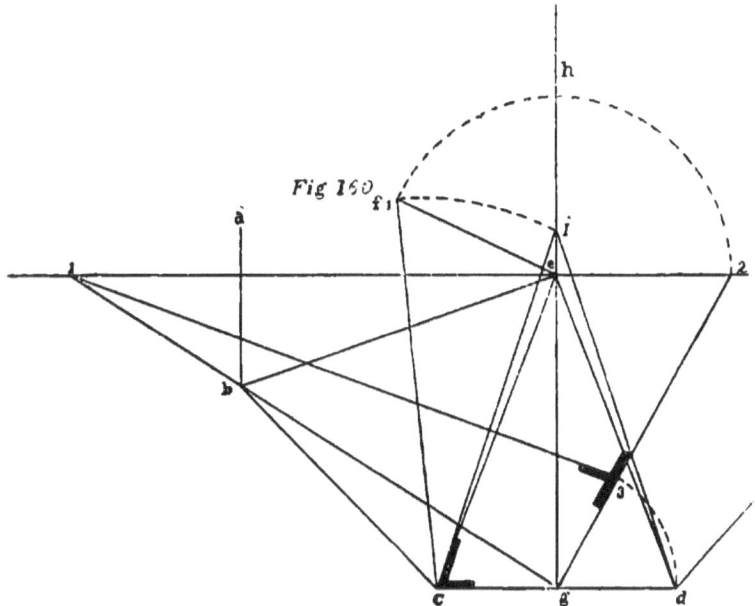

Fig 160

as centre and *e f* as radius, find point 2; then connect 2 and *g;* now draw a line at right angles to 2 *g* from *g* until it strikes the line 1 2; then, with *g* as centre and *g d* as radius, find point 3 on *g* 2; connect 1 and 3, thus giving the bevel for the edge of the work, as shown at 3. This rule applies to hoppers of any number of sides and may also be used for cutting sheathing for any roof.

139—To Find the Bevels for a Hopper with Butt Joints.—*A* and *b* represent the bottom, *c a* the slope of

the side, Fig. 161, which continue indefinitely, as shown ;
let fall a perpendicular from the top of the slope line until

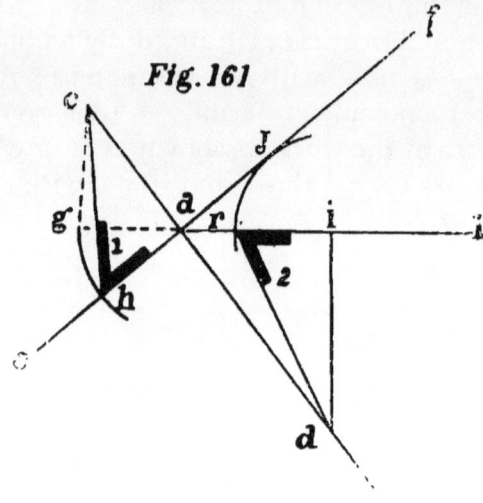

Fig. 161

it strikes the base
line, as *c g;* then
draw a line through
a at right angles to
c d, as *e f;* then,
with *a* as centre and
a g as radius, find
point *h;* connect *c*
and *h*, thus giving
the bevel for the face
of work ; then draw
a perpendicular from
any point on *a b*, as
i d; then, with *i* as
centre and *i j* as
radius, find point *k;* connect *k* and *d*, thus giving the
bevel for the edge of board, the board being jointed square.

140—To Find Hopper Bevels.—Draw an elevation
of the box or hopper, Fig. 161, as *a b c d;* then, with *b d*

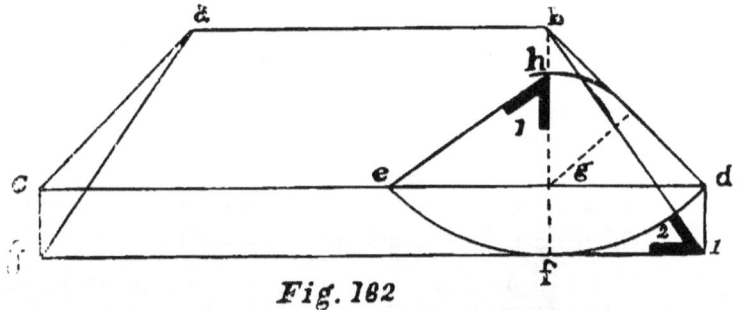

Fig. 182

as radius and *b* as centre, strike arc *c f d;* then draw line
j i parallel to *c d* and touching the arc at *f;* connect *c j*
and *d i;* then draw line from *b* to *i*, which gives the bevel
for the face cut, as shown at 2 ; then draw perpendicular

from *b* intersecting arc at *f;* then, with *g* as centre and the distance from *g* to the line *b d* as radius, strike arc at

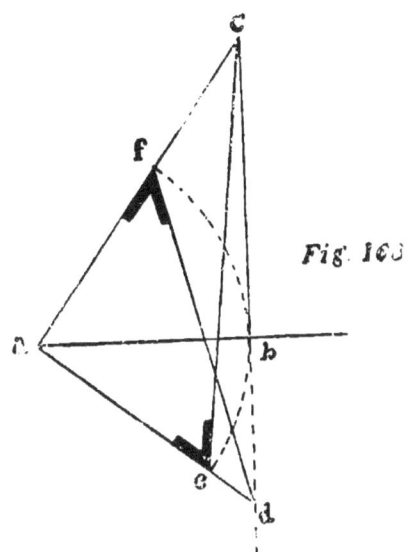

Fig. 163

h, intersecting *b f;* then draw line from *e* to *h*, thus giving the bevel at 1 for the edge of the work. In this diagram the sides have a slope of 45°, as shown by the elevation *a b c d.*

141—A Simple Way to Obtain the Cuts of a Square Hopper with Mitre Joints.—On the base *a b* draw the rise *b c*, Fig. 163, and the slant *a c;* draw a line from *a* at right angles to *a c* to strike a continuation of *c b*, as *a d;* now, with *a b* as radius and *a* as centre, draw the arc *e f;* connect *e e* and *e* will be the bevel for the face of the work. Now connect *d* and *f*, and the bevel at *f* is the bevel for the edge of the work. The above rule can be used for a hopper of any number of sides by taking for the radius *a b* one-half the width of one side of the hopper at its widest part.

142—To Lay Out a Rake Moulding to Join the Moulding on the Square Set on a Plumb Facia.—

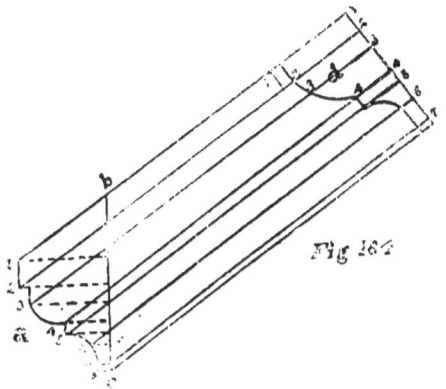

Fig. 164

Mark out the square moulding, as *a*, with *b c* as the facia, Fig. 164; then draw lines at right angles to the facia, joining all the breaks in the moulding, as 1, 2, 3, 4, etc ; then draw lines from these points on the moulding with the rake of the roof, as 1 1, 2 2, 3 3, etc., and draw a line at right angles to these, as 1 7 at *d;* make line 1 1 at *d* the same length as 1 1 at *a* and 2 2 at *d* same as at *a*, etc. ; then join these points, as shown, thus giving the profile of the rake moulding.

143—To Lay Off an Octagon Bay when the Length of One Side is Given.—First draw a line to

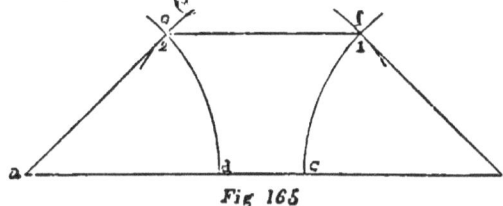

Fig 165

represent the side of the house, as *a b*, Fig. 165 ; then with the trammel set the length of the side, place the foot at *a* and find point *d;* make the distance from *d* to *c* five-twelfths of *a d;* then, with the foot of the compasses

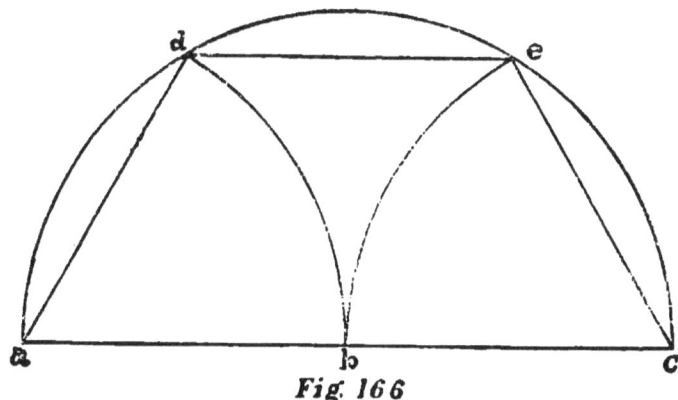

Fig. 166

at *c*, find point *b;* with the foot at *b*, strike the arc *c f;* with the foot at *d*, find point 1 ; with the foot at *a*, strike the

arc *d c;* with the foot at *c,* find point 2 ; then connect *a e,*
c f and *f b.*

144—To Lay Out a Hexagon Bay Window when
the Length of One Side is Given.—Draw the line *a c*
as side of the house, Fig. 166 ; then, with *a* as centre and

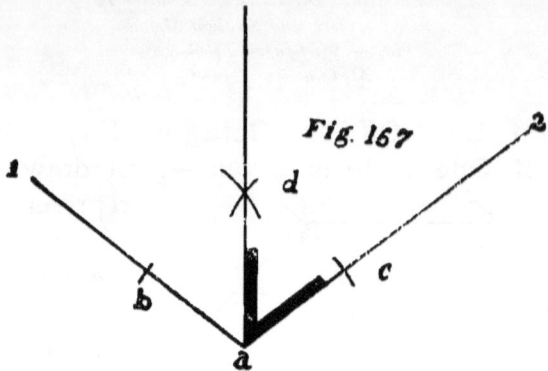

Fig. 167

the given side as radius, strike arc *d b;* then, with *b* as
centre, find point *c;* then, with *c* as centre, strike arc *e b;*
then, with *b* as centre, strike semi-circle *a d e c;* connect
a d, d e and *e c.*

**145—To Find the Side of an
Octagon when the Length on
the House is Given.**—Divide the
distance on the house by $2\frac{5}{12}$, and
the answer will be the length of the
side.

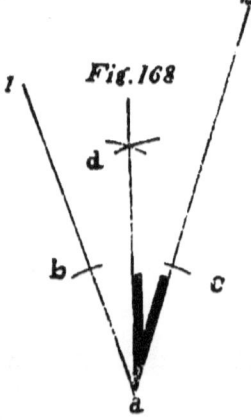

Fig. 168

To find the distance on the house
when the side is given, multiply the
side by $2\frac{5}{12}$, and the answer will be
the diameter of the octagon.

**146—To Find the Mitre Cut
for any Angle.**—Draw the angle as
1, *a,* 2, Figs. 167 and 168 ; then, with
the compasses and any radius, take *a* as centre and strike
arcs intersecting lines 1 *a* and 2 *a* at *b c;* then, with same

radius and *b c* as centres, strike arcs intersecting at *d;* then draw line from *a* through this intersection, thus giving the cut.

147—To Strike an Ogee for a Bracket.—Lay off the width and length of the bracket, as *a c* and *a b*, Fig. 169 ; then draw the line shown at the back of bracket an inch, or more if desired, from the edge of board ; then draw the diagonal *c d;* then divide *c d* into two equal parts at 3 ; then, with 3 as centre and 3 *c* as radius, strike

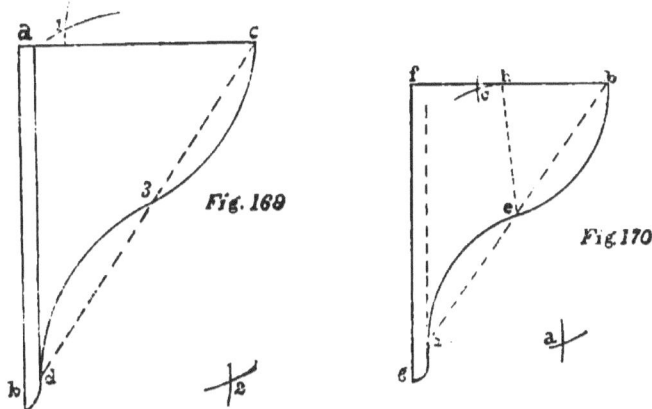

Fig. 169

Fig 170

arc at 1 ; then, with *c* as centre and same radius, strike arc intersecting at 1 ; then, with 1 as centre, strike arc *c* 3 ; then, with 3 *d* as centre, strike arcs intersecting at 2 ; then, with 2 as centre, strike arc 3 *d*.

148—Another Way to Lay Off a Bracket.—With *f g* as edge of board and *f b* as end or top of bracket, Fig. 170, draw the dotted line, as shown ; then draw the diagonal *a b* and divide it into two equal parts at *c;* then, with *c b* as centres and *c h* as radius, strike arcs intersecting at *c;* then, with same radius and *c* as centre, strike arc *b c;* then, with same radius and *a c* as centres, strike arcs intersecting at *d;* then, with *d* as centre, strike arc *c a*.

149—To Lay Out the Ventilating Hole of a Privy Door.—*B a c* represents the top edge of the door, Fig.

171; with *a* as centre and the desired radius, draw the semi-circle *b* 1 2 *c;* now, with *b c* as radius and *b* and *c* as centres, draw arcs intersecting at *e;* then, with same radius

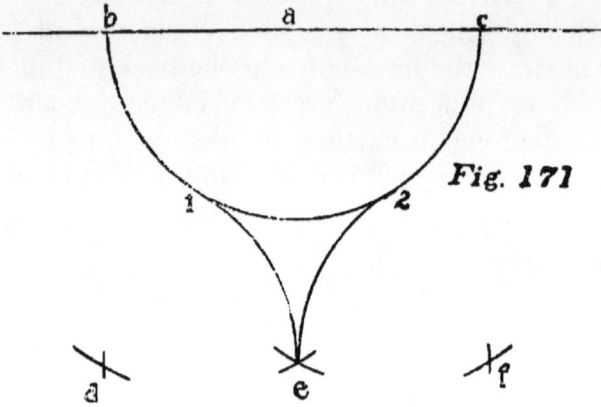

Fig. 171

and *a* as centre, draw arcs at *d* and *f;* now, with *a c* as radius and *e* as centre, draw arcs intersecting these at *d* and *f,* and with same radius and these intersections as centres, draw the arcs 1 *e* and 2 *c.*

150—To Lay Out a Privy Seat.—Draw two lines at right angles to each other, as 2 4 and 3 8, Fig. 172; make 2 4 about eight inches long; with 1 as centre and 1 4 as radius, draw a circle; now draw lines from 2 and 4 through 7; then, with 2 4 as radius and

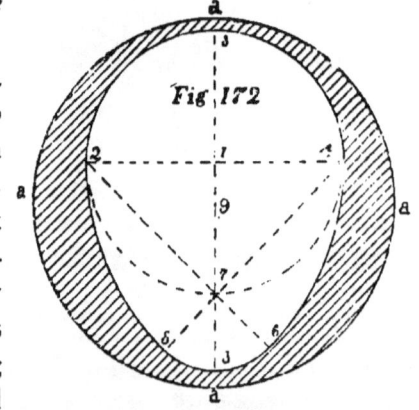

Fig. 172

2 4 as centre, draw the arcs 4 6 and 2 5; now, with 7 as centre and 7 6 as radius, draw the arc 5 6, completing the oval; now find the centre of the line 3 8, as 9, and with this point as centre and 2 7 as radius, draw the circle *a a a a;* saw out to the oval line and round off to the circle.

151—To Lay Out a Hole in a Roof for a Stovepipe or Flagstaff.

—Draw a section of the pipe or staff, as *c*, and lay off the slope of the roof, as *a b*, and the run as *d b*, Fig. 173; now, with *a b* and *d b* as axis, draw an ellipse, as shown at Fig. 174, which will be the shape and size of the hole.

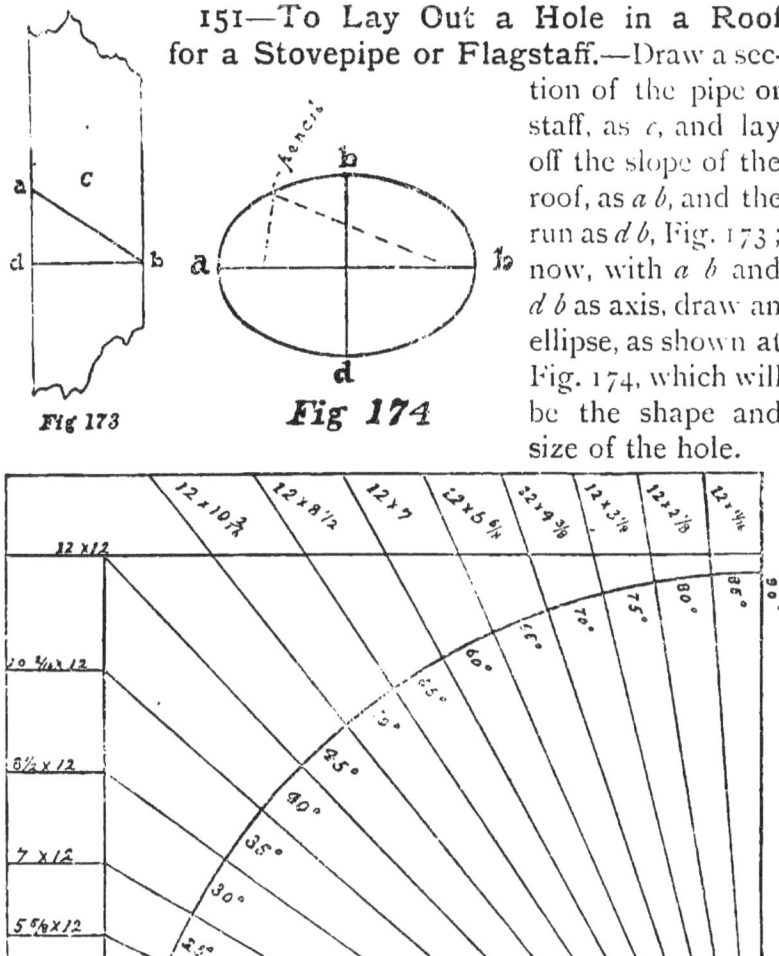

Fig 173

Fig 174

Fig 175

152—Diagram to Obtain Degrees on the Square.—
For instance, if a pitch of 25° is required, use 5⅝ on the
tongue of the square and 12 on the blade; for 65° it is
just the reverse, or 12 on the tongue and 5⅝ on the blade.
See Fig. 175.

153—To Mitre a Circle and Straight Moulding.—
Draw a full-size plan of the two mouldings, as shown in
Fig. 176; draw *a b c*, as shown, in the centre of the space

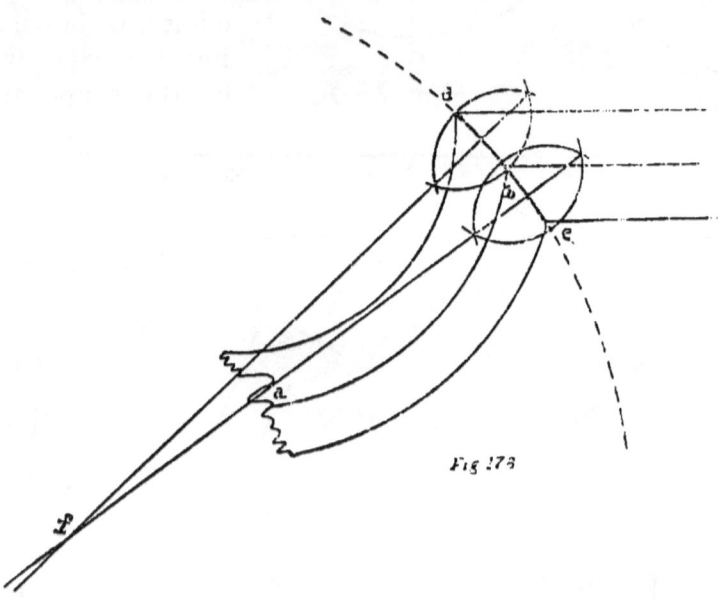

Fig 176

between the two outside lines: connect *d* and *b* and *b* and
c; bisect *d b* and *b c* and draw lines at right angles to them
to meet at *f;* then *f d* is the radius of the mitre joint.

154—Sand-paper File.—A convenient sand-paper file
or rasp is made by dressing a stick to the desired shape
and rip it in two up to the handle; then take a piece of
sand-paper and wrap around the stick, placing the two
edges in the split; place a small screw in the end to keep
in place, as shown in Figs. 178 and 179.

155—To Make a Saw Jointer.—Take a block of wood—say, 1x2x3—and bore a hole through it, as shown in Fig. 180; then run a saw cut from the edge to the hole;

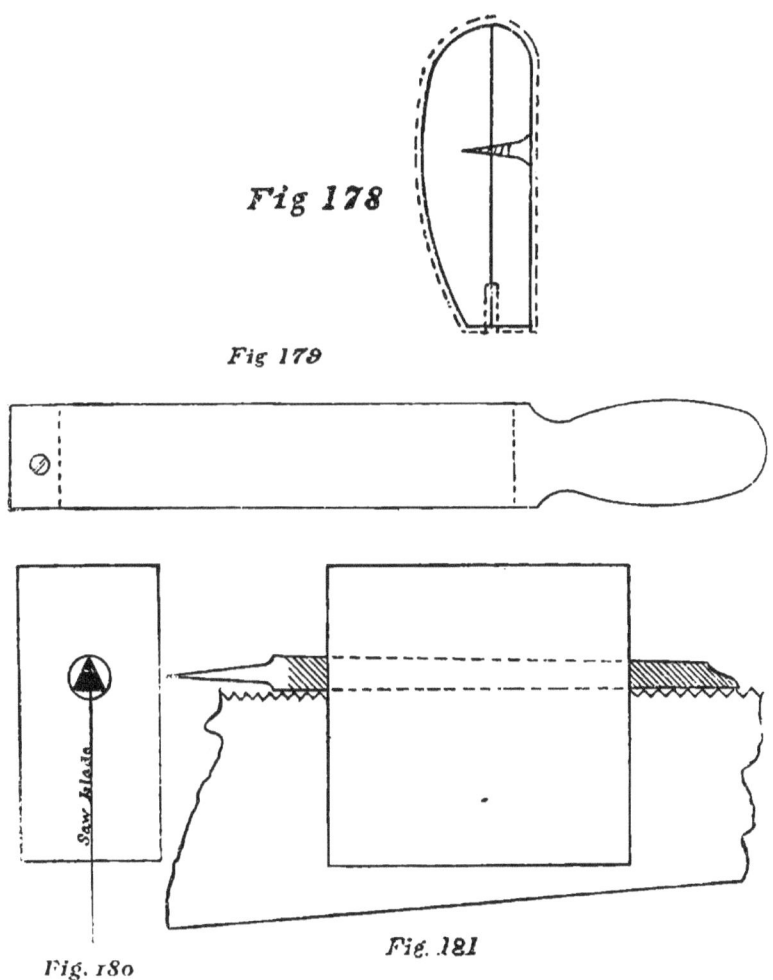

Fig 178

Fig 179

Fig. 180

Fig. 181

now insert a file in the hole, keeping one side square with the saw cut; now place the block on the tooth edge, Fig. 181, of the saw blade, and by running it from end to end all the teeth may be jointed to a uniform length.

156—To Find the Cut on the Square of any Angle.—*A b c* represents the angle, Fig. 182 ; then draw lines parallel to *a b* and *b c*, making them equally distant from *a b* and *b c;* then draw a line from angle *b* through intersection *d*, which is the bevel ; then apply the square, as shown.

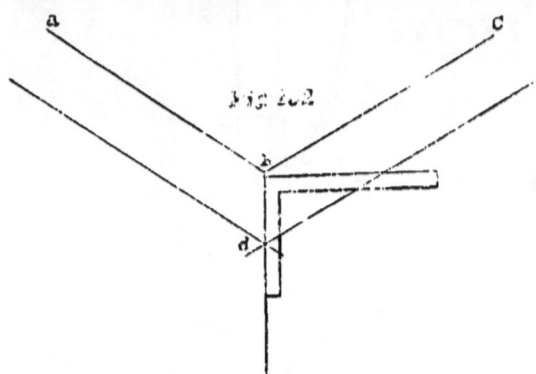

Fig. 182.

157—To Fit Corner Washstands.—Mark on the floor the position the stand is to occupy, as shown by the dotted lines, Fig. 183 ; then place the stand in position, as shown, and the distance from the stand along the wall to the position it is to set is the space to compass

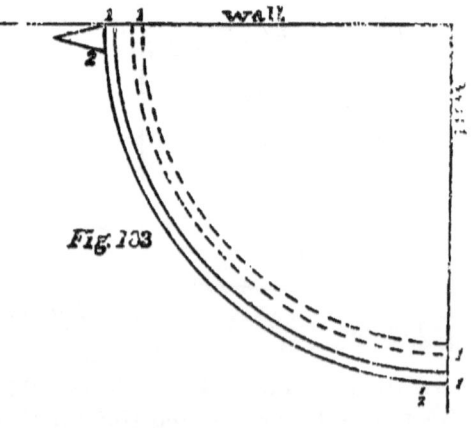

Fig. 183.

wall

off each side, as shown ; the distance from 1 to 2 is made equal to 1 1.

158—To Bend a Straight Piece of Moulding Over a Circle or Segmental Head.

—Take a soft piece of the moulding and rip it into strips, as shown, keeping

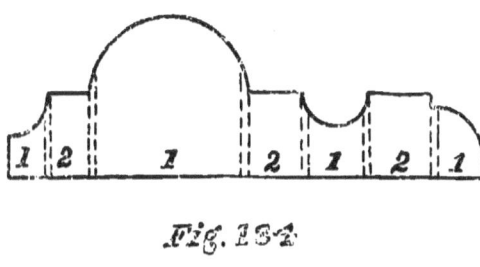

each member of the moulding separate ; use two pieces of moulding the desired length ; rip the one piece so as to have one-half the members whole, as

Fig. 184.

2, 2, 2 in Fig. 184 ; then rip the other piece so as to have the other members whole, as 1, 1, 1. The strips can be steamed or wet, when each piece can be bent on separate and sand-papered off, when the joints are hardly noticeable, as they come at the intersection of the different members of the moulding.

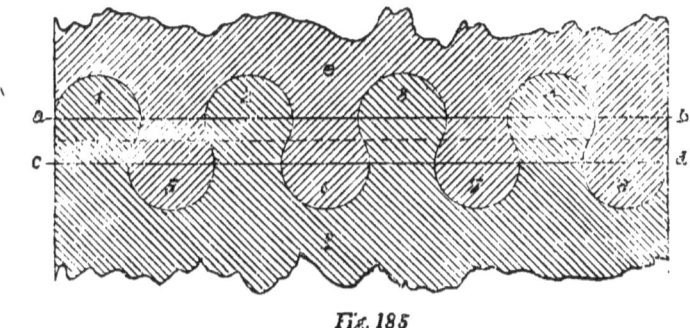

Fig. 185

159—Splicing Counter Tops.

—The following shows a very good method of splicing counter tops, etc., Fig. 185. Draw two lines square across the end of each board, as *a b* and *c d*—say half an inch apart ; then, with *a c* as radius, draw the arcs, as shown, with the centres on the lines *a b* and *c d;* then bore the holes 1, 2, 3, 4 in board *c*, using an inch bit, and trim the dovetails 5, 6, 7, 8; 1, 2, 3, 4 is the dovetail of board f and 5, 6, 7, 8 are the holes. The diagram shows the splice after the boards have been put together.

160—To Mark Inside Blinds.—The following diagrams, Figs. 186, 187 and 188, will explain how to mark

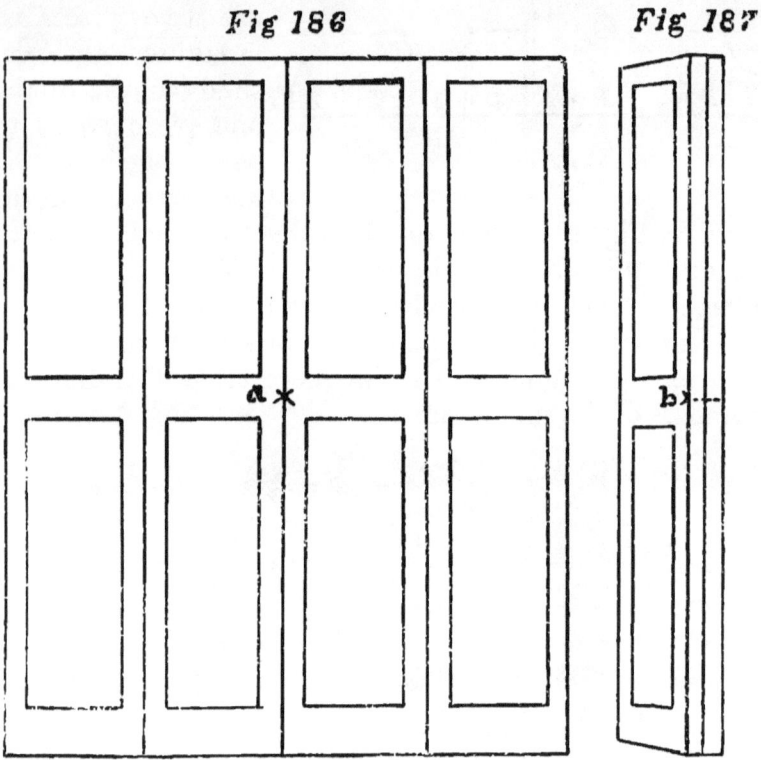

Fig 186   *Fig 187*

inside blinds for cutting them in two: After they are hung shut them together and mark on the edge of the meeting stiles the centre of the meeting rail, as a in Fig. 186; shut each flap together and square the mark over to the hanging stile, as b, Fig. 187; then open the flap and with a straight-edge mark them as shown in Fig. 188.

161—To Mark Hinges on Doors and Jambs.—

A quick and easy way to mark the hinges on doors and jambs is to take a stick or strip the length of the door and mark on it the position of the hinges and drive in wire brads so that the points stick through about one-eighth of an inch, as shown in Fig. 189. To mark the door, place the stick on the edge of the door, keeping the top end of the stick and the top end of the door even ; press the stick on the door and the brad points will mark the position of the hinge, as Fig. 190. In marking the jamb, keep the stick down one-sixteenth of an inch to give a little "play" above the door, as shown in Fig. 191.

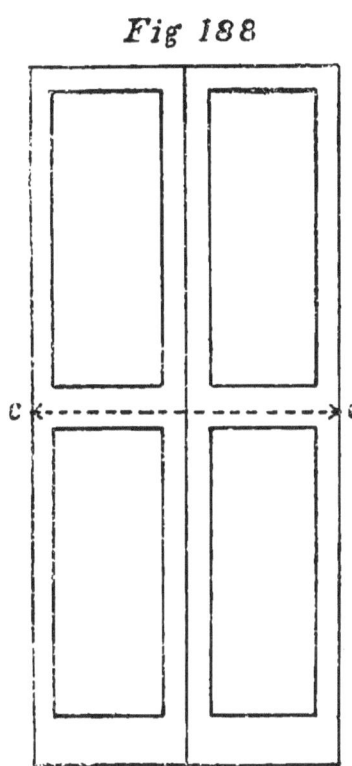

Fig 188

162—To Make a Saw Clamp.

—A convenient saw clamp for outside use is made by taking two pieces of 2x3 or 2x4 about three feet long and cutting a V in one end, as shown in Fig. 192; nail them together with a couple of strips, as Fig. 194; now take two pieces of 1x4 the length of the saw and bevel them to fit in the V ; place the saw in the clamps and place them in the frame and a couple of taps with a hammer will tighten them.

163—Knots Used by Carpenters.

—*a* and *g*, mooring knots; *b*, knot used by sailors and horsemen which will not slip ; *c*, square knot ; *d*, timber hitch ; *e* and *f*, knots used to fasten the centre of a line to the top of a

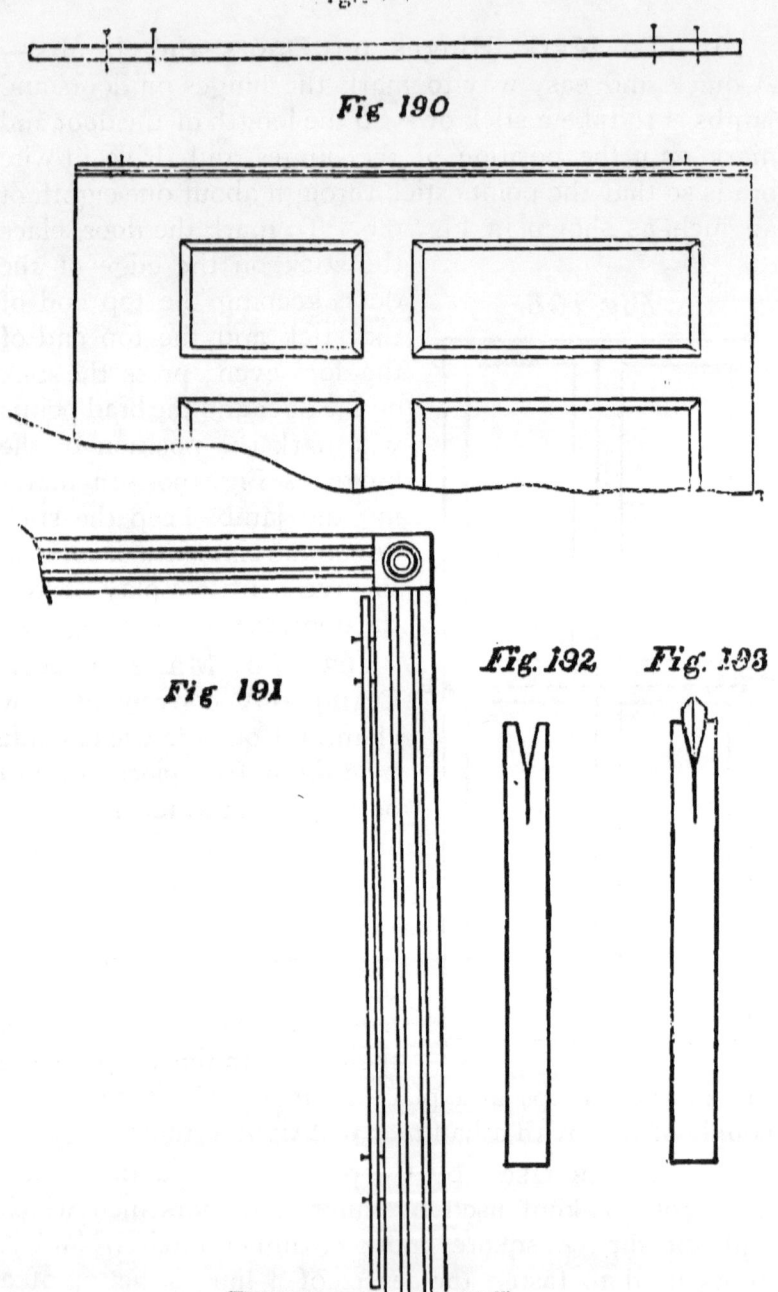

Fig. 189

Fig 190

Fig 191

Fig. 192

Fig. 193

mast when both ends of the rope are used as guy lines; *h*, blackwall hitch. Fig. 195.

164—Methods of Splicing Timbers.—Fig. 196.

165—To Find the Contents of a Round Taper-ing Stick of Timber.—Multiply the diameter of one

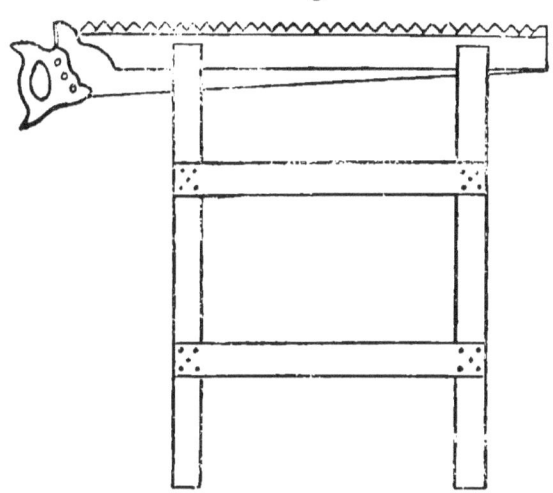

Fig. 194

end by the diameter of the other end, and to this product add one-third of the square of the difference of the diame-ters; then multiply this answer by .7854, which gives the mean area between the two ends, which multiplied by the height gives the cubical contents, as: Find the contents of a round stick 6″ in diameter at one end and 12″ at the other and 10′ long: 12×6=72, 12-6=6, 6×6=36, 36÷3=12, 72+12=84, 84×.7854=65.97″, the mean area between the ends; 65.97″×10′=7916.4 cubic inches, which reduced to feet equals 7916.4÷1728=4.5 cubic feet, the contents of the stick. If the stick tapers to a point, to find the contents, multiply the area of the base by one-third the height. This rule applies also to square timber tapering to a point.

166—To Find the Contents of Tapering Tim-ber.—Multiply the side of the large end by the side of the

small end and to the product add one-third of the square
of the difference of the sides, which gives the mean area

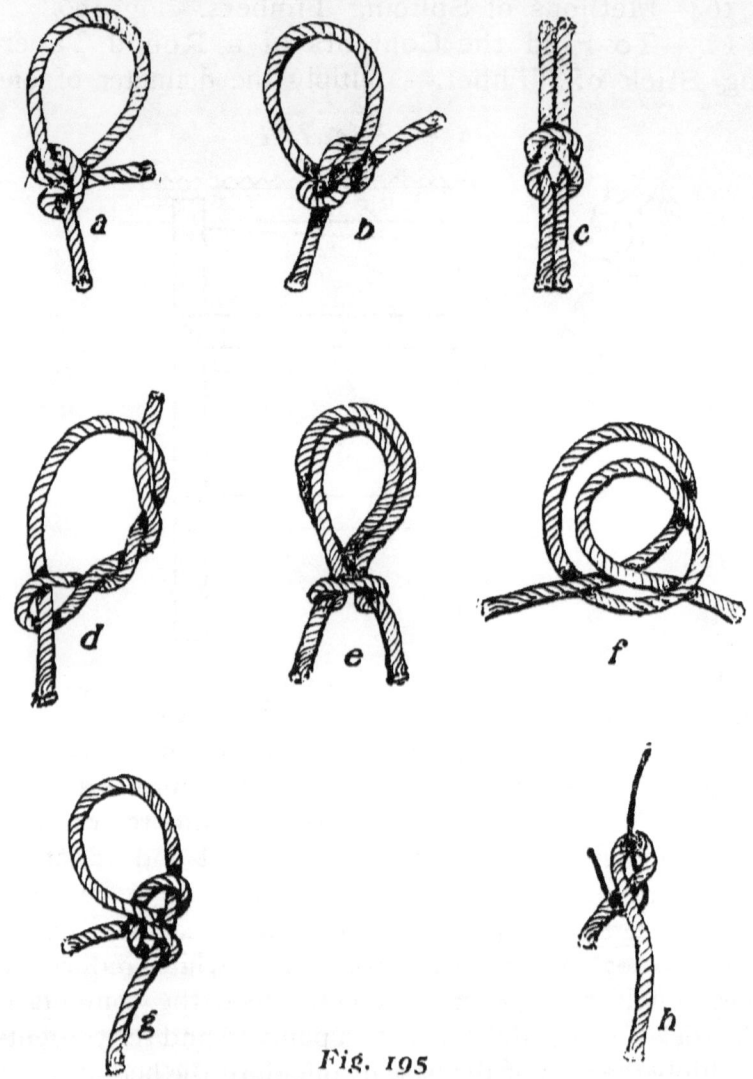

Fig. 195

between the two ends, which multiplied by the length
gives the cubical contents, as the following: Find the contents of a stick 18″ square at one end and 6″ square at the

other and 12′ long—18″×6″=108″, 18″-6″= 12, 12×12=144, 144÷3=48, 108″+48″=156″, the mean area between the two ends; 12′, the length, reduced to inches equals 144″;

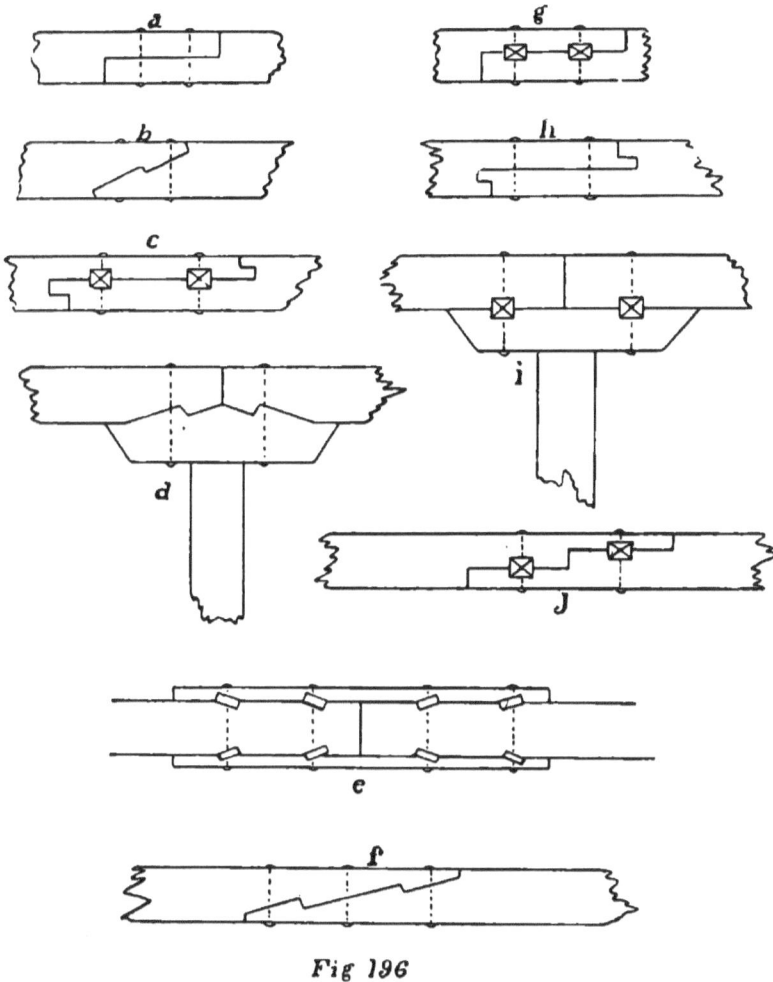

Fig 196

156″×144″=22464 cubic inches, which reduced to feet equals 22464÷1728=13 cubic feet, the contents of the stick (13×12=156′, board measure.)

CHAPTER XVI.

167—To Find Mitres on the Steel Square.—
12×12 equals square mitre; 7×4 equals triangle mitre; $13\frac{3}{4} \times 10$ equals pentagon mitre; 4×7 equals hexagon mitre; $12\frac{1}{2} \times 6$ equals heptagon mitre; 7×17 equals octagon mitre; $22\frac{1}{2} \times 9$ equals nonagon mitre; $9\frac{1}{2} \times 3$ equals decagon mitre.

All plumb lines radiate from the centre of the earth, showing that if it were possible to make walls perfectly plumb they would not be parallel.

All level lines are at right angles to an imaginary line from the centre of the level to the centre of the earth. If a line is drawn parallel to the earth's surface it has a curve of eight inches to the mile.

168—Table for Finding the Area of Angles Cut on the Square or Number of Sides of any Polygon.—
To find the cut, use the figures in column 5 on the blade and column 6 on the tongue, and the tongue will give the cut. To find the area, multiply the square of the side by the factor in column 4

No. of sides.	Name of polygon.	Angle of polygon.	Factor of area.	Figure on blade of square.	Figure on tongue of square.
3	Triangle...............	60°	0.4330	4	7
4	Square...............	90°	1.	12	12
5	Pentagon...............	108°	1.7204	9 ½	7
6	Hexagon...............	120°	2.5981	10 ½	6
7	Heptagon...............	128⅝°	3.6339	10 ½	5
8	Octagon...............	135°	4.8284	17	7
9	Nonagon...............	140°	6.1818	11 ½	4
10	Decagon...............	144°	7.6942	12'	4
11	Undecagon...............	148°	9.3656	10 ¼	3
12	Dodecagon...............	150°	11.1962	11 ½	3

169—To Cut a Stick Square or on an Angle of 45° Without a Square.—Place the saw on the stick in a position to saw and note the reflection of the stick on the side of the saw. If the reflection and the stick are in a line, then the saw is in a position to make a square cut. If the reflection and the stick are at right angles, then the saw is in position for a square mitre or angle of 45°.

170—To Find the Power of a Lever.—RULE: As the distance between the weight and the fulcrum is to the distance between the power and the fulcrum, so is the power to the weight.

To find the power of pulleys or set of blocks. RULE: As one is to twice the number of movable pulleys, so is the power to the weight.

To clear lime stains from windows: after the lime has been scraped off, wash the window with diluted muriatic acid, care being taken to keep the acid off the paint or sash.

171—To Find the Safe Loads on Pine Beams.— When the beam is supported at each end and the load uniformly distributed: Twice the breadth by the square of the depth by 85; this answer divided by the span in feet equals the safe load in pounds. When the load is concentrated at the centre: The breadth by the square of

the depth by 85 ; this answer divided by the span in feet equals the safe load in pounds.

For the strength of yellow pine use 100 as co-efficient instead of 85 ; wrought iron, 666 ; steel, 1333 ; hemlock, 66.

172—To Find the Strength of Cast Iron Beams.— RULE: Multiply the sectional area of the bottom flanges in square inches by the depth of the beam in inches, and divide the product by the length between the supports, also in inches; then 514 times the quotient will be the breaking weight in pounds.

173—To Find the Breaking Stress of Pine Timber.—Multiply the square of the depth by the breadth in inches, and this product by 10.840; divide this product by the length between bearings in feet, multiplied by the depth in inches; the quotient is the breaking weight in pounds.   One-tenth is a safe load.

174—The Tensile Strength of Wrought Iron Wire is 100,000 pounds per square inch; of steel, 100,-000; brass wire, 50,000; iron, 75,000; cast iron, 18,000. In use take one-quarter of the above as breaking weight.

175—The Crushing Strength of Cast Iron is 75,-000 to 100,000 pounds per square inch.

176—To Find the Depth of a Flitch Plate Girder to Carry a Given Distributed Weight.—RULE: Multiply the weight by the span and divide the answer by 2 by 100 by the thickness of the wooden beams plus 1500 by the thickness of the flitch plate; the square root of this product will be the required depth of the girder. Example: Find the depth of a flitch plate girder to carry a distributed weight of 14,000 pounds with a span of 30 feet; thickness of wooden beams 12 inches and plate 1 inch.

$$14000 \times 30 = 420000$$
$$2 \times 100 \times 12 = 2400$$
$$2400 + 1500 \times 1 = 3900$$
$$420000 \div 3900 = 107.68$$
$$\sqrt{107.68} = 10.3,$$ or 10.3 inches, the depth of the girder.

177—To Find the Depth of a Flitch Plate Girder to Carry a Given Weight at the Centre.—RULE: Multiply the weight by the span, and divide this answer by 100 by the thickness of wooden beams, plus 750 by the thickness of the flitch plate; the square root of this product is the required depth. Example: Find the depth of a flitch plate girder to carry a weight of 14,0co pounds at the centre of span, the span being 30 feet and the width of timbers 12 inches; the thickness of plate being 1 inch.

Weight Span
14000 × 30 = 420000
Thickness of two 6-in. timbers

100 × 12 = 1200
1200 + 750 × 1 = 1950
420000 ÷ 1950 = 215.38
$\sqrt{215.38} = 14.6$, or 14.6 inches, the depth of the girder.

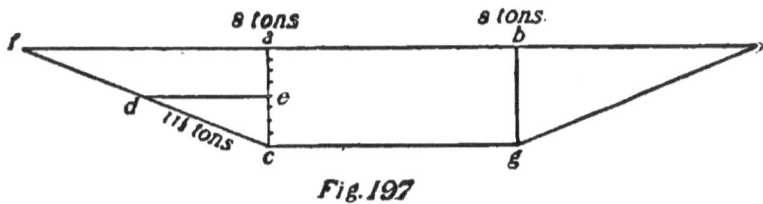

Fig. 197

178—To Find the Strain on Hog Chains (Mechanical method).—Draw to a scale a plan of the hog chain or truss, as Fig. 197; find the weight to be carried at the two points a and b, in this case eight tons; bisect the line $a c$ at e and draw $d e$ parallel to $f a$; divide the line $a e$ into as many equal parts as there are tons in the weight, which is eight; each space represents a ton of weight; find how many of these spaces there are in the line $d e$, which is $11\frac{1}{3}$, or $11\frac{1}{3}$ tons stress on the rod $f c$. RULE: As the length of the line $a e$ is to the weight to be supported, so is half the length of $f c$ to the stress on the rod.

179—To Find the Strain on Roof Truss with Single Rod.—The strains on a truss built as shown in Fig. 198 are found as follows: Three-tenths of the distributed

weight by half the length of the chord divided by the
length of *a b* equals the tensile strain on the chord; five-
eighths of weight equals tensile strain on the rod; three-
tenths of the distributed weight by the length of the
rafter divided by the length of *a b* equals the compression in the rafter. For concentrated weight at the cen-

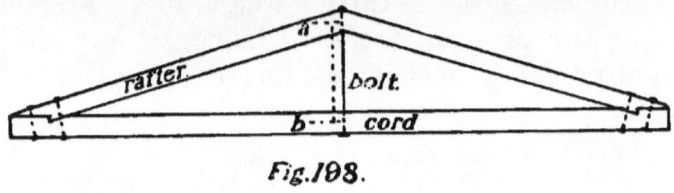

Fig. 198.

tre: One-half the weight by half the length of the chord
divided by the length of *a b* equals the strain on the
chord; the strain on the rod is equal to the weight; one-
half the weight by the length of the rafter divided by
the length of *a b* equals the compression in the rafter.

**180—To Find the Strain on Roof Truss with
Two Rods.**—The strains on a truss built as shown in
Fig. 199 are as follows: The distributed weight by 0.367

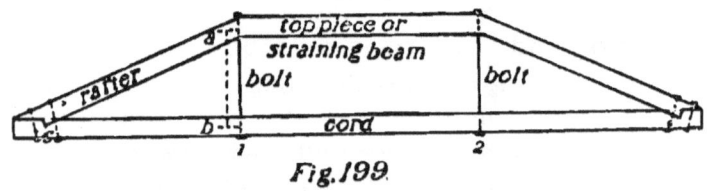

Fig. 199.

by one-third the length of the chord, or *c b*, divided by
the length of *a b* equals the strain on the chord or the compression of top piece; the weight by 0.367 equals the
strain on the rods; the distributed weight by 0.367 by the
length of the rafter divided by the length of *a b* equals
the compression in the rafter. When the weight is concentrated at 1 and 2: The weight by one-third the length
of the chord or *c b* divided by the length of *a b* equals
the strain on the chord or the compression of the top piece;

the weight equals the strain on the rods; the weight by the length of the rafter divided by the length of $a\ b$ equals the compression of the rafter.

The diameter of a single rod to carry a given weight may be found by dividing the weight by 9425, and the

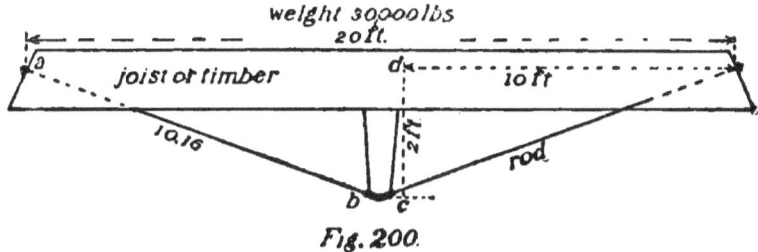

Fig. 200.

square root of the product will be the diameter of the roa allowing 12,000 pounds per square inch in the rod.

When two rods carry a given weight, take half the weight and proceed as above.

181—To Find the Strain on the Rods of a Hog Chain Girder.—RULE: Three-tenths of the distributed weight by the length of the rod $a\ b$ multiplied by the length of $c\ d$ equals the strain on the rod. Example, Fig.

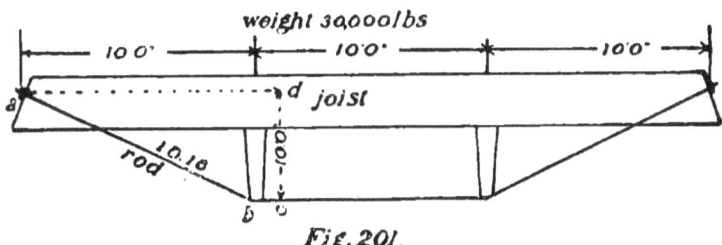

Fig. 201.

200: Find the strain on the above rods; length of $a\ b$, 10.16 feet; length of $c\ d$, two feet; weight, 30,000 pounds; $\frac{3}{10}$ of 30,000 = 9,000, 10.16 ÷ 2 = 5.08, 9,000 × 5.08 = 45.720 pounds, the strain on the rod. For concentrated load at centre, the strain on the rod equals one-half the weight by the length of $a\ b$ divided by the length of $c\ d$.

182—To Find the Strain on the Rods of a Hog Chain Girder with Two Struts or Bearings.—RULE: Multiply the distributed weight by 0.367 and multiply this answer by the length of *a b* divided by *c d;* the answer will be the strain on the rod. Example, Fig. 201 : Find the strain on the above rods; length of *a b*, 10.16 feet; length of *c d*, 2 feet; distributed weight, 30,000 pounds ; 30,000×0.367=11010, 10.16÷2=5.08, 11010×5.08= 50850 pounds, the strain on the rod. With concentrated load over each of the bearings, the strain equals the weight by the length of *a b* divided by the length of *c d*.

CHAPTER XVII.

183—Soundness of Timbers.—The soundness of timber may be ascertained by placing the ear close to one end of the log, while another person strikes a succession of blows on the other end, using a hammer or mallet. If only a dull sound is heard, then the stick is unsound.

184—Age of Trees.—It has been estimated that the age attained by the elm is 335 years; of a palm, 600 to 700; of an olive, 700; of a plane tree, 720; of a cedar, 800; of an oak, 1,500; of a yew, 2,880; of a taxodium, 4,000; of a baobab, 5,000.

185—To Remove Old Glass from Sash.—Take a hot iron and run along the surface of the putty, when it can easily be removed with a chisel.

186—Penny as Applied to Nails.—The term penny is derived from pound. It originally meant so many pounds to the thousand. Three-penny nails would mean three pounds to the thousand nails; eight-penny, eight pounds to the thousand nails, etc.

187—To Mark Tools.—Take seven ounces of nitric acid and one ounce of muriatic acid; mix and shake together; then cover the tool where you wish to put your name with beeswax; then take a needle or some sharp instrument and scratch the name plainly in the beeswax, and apply the acid with a feather, filling each letter in the wax; let it remain from two to eight minutes, then dip in water and clean off; then rub with oil.

188—Waterproof Glue.—Waterproof glue is made by boiling one pound of glue in two quarts of skim milk.

189—Number of Shingles in a Roof.—If laid 4″ to the weather it takes 9 to the square foot; if laid 4½″, it takes 8; if laid 5″, it takes 7½; if laid 6″, it takes 6.

190—To Find the Weight of Grindstones.—Square the diameter (in inches) and multiply this answer by the thickness (in inches); then multiply by .06363 (decimal); the answer will be the weight of the stone in pounds.

191—Standard of Specific Gravity.—The standard of specific gravity is water, which weighs 1,000 ounces to the cubic foot.

192—Hollow Columns.—A hollow cast iron column will carry as much weight as a solid one of the same weight.

193—Hints and Recipes.—Lime water is a fire-proof protection for shingles.

Common brick will absorb a pint of water each.

A closet finished with red cedar is death to moths and insects.

Timber for posts is made almost rot-proof by a coat of hot coal tar.

To make chimneys soot-proof use salt in the lime to plaster the flues—one part of salt to three of lime.

In leading hinges into stone if you put a few drops of oil in the hole before running in the lead there will be no danger of it exploding and flying into your face.   2. Or put a piece of resin the size of the end of a man's thumb in the lead before pouring.

Corner blocks, when the trimmings are to be stained or finished natural, should always be placed with the grain perpendicular, as the end wood turns black when stained, and if the grain was placed horizontal would show at the side.

Marine Glue.—Glue twelve parts, water sufficient to

dissolve; add yellow resin three parts; melt, and then add turpentine four parts and mix well together.

MOISTURE-PROOF GLUE.—Glue, five parts; resin, four parts; red ochre, two parts; mix well with the least possible amount of water.

To PETRIFY WOOD.—Gum salt, rock alum, white vinegar, chalk and Pebbel's powder of equal quantities; mix well together; after the ebullition is over, throw in the wood and it will become petrified.

To BEND LEAD PIPE.—Fill the pipe with dry sand and bend gradually into the desired shape.

To MAKE GRINDSTONES FROM SAND.—Take sharp sand thirty-two parts, shellac ten parts, powdered glass two parts; melt in an iron pot and cast into moulds.

The largest iron girder in the United States is 105 feet long and weighs seventy tons. It was built by the Keystone Bridge Co., of Pittsburgh, Pa., for the City Hall, San Francisco.

Bicromate of potash is used to darken new mahogany. It gives it the shade of old mahogany furniture.

The following process of impregnating wood for its preservation has been patented in Germany: First coat the wood with a solution of zinc vitriol and then with a solution of chloride of calcium.

Paint for shingle roofs: One barrel coal tar, ten pounds asphaltum, ten pounds ground slate, two gallons dead oil; add the oil after heating the mixture.

To remove old paint wash with a solution of caustic potash; it will loosen the paint in a few hours.

To preserve sandstone saturate the stone as deeply as possible with a solution of silicate of soda, then wash with chloride of calcium. It should be applied with great care and very weak. If the silicate of soda is too strong it will form a gummy coating. The washes should be applied several times.

There are stones in the pyramids of Egypt thirty feet long, weighing eight hundred tons. The stones fit so close together that a knife blade can be passed over the surface without discovering the joints, in which no mortar was used.

In the United States there are ten States which produce marble, of which Vermont furnishes more than all the rest combined. There are 103 quarries in operation and the total value of the annual output is $3,488,170, of which Vermont produces $2,169,560; California, $87,030; Georgia, $196,250; Maryland, $139,816; Tennessee, $419,467; Massachusetts, $35,000; Idaho, $2,500; New York, $354,-197; Pennsylvania, $41,850; Virginia, $42,500.

To remove rust stains from wood wash the disfigured parts with a solution of two ounces of oxalic acid to one pint of hot water.

In fitting doors always keep the hollow side next the stop or rebate strip.

To make paint stick to metal sandpaper the metal before applying the paint.

When hanging transoms where possible, if the transom is to be hung at the top, hang them so that when they are open the glass will lay on the wood and not on the putty.

The largest plank in the world (up to date) is sixteen feet five inches wide, twelve feet nine inches long and five inches thick, and was taken from a California redwood tree, thirty-five feet in diameter, for exhibition at the World's Fair.

A strong glue for inlaying or veneering is made by selecting the best light brown glue; dissolve this in water and to every pint add half a gill of the best vinegar and half an ounce of isinglass.

Washstands are usually set two feet six inches from the floor.

The relative strength of timbers is estimated by multi-

plying the breadth by the square of the depth. Example—
How many times as strong is a joist $2\frac{1}{2}'' \times 15''$ when supported on its narrow side as when supported on its broad
side : $2\frac{1}{2} \times 2\frac{1}{2} = 6\frac{1}{4}$, $6\frac{1}{4} \times 15 = 93\frac{7}{10}$, $15 \times 15 = 225$, $225 \times 2\frac{1}{2} = 562\frac{1}{2}$,
$562\frac{1}{2} \div 93\frac{7}{10} = 6$. or six times stronger.

A good oil for oil stones is made by mixing equal
quantities of sperm and carbon oil (coal oil).

To fit keys in locks, where the lock cannot be taken out,
hold the key over a flame until it is well smoked, then
place in lock and turn carefully ; then take out, and where
it strikes and needs filing will be marked in the soot.

When working in hard woods bore a hole in the end
of your hammer handle and fill with soap or beeswax.
When you wish to drive in a nail place the point of the
nail in the soap or beeswax and it will drive much easier.

When filing a saw always file with the point of the file
toward the handle of the saw, as this leaves the ragged
edge on the back of the tooth.

A flour barrel is twenty-eight to thirty inches high and
twenty to twenty-one inches in diameter.

To prevent logs and planks splitting at the end when
drying saturate muriatic acid with lime and apply to the
end like whitewash.

To soften ivory so it will cut easy soak three or four
days in a mixture of three ounces nitric acid and fifteen
ounces water.

To harden ivory after it has been softened wrap in a
piece of white paper and cover with dry decrepitated salt ;
let stand for twenty-four hours.

The United States standard bushel contains 2,150.42
cubic inches.

The United States standard gallon contains 231 cubic
inches.

To find the length of one side of an octagon when the
diameter is given multiply the diameter by .4141.

Woods which are heavier than water are : Irish bog oak, ebony, mahogany, heart of oak, French box, pomegranate and lignum-vitæ.

To measure square timber (board measure) multiply the length, width and thickness together and divide the product by twelve. Example—How many feet in a stick 8"×10", 18' long : 8×10×18=1440, 1440÷12==120'.

The radius of segment window or door frames is generally equal to the width of the frame.

Beams of timber, when laid with their concentric layers vertical, are stronger than when laid horizontal in the proportion of eight to seven.

194—A Preparation to Render Wood Fire-proof.—
Sal-ammoniæ, fifteen parts ; boracic acid, five parts ; glue, fifty parts ; gelatine, one and one-half parts ; water, one hundred parts ; add powdered talc to give the mixture the necessary consistency. Heat to 120° to 140° Fahr. and apply with a brush.

195—How to Make Different Kinds of Varnish.—
(1) Resin, four pounds ; beeswax, one-half pound ; boiled oil, one gallon ; mix with heat, and then add spirits of turpentine, two quarts.

(2) COPAL VARNISH.—African copal, one part ; melt and then add hot oil, two parts ; boil till the mixture becomes stringy, then cool a little and add spirits of turpentine, three parts.

(3) TURPENTINE VARNISH.—Resin, one pound ; boiled oil, one pound ; melt and add turpentine, two pounds ; mix well.

(4) MASTIC VARNISH.—Mastic, one pound ; white wax, one ounce ; oil turpentine, one gallon ; reduce the gums small and heat in a closed vessel till dissolved.

(5) CABINET MAKERS' VARNISH—Pale shellac, seven parts ; mastic, six-tenths of a part ; strong alcohol, ten parts ; dissolve and dilute with alcohol.

196—How to Make Stains of Different Kinds.—

CHERRY.—Rain water, three quarts; annetto, four ounces; boil in a copper kettle till the annetto is dissolved; then put in a piece of potash the size of a walnut; keep on the fire half an hour and it is then ready for use.

MAHOGANY.—(1) Put two ounces of dragon's blood, bruised, into a quart of oil of turpentine; let stand in a warm place until dissolved, when it is ready for use.

(2) Dragon's blood, one-half ounce; alkanet, one-quarter ounce; aloes, one drachm; spirits of wine, sixteen ounces.

RED.—Brazil wood, eleven parts; alum, four parts; water, eighty-five parts; boil together.

BLUE.—Logwood, seven parts; blue vitriol, one part; water, twenty-two parts; boil.

BLACK.—Logwood, nine parts; sulphate of iron, one part; water, twenty-five parts; boil.

GREEN.—Verdigris, one part; vinegar, three parts; dissolve.

YELLOW.—French berries, seven parts; alum, one part; water, ten parts; boil.

PURPLE.—Logwood, eleven parts; alum, three parts; water, twenty-nine parts; boil.

BLACK WALNUT.—Burnt umber, two parts; rose pink, one part; glue, one part; water sufficient to mix; heat and dissolve completely.

EBONY.—Drop black, two parts; rose pink, one part; turpentine sufficient to mix.

SATINWOOD.—Alcohol, two parts; powdered gamboge, three ounces; ground turmeric, six ounces; steep and strain through muslin.

ROSEWOOD.—Alcohol, one gallon; cam wood, two ounces; set in a warm place twenty-four hours, then add aquafortis, one ounce; extract logwood, three ounces; when dissolved is ready for use.

197—Colors Used to Mix Paints for Tints.—Red

and black make brown ; white and brown make chestnut ; white, blue and lake make purple ; white and carmine make pink ; white and green make bright green ; white and yellow make straw color ; white, blue and black make pearl gray ; white, lake and vermillion make flesh color ; white, yellow and Venetian red make cream ; yellow, white and a little Venetian red make buff ; umber, white and Venetian red make drab ; white and emerald green make brilliant green ; light green and black make dark green ; black and Venetian red make chocolate ; purple and white make French white ; indigo and lampblack make silver gray ; lake and white make rose ; red and yellow make orange ; blue and lead color make pearl.

198—Different Kinds of Wood and Where Found.

NAME.	WHERE FOUND.	NAME.	WHERE FOUND.
Acacia	Warm climates.	Buttonwood	(See Sycamore.)
Alder	Europe, etc.	Calamander	Ceylon.
Almond	South of Europe.	Camphor	Warm climates.
Amboine	Africa.	Camwood	Africa.
Apple	Europe, America.	Canary Wood	Brazil.
Apple (crab)	East. United States.	Caugica Wood	"
Arbor vitæ	Temperate climates.	Catalpa	East. United States.
Ash	Britain, etc.	Cedar, Bastard	SouthernCalifornia.
" Black	East. United States.	" Red	East. United States.
" Blue	" " "	" Yellow	Utah to Pacific Coast.
" White	" " "		
Bamboo	China and India.	" Spanish	West Indies and South America.
Barwood	Africa.		
Basswood	East. United States.	" Western	Utah to Oregon.
Beech	" " "	" White	United States.
Birch	Europe, America	" West In-	
Bite	India.	dia	West Indies.
Black Botany		Cherry	Europe, America.
Baywood	Australia.	Cherry, Wild	
Blue Gum	"	Black	East. United States.
Bog Oak	England, Ireland.	Cherry Tree	Australia.
Boxwood	Southern and Western Europe.	Chestnut	America, Europe.
		Cocoa Wood	West Indies.
Brazil Wood	Brazil.	Coquilla Nut	Brazil.
Buckeye	Tennessee and North.	Cork Oak	Southwest Europe.
		Cottonwood	West. United States.
Bullet Tree	Jamaica.	Cowdi Pine	Temperate climates

DIFFERENT KINDS OF WOOD AND WHERE FOUND—Continued.

NAME.	WHERE FOUND.	NAME.	WHERE FOUND.
Cypress	South. United States.	Linn	East. United States.
"	New Zealand.	Locust	West Indies.
Deodar	India.	"	East of Mississippi
Dogwood	Tasmania, Jamaica		River.
	and East. United	Mahogany	Central America
	States.		and Cuba.
East India		" Moun-	
Blackwood	East Indies.	tain	Rocky Mountains.
Ebony	Ceylon, Africa, In-	" White	(See Prima Vera.)
	dia.	Mangrove	Tropics.
Elder	Jamaica.	Maple, Black	East. United States.
Elm	Europe.	" Red	" " "
" Red	East. United States.	" Sugar	" " "
" White	" " "	Mountain Ash	Australia, Britain,
Fir, Red Silver	Sierra Nevada Mts.		etc.
" Scotch	Europe.	Mulberry	Europe and China.
" Silver	California.	" Red	East. United States.
Fustic	North and South	Muskwood	Tasmania, New
	America.		South Wales.
Greenheart	Guiana, Trinidad.	Mustaiba	Brazil.
Gum, Black and		Myrtle	Southern Europe,
Red	East. United States.		Tasmania.
Hawthorn	Europe, etc.	Nellec	India.
Hazel	" "	Nettle Tree	South of Europe.
Hemlock		Norfolk Island	
(Spruce)	North America.	Pine	Norfolk Island.
Hickory	America.	Norway Spruce	Norway.
Holly	Europe, Southeast-	Novaladdi	India.
	ern United States.	Oak	Europe, etc.
Hoonsay	India.	" African	Africa.
Ironwood	East. United States.	" Black	East. United States
" Red	Jamaica.	" White	" " "
Jackwood	Asia, Ceylon.	" Red	" " "
Juniper	(See Cedar.)	" Chestnut	" " "
Kiaboca	East Indies.	Olive	Europe, Syria, Cali-
Kingwood	Brazil.		fornia.
Laburnum	Europe.	Osage Orange	Arkansas and South
Lancewood	South America.	Osiers	Europe.
" Black	Jamaica.	Oyster Bay-	
Larch	Europe.	wood	Tasmania.
" Western	Oregon.	Paddle Wood	Guiana.
Laurel,		Palm	Tropical climates.
Mountain	Penn. and South.	Partridge Wood	West Indies, South
Leopard Wood	Central America.		America.
Lignum-vitæ	West Indies and	Pine	Europe and Asia.
	Florida.	" Yellow	North America.
Lime	Europe.	" Red	" "

DIFFERENT KINDS OF WOOD AND WHERE FOUND—Concluded.

NAME.	WHERE FOUND.	NAME.	WHERE FOUND.
Pine, White	North America.	Spruce, Engle-	
" Spruce	" "	man's	Rocky Mountains.
Plane	North America,	Stringy Bark	Australia.
	Asia, Britain.	Sycamore	Temperate climates
Plum	Britain, etc.	"	East. United States.
Poon	West Indies.	" (Fig)	Egypt.
Poplar	Europe, Asia.	Tamarac (Amer-	
"	East. United States.	ican Larch)	Northern and
PorcupineWood,	Tropical climates.		Northeastern
Prima Vera	Mexico.		United States.
Purple Heart	Brazil.	Teak, African	Africa.
Quassia	Tropical climates.	" Indian	India.
Rattans	" "	Thorn	East. United States.
Red Sanders	India.	Toonwood	India.
Redwood	California.	Toqua	Himalaya.
Rhododendron	Himalaya.	Tulip Wood	Australia.
Rosewood	Tasmania.	Vegetable Ivory.	Central America.
Sandalwood	India.	Walnut, Black	East. United States.
Sapan Wood	"	White (Butter-	
Sassafras	America, Tasmania.	nut	" " "
Satinwood	East Indies.	" English,	Europe.
Saul	" "	" French,	Persia, Asia Minor.
Scotch Fir	Scotland.	Whitewood	New South Wales.
Service Tree	East. United States.	Willow	Europe, America.
She Oak	Tasmania.	Yacca Wood	Jamaica.
Silverwood	Cape of Good Hope.	Yew Wood	Britain, California,
Snakewood	West Indies.		Oregon.
Spindle Tree	Britain, etc.	Zebray	Brazil.
Spruce, Black	Sierra Nevada Mts.		

CHAPTER XVIII.

199—Capacity of Cisterns to Each Ten Inches of Depth.—Twenty-five feet in diameter holds 3,059 gallons; twenty feet in diameter holds 1,958 gallons; fifteen feet in diameter holds 1,101 gallons; fourteen feet in diameter holds 959 gallons; thirteen feet in diameter holds 827 gallons; twelve feet in diameter holds 705 gallons; eleven feet in diameter holds 592 gallons; ten feet in diameter holds 489 gallons; nine feet in diameter holds 396 gallons; eight feet in diameter holds 313 gallons; seven feet in diameter holds 239 gallons; six feet in diameter holds 176 gallons; five feet in diameter holds 122 gallons; four feet in diameter holds 78 gallons; three feet in diameter holds 44 gallons; two feet in diameter holds 19 gallons.

200—To Find the Capacity of a Cistern.—Multiply the square of the diameter by .7854, which will give the area in feet; multiply this by 1728 and divide by 231, which will give the number of gallons the cistern will hold to each foot of depth.

For a square cistern multiply the length by the breadth, which gives the area; then multiply by 1728 and divide by 231, which gives the contents of the cistern in gallons.

In calculating the capacity of cisterns, 231 cubic inches equals one gallon, 31½ gallons equal one barrel and two barrels equal one hogshead.

201—Size of Boxes.—A box 4″x4″ square and 4⅛″ deep will hold one quart ; a box 7″x4″ square and 4¼″ deep will hold half a gallon ; a box 8″x8″ square and 4⅛″ deep will hold one gallon ; a box 8″x8″ square and 8¾″ deep will hold one peck ; a box 16″x8¾″ square and 8″ deep will hold half a bushel ; a box 24″x16″ square and 14″ deep will hold half a barrel ; a box 24″x16″ square and 28″ deep will hold one barrel, or three bushels.

202—To Find the Solid Contents of an Irregular Body.—Immerse it in a vessel partly filled with water ; then the contents of that part of the vessel filled by the rising water will be the cubical contents of the body.

203—Weights and Measures.

CUBIC MEASURE.
1728 cubic inches = 1 cubic foot.
27 cubic feet   = 1 cubic yard.
231 cubic inches = 1 gallon.

SQUARE MEASURE.
144 square inches = 1 square foot.
9 square feet   = 1 square yard.
30¼ square yards = 1 square rod.
40 square rods   = 1 square rood.
4 square roods   = 1 square acre.
640 square acres = 1 square mile.

GUNTER'S CHAIN.
7.92 inches = 1 link.
100 links = 1 chain.
80 chains = 1 mile.

MEASURE OF LENGTH.
3 feet   = 1 yard.
5½ yards   = 1 rod.
40 rods   = 1 furlong.
8 furlongs = 1 mile.
69⅟₂ miles = 1 degree.
60 geographical miles = 1 degree.

4 inches = 1 hand.
7.92 inches = 1 link.
18 inches = 1 cubit.
6 feet   = 1 fathom.

LIQUID MEASURE.
4 gills   = 1 pint.
2 pints   = 1 quart.
4 quarts = 1 gallon.
2 gallons = 1 peck.
31½ gallons = 1 barrel.
63 gallons = 1 hogshead.

The hair's breadth is the smallest measure of length; 48 = 1 inch.

Four barleycorns laid breadthways = ¾ of an inch, or 1 digit.

One barleycorn lengthways = ⅓ of an inch.

A palm is 3 inches.

A hand is four inches.

204—Metric System of Measures.

MEASURE OF LENGTH.
10,000 meters = 1 myriameter.
1,000 ″   = 1 kilometer.
100 ″   = 1 hectometer.
10 ″   = 1 decameter.

1 meter = 1 meter.
.1 ″   = 1 decimeter.
.01 ″   = 1 centimeter.
.001 ″   = 1 millimeter.

MEASURE OF SURFACE.

10,000 square meters = 1 hectare.	Hectare = 2.471 acres.
100 " " = 1 are.	Are = 119.6 square yards.
1 " " = 1 centare.	Centare = 1550 square inches.

MEASURE OF LENGTH.

Myriameter = 6.2137 miles.	Meter = 39.37 inches.
Kilometer = 0.62137 mile = 3280	Decimeter = 3.937 inches.
feet 10 inches.	Centimeter = .3937 inch.
Hectometer= 328 feet 1 inch.	Millimeter = .0394 inch.
Decameter = 393.7 inches.	

MEASURES OF CAPACITY.

1,000 liters= 1 kiloliter or 1 cubic meter.
100 " = 1 hectoliter or .1 cubic meter.
10 " = 1 decaliter or 10 cubic decimeters.
1 liter = 1 liter or 1 cubic decimeter.
.1 " = 1 deciliter or .1 cubic decimeter.
.01 " = 1 centiliter or 10 cubic centimeters.
.001 " = 1 milliliter or .1 cubic centimeter.

205—Equivalents of Denominations in Use.

DRY MEASURE.

1 kiloliter = 1.308 cubic yards.	
1 hectoliter= 2 bushels, 3.35 pecks.	
1 decaliter = 9.08 quarts.	
1 liter = .908 quart.	
1 deciliter = 6.1022 cubic inches.	
1 centiliter = .6102 " "	
1 milliliter = .061 " "	

LIQUID MEASURE.

1 kiloliter = 264.17 gallons.	
1 hectoliter = 26.417 "	
1 decaliter = 2.6417 "	
1 liter = 1.0567 quarts.	
1 deciliter = .845 gill.	
1 centiliter = .368 fluid ounce.	
1 milliliter = .27 " dram.	

WEIGHTS.

1,000,000 grains = 1 millier or tonneau.
100,000 " = 1 quintal.
10,000 " = 1 myriagram.
1,000 " = 1 kilogram.
100 " = 1 hectogram.
10 " = 1 decagram.
1 " = 1 gram.
.1 " = 1 decigram.
.01 " = centigram.
.001 " = milligram.

1 millier	= 2,204.6 lbs. avoirdupois.
1 quintal	= 220.46 " "
1 myriagram	= 22.046 " "
1 kilogram	= 2.2046 " "
1 hectogram	= 3.5274 ounces "
1 decagram	= .3527 " "
1 gram	= 15.432 grains "
1 decigram	= 1.5432 " "
1 centigram	= .1543 " "
1 milligram	= .0154 " "

In the metric system the meter is the base of all weights and measures which it employs. The meter is one ten-millionth part of the distance measured on a meridian of the earth from the equator to the pole, and equals about 39.37 inches, or nearly 3 feet 3⅜ inches.

206—Common Weights and Measures and Their Metric Equivalents.

An inch = 2.54 centimeters.
A foot = .3048 meter.
A yard = .9144 meter.
A rod = 5.029 meters.
A mile = 1.6093 kilometers.
A square inch = 6.452 square centimeters.
A square foot = .0929 square meter.
A square yard = .8361 "   "
An acre = .4047 hectare.
A square mile = 259 hectare.
A cubic foot = .02832 cubic meter.
A cubic yard = .7646 "   "
A cord = 3.624 steres.

A liquid quart = .9465 liter.
A gallon = 3.786 liter.
A dry quart = 1.101 liter.
A peck = 8.811 liter.
A bushel = 35.24 liter.
An ounce avoirdupois = 28.35 grams.
A pound avoirdupois = .4336 kilogram.
A ton = .9072 tonneau.
A grain troy = .0648 gram.
An ounce troy = 31.104 grams.
A pound troy = .3732 kilogram.

207—The Weight a Good Hemp Rope Will Bear in Safety.

DIAMETER.	CIRCUMFERENCE.	POUNDS.	DIAMETER.	CIRCUMFERENCE	POUNDS.
.315	1	200	1.510	4.75	4512.5
.397	1.25	312.5	1.590	5	5000
.477	1.50	450	1 670	5.25	5512.5
.557	1.75	612.5	1.750	5.50	6050
.636	2	800	1.830	5.75	6612.5
.715	2.25	1012.5	1.910	6	7200
.797	2.50	1250	1.990	6.25	7812.5
.874	2.75	1512.5	2.070	6.50	8450
.954	3	1800	2.150	6.75	9112.5
1.030	3.25	2112.5	2.230	7	9800
1.110	3.50	2450	2.310	7.25	10512 5
1.190	3.75	2812.5	2.390	7.50	11250
1.270	4	3200	2.470	7.75	12012.5
1.350	4.25	3612.5	2.540	8	12800
1.430	4.50	4050			

208—Weight of Woods per Cubic Foot.

	Lbs.		Lbs.
Apple	59	Lignum Vitæ	83
Ash	43	Logwood	57
Alder	50	Mahogany, Spanish	53
Bullet Wood	58	" Honduras	35
Box	62	Maple	47
Birch	43	Oak, English	58
Birch, Black	46	" Canadian	54
Beech	45	" Green	78
Butternut	25	" Live, seasoned	66
Cherry	45	Pear	41
Chestnut	38	Plum	49
Cork	15	Poplar	26
Ebony	40	Pine, Pitch, dry	41
Elm	38	" White	34
Fir	34	" Well-seasoned	30
Gum	53	" Yellow	33
Hazel	54	" " dry	30
Holly	47	Rosewood	45
Hickory, Pig Nut	49	Satin Wood	55
" Shellbark	44	Spruce	31
Hemlock	23	Tamarack	23
Hackmatack	37	Teak	46
Juniper	35	Walnut, dry	41
Lancewood	46	Willow	35
Larch	34		

209—The Weight Required to Tear Asunder a Stick One Inch Square of the Following Woods:

	Lbs.		Lbs.
African Oak	14,500	Larch	9,500
Ash	14,000	Maple	10,000
Box	20,000	Mahogany	8,000
Bay	14,500	Oak	11,000
Beech	11,500	Pine, White	11,000
Cedar	14,000	" Pitch	12,000
Chestnut	10,500	Pear	9,800
Cypress	6,000	Poplar	7,000
Elm	13,500	Sycamore	13,000
Lance	23,000	Teak	14,000
Locust	25,000	Willow	13,000
Lignum Vitæ	11,900	Walnut	7,500

210—Crushing Strength per Square Inch of Different Woods.

	Lbs.		Lbs.
Ash	8,900	Larch	6,200
Alder	6,875	Lignum Vitæ	10,000
Box	10,000	Mahogany	8,100
Bay	7,500	Oak	8,000
Beech	7,400	Pine	6,800
Birch	9,750	Poplar	4,100
Cedar	5,700	Plum	9,000
Deal	6,000	Sycamore	6,000
Elder	7,500	Teak	9,000
Elm	8,000	Walnut	6,500
Fir	6,500	Willow	4,500

211—Relative Hardness of Woods, Taking Shellbark Hickory as a Base.

Hickory, Shellbark	1,000	Birch	630
" Pig Nut	950	Maple	550
Oak, White	850	Elm	55·
Ash, White	775	Cedar	54·
Dogwood	750	Wild Cherry	540
Scrub Oak	740	Yellow Pine	530
White Hazel	720	Chestnut	520
Apple	700	Poplar	510
Red Oak	700	Butternut	440
Beech	660	White Pine	300
Walnut	650		

212—Lasting Qualities of Wood in the Earth.—

Experiments have been made by driving sticks of different woods into the ground, by which it is ascertained that in five years all of those made of oak, elm, fir, ash, soft mahogany and all varieties of pine were almost totally rotten ; larch and teak were decayed on the outside ; acacia was only slightly decayed on the outside ; hard mahogany and cedar of Lebanon were in good condition ; Virginia cedar was as good as when put in.

CHAPTER XIX.

213—To Find the Weight of Grindstones.—Multiply the square of the diameter (in inches) by the thickness (in inches), then by the decimal .06363; the product will be the weight of the stone in pounds.

214—Strength of Cast Iron Columns, with Iron One Inch Thick.

No. of Inches in Diameter.	WEIGHT IN HUNDREDWEIGHTS.										
	4 FT. HIGH.	6 FT. HIGH.	8 FT. HIGH.	10 FT. HIGH.	12 FT. HIGH.	14 FT. HIGH.	16 FT. HIGH.	18 FT. HIGH.	20 FT. HIGH.	22 FT. HIGH.	24 FT. HIGH.
2	72	60	49	40	32	26	22	18	15	13	11
2½	119	105	91	77	65	55	47	40	34	29	25
3	178	143	145	128	111	97	84	73	64	56	49
3½	247	232	214	191	172	156	135	119	106	94	83
4	326	318	288	266	242	220	198	178	160	144	130
4½	418	400	379	354	327	301	275	215	229	208	189
5	522	501	479	452	427	394	365	337	310	285	262
6	607	592	573	550	525	407	469	440	413	386	360
7	1,032	1,013	989	959	924	887	848	808	765	725	686
8	1,333	1,315	1,289	1,259	1,224	1,185	1,142	1,097	1,052	1,005	959
9	1,716	1,697	1,672	1,640	1,603	1,561	1,515	1,467	1,416	1,364	1,311
10	2,119	2,100	2,077	2,045	2,007	1,964	1,916	1,865	1,811	1,755	1,697
11	2,570	2,550	2,520	2,490	2,450	2,410	2,358	2,305	2,248	2,189	2,127

215—Weight Per Foot of Flat Iron.

Size.	Weight.	Size.	Weight.	Size.	Weight.
1 x $\frac{1}{8}$	.833	1 x $\frac{1}{2}$	1.66	1 x $\frac{3}{4}$	2.50
$1\frac{1}{4}$ x $\frac{1}{4}$	1.04	$1\frac{1}{2}$ x $\frac{1}{2}$	2.50	$1\frac{1}{2}$ x $\frac{3}{4}$	3.75
$1\frac{1}{2}$ x $\frac{1}{4}$	1.25	2 x $\frac{1}{2}$	3.33	2 x $\frac{3}{4}$	5.00
2 x $\frac{1}{4}$	1.66	$2\frac{1}{2}$ x $\frac{1}{2}$	4.16	$2\frac{1}{2}$ x $\frac{3}{4}$	6.25
$2\frac{1}{4}$ x $\frac{1}{4}$	1.87	3 x $\frac{1}{2}$	5.00	3 x $\frac{3}{4}$	7.50
$2\frac{1}{2}$ x $\frac{1}{4}$	2.08	$3\frac{1}{2}$ x $\frac{1}{2}$	5.83	$3\frac{1}{2}$ x $\frac{3}{4}$	8.75
$2\frac{3}{4}$ x $\frac{1}{4}$	2.29	4 x $\frac{1}{2}$	6.66	4 x $\frac{3}{4}$	10.00
3 x $\frac{1}{4}$	2.50	5 x $\frac{1}{2}$	8.33	5 x $\frac{3}{4}$	12.50
1 x $\frac{3}{8}$	1.25	1 x $\frac{5}{8}$	2.08	$1\frac{1}{2}$ x 1	5.00
$1\frac{1}{4}$ x $\frac{3}{8}$	1.56	$1\frac{1}{2}$ x $\frac{5}{8}$	3.12	2 x 1	6.66
$1\frac{1}{2}$ x $\frac{3}{8}$	1.87	2 x $\frac{5}{8}$	4.16	$2\frac{1}{2}$ x 1	8.33
2 x $\frac{3}{8}$	2.50	$2\frac{1}{2}$ x $\frac{5}{8}$	5.20	3 x 1	10.00
$2\frac{1}{2}$ x $\frac{3}{8}$	3.12	3 x $\frac{5}{8}$	6.25	$3\frac{1}{2}$ x 1	11.66
3 x $\frac{3}{8}$	3.75	$3\frac{1}{2}$ x $\frac{5}{8}$	7.29	4 x 1	13.33
4 x $\frac{3}{8}$	5.00	4 x $\frac{5}{8}$	8.33	5 x 1	16.66
5 x $\frac{3}{8}$	6.25	5 x $\frac{5}{8}$	10.41	6 x 1	20.00

216—Weight of Iron Rods Per Foot.

ROUND.				SQUARE.			
Size.	Weight.	Size.	Weight.	Size.	Weight.	Size.	Weight.
$\frac{1}{4}$	.163	$2\frac{3}{8}$	14.76	$\frac{1}{4}$	.208	$2\frac{1}{2}$	20.80
$\frac{5}{16}$	.368	$2\frac{1}{2}$	16.36	$\frac{5}{16}$	.468	$2\frac{3}{4}$	25.20
$\frac{3}{8}$	.654	$2\frac{3}{4}$	19.79	$\frac{3}{8}$	.833	3	30.00
$\frac{7}{16}$	1.02	3	23.56	$\frac{1}{2}$	1.30	$3\frac{1}{8}$	32.55
$\frac{1}{2}$	1.47	$3\frac{1}{8}$	25.56	$\frac{5}{8}$	1.87	$3\frac{1}{4}$	35.20
$\frac{3}{4}$	2.00	$3\frac{1}{4}$	27.65	$\frac{3}{4}$	2.55	$3\frac{3}{8}$	37.96
1	2.61	$3\frac{3}{8}$	29.82	1	3.33	$3\frac{1}{2}$	40.80
$1\frac{1}{8}$	3.31	$3\frac{1}{2}$	32.07	$1\frac{1}{8}$	4.21	$3\frac{3}{4}$	46.87
$1\frac{1}{4}$	4.09	$3\frac{3}{4}$	36.81	$1\frac{1}{4}$	5.20	4	53.33
$1\frac{3}{8}$	4.95	4	41.88	$1\frac{3}{8}$	6.30	$4\frac{1}{4}$	60.20
$1\frac{1}{2}$	5.81	$4\frac{1}{8}$	44.54	$1\frac{1}{2}$	7.50	$4\frac{1}{2}$	67.50
$1\frac{5}{8}$	6.91	$4\frac{1}{4}$	47.28	$1\frac{5}{8}$	8.80	$4\frac{3}{4}$	75.20
$1\frac{3}{4}$	8.01	$4\frac{3}{8}$	50.11	$1\frac{3}{4}$	10.20	5	83.33
$1\frac{7}{8}$	9.20	$4\frac{1}{2}$	53.01	$1\frac{7}{8}$	11.71		
2	10.47	$4\frac{3}{4}$	59.06	2	13.33		
$2\frac{1}{8}$	11.82	5	65.45	$2\frac{1}{8}$	15.05		
$2\frac{1}{4}$	13.25			$2\frac{1}{4}$	16.87		

217—Weight and Size of Iron I Beams.

Depth of Beam in Inches	Width of Flange in Inches	Thickness of Web in Inches	Weight per Ft. in Pounds	Depth of Beam in Inches	Width of Flange in Inches	Thickness of Web in Inches	Weight per Ft. in Pounds
15	6.08	.76	80	8	4.50	.50	34
15	5.45	.57	60	8	4.09	.41	27
15	5.05	.49	50	8	3.71	.33	$21\frac{1}{2}$
12	5.16	.78	$56\frac{1}{2}$	7	3.82	.38	22
12	4.63	.51	42	7	3.52	.26	18
$10\frac{1}{2}$	4.80	.55	40	6	3.44	.25	16
$10\frac{1}{2}$	4.53	.41	$31\frac{1}{2}$	6	3.24	.24	$13\frac{1}{2}$
10	4.75	.50	42	5	2.96	.28	12
10	4.50	.44	36	5	2.85	.23	10
10	4.31	.37	30	4	2.50	.18	7
9	4.71	.46	$38\frac{1}{2}$	4	2.18	.18	6
9	4.16	.40	$28\frac{1}{2}$	3	2.58	.40	9
9	3.96	.34	$23\frac{1}{2}$	3	2.22	.16	$5\frac{1}{4}$

218—Weight and Size of Steel I Beams.

Depth of Beam in Inches	Width of Flange in Inches	Thickness of Web in Inches	Weight per Ft. in Pounds	Depth of Beam in Inches	Width of Flange in Inches	Thickness of Web in Inches	Weight per Ft. in Pounds
24	6.95	.50	80	9	4.5	.27	21
24	7.20	.75	100	9	4.75	.31	27
20	6.25	.50	64	8	4.25	.25	18
20	7.	.60	80	8	4.5	.27	22
15	5.5	.40	41	7	4.	.23	15.5
15	5.75	.45	50	7	4.25	.27	20
15	6 04	.54	60	6	3.5	.23	13
15	6.31	.67	75	6	3.62	.26	16
12	5.25	.35	32	5	3.	.22	10
12	5.5	.39	40	5	3.13	.26	13
10	4.75	.32	25.5	4	2.62	.20	7.5
10	5.	.37	33	4	2.75	.24	10

219—Crushing Weight Per Square Inch of Various Materials.

	Lbs.		Lbs.
Massachusetts Marble	22,702	Quincy Granite	15,300
Baltimore Marble	18,061	Italian Marble	12,600
Portland Cement	2,500	Aberdeen Granite	10,260

CRUSHING WEIGHT PER SQUARE INCH OF VARIOUS MATERIALS.

(Continued.)

	LBS.		LBS.
Seneca Sandstone.........	10,760	Good Mortar.............	240
Acquia Creek Sandstone...	5,340	Common Masonry........	800
Hard Brick...............	4,368	Fire Brick................	1,717
Common Brick...........	4,000		

220—Weight of a Cubic Foot of Various Materials.

	LBS.		LBS.
One cubic foot of sand, solid,	112½	One cubic foot of brick..	95 to 120
" " " loose,	95	" " granite,	170 to 180
" " earth, "	94	" " marble.....	168
" " common soil,	124	One cubic yard of sand......	3,037
" " strong "	127	" " soil.......	3,429
" " clay.......	130	One cubic foot of lead.......	709
" " clay and stone....................	160	" " water.....	62
One cubic foot of common stone,	160	" " cast-iron...	450
		" " steel.......	489

221—Strength of Wire Ropes (Iron).

DIAMETER.	CIRCUMFERENCE.	WEIGHT PER FOOT IN POUNDS.	BREAKING WEIGHT IN TONS.	SAFE WORKING LOAD IN TONS.	CIRCUMFERENCE OF HEMP ROPE OF EQUAL STRENGTH.
2¼	7	8.	74	15	15½
2	6¼	6.30	65	13	14½
1¾	5½	5.60	54	11	13
1⅝	5⅛	5.25	44	9	12
1½	4¾	4.10	39	8	11½
1⅜	4¼	3.65	33	6½	10¼
1¼	4	3.00	27	5½	9½
1⅛	3½	2.50	20	4	8
1	3⅛	2.00	16	3	7
⅞	2¾	1.58	11½	2½	6
¾	2⅜	1.20	8.64	1¾	5
⅝	2	.88	5.13	1¼	4½
9/16	1¾	.70	4.27	¾	4
½	1⅝	.44	3.48	½	3½
7/16	1⅜	.35	2.70	⅜	3
⅜	1⅛	.28	2.50	¼	3

222—Strength of Wire Ropes (Crucible Cast Steel).

Diameter.	Circumference.	Weight per Foot in Pounds.	Breaking Weight in Tons.	Safe Working Load in Tons.	Circumference of Hemp Rope of Equal Strength.
2¼	7	8.00	160	26	
2	6¼	6.30	122	21	
1¾	5½	5.60	103	17	15¾
1⅝	5⅛	5.25	82	13	14½
1½	4¾	4.10	75	11	13½
1⅜	4¼	3.65	60	9	12½
1¼	4	3.00	51	8	11½
1⅛	3½	2.50	40	6	10
1	3⅛	2.00	32	5	9¼
⅞	2¾	1.58	24	4	8
¾	2⅜	1.20	18	3	6¼
⅝	2	.88	14	2	5¼
9/16	1¾	.70	9½	1½	4¾
½	1⅝	.44	7½	1	4½
7/16	1⅜	.35	6	¾	4
⅜	1⅛	.28	5	⅝	3¾

223—Shrinkage of Timber.—Pitch pine, 18⅜ to 18¼; spruce, 8½ to 8⅜; white pine, 12 to 11⅞; yellow pine, 18 to 17⅞; oak, 12½ to 12⅜; cedar, 14 to 13⅜; elm, 11 to 10¾.

224—Moulders' and Pattern Makers' Table.

White Pine being 1.		Cast Iron being 1.		Bar Iron being 1.	
Cast Iron =	13.	Bar Iron =	1.07	Cast Iron =	.95
Copper =	13.4	Steel =	1.08	Steel =	1.03
Brass =	12.7	Brass =	1.16	Copper =	1.16
Lead =	18.1	Copper =	1.21	Brass =	1.09
Steel =	14.	Lead =	1.55	Lead =	1.48

In making patterns for iron castings the casting will weigh as many pounds as the pattern ounces.

225—Sizes, Lengths and Number to the Pound of Standard Steel Wire Nails.

Sizes.	Length, Inch.	Common.	Barbed Common.	Clinch.	Fence.	Smooth and Barbed Finishing.	Common Brads.	Fine.	Barrel.	Casing.	Smooth Box.	Barbed Box.	Flooring Brads.	Barbed Oval Head Car Nails. Light.	Barbed Oval Head Car Nails. Heav.	Slating.	Barbed Roofing.	Shingle	Tobacco.	Lining.	Wire Spikes.	Length, Inch.	Sizes.
	$\frac{3}{4}$								1500								714			2100		$\frac{3}{4}$	
	$\frac{7}{8}$								1000								469			1780		$\frac{7}{8}$	
2d	1	1200	876	710		1558	1200	1550	875	1350	1350	1350				411	411			1500		1	2d
3d fine.	$1\frac{1}{8}$							1140	775													$1\frac{1}{8}$	3d fine.
3d com	$1\frac{1}{4}$	720	568	429		980	720		560	913	913	913				251	251					$1\frac{1}{4}$	3d com
	$1\frac{3}{8}$								390													$1\frac{3}{8}$	
4d	$1\frac{1}{2}$	432	357	274		760	432	760	350	584	583	584		274	165	209	165		274			$1\frac{1}{2}$	4d
5d	$1\frac{3}{4}$	300	235	235	142	575	300			410	410	410		142	118	142	142	270	235			$1\frac{3}{4}$	5d
6d	2	252	204	157	124	350	252			310	310	310	157	124	103		103	204	157			2	6d
7d	$2\frac{1}{4}$	186	139	639	92	275	186			238	238	238	139	92	76			182	139			$2\frac{1}{4}$	7d
8d	$2\frac{1}{2}$	132	99	99	82	190	132			170	170	170	99	82	69			125	99			$2\frac{1}{2}$	8d
9d	$2\frac{3}{4}$	105	90	90	62	173	105			150	150	150	90	62	54			114	90			$2\frac{3}{4}$	9d
10d	3	87	69	83	50	137	87			121	121	121	67	57	50			83	69		50	3	10d
12d	$3\frac{1}{4}$	66	53	64	38	98	66			97	97	97	53	47	38							$3\frac{1}{4}$	12d
16d	$3\frac{1}{2}$	51	43	59	30	81	51			72	72	72	43	43	35						35	$3\frac{1}{2}$	16d
20d	4	35	31	43	23	71	35			54	54	54		31	26						26	4	20d
30d	$4\frac{1}{2}$	27	24				27			46	46	46		28	24						20	$4\frac{1}{2}$	30d
40d	5	21	18				21			36	36	36		21	18						15	5	40d
50d	$5\frac{1}{2}$	15					15							17	14						12	$5\frac{1}{2}$	50d
60d	6	12					12							15	13						10	6	60d
	$6\frac{1}{2}$																				9	$6\frac{1}{2}$	
	7																				7	7	
	8																				5	8	
	9																				$4\frac{1}{2}$	9	

$3\frac{1}{3}$ lbs. of 4d Common, or $2\frac{3}{8}$ lbs. of 3d common will lay 1,000 shingles; $3\frac{1}{4}$ lbs. of 3d Fine will put on 1,000 laths, 4 nails to the lath.

226—Lengths and Gauges of Standard Steel Wire Nails.

	Spikes	Lining	Tobacco	Shingle	Barbed Roofing	Slating	Barbed Car. Light	Barbed Car. Heavy	Flooring Brads	Barbed Box	Smooth Box	Casing	Barrel	Fine	Smooth and Barbed Finishing	Common Brads	Fence	Clinch	Barbed Common	Common	Length, Inch	Sizes
		17											16							16	1	2d
		17			13			12		16½	16½	16½	15	17	17	16		14	15	15½	1¼	3d fine
		17			12	12		10		16	16	16	15	16¼	16½	15½		13	14		1¼	3d
			12	12	12	11	9	10	11	15	15	15	15	16	16	13	10	12	13	13	1½	4d
			12	12	11	11	9	9	11	14	14	14	14		15	13	10	12	12	13	1¾	5d
			11	11		11	8	9	10	13	13	13	13		14	12	9	11	11	12	2	6d
			11	11	10	10	8	8	10	12	12	12			13	12	8	11	11	12	2¼	7d
	7		10	11	9		7	7	9	12	12	12			12	11	7	10	10	11	2½	8d
	6		10	10			7	7	8	11	11	11			12	11		10	10	10	2¾	9d
	5	1	9				6	6	7	10	10	10			11	10	5	9	9	9	3	10d
	4	0					6	6		9	9	9			10	9	4	9	8	8	3¼	12d
	3	0					5	5		9	9	9			10	8			7	7	3½	16d
	2	0	6½				5	4		8	8	8				6			6	6	4	20d
	1	0	7				4	4								4			5	4	4½	30d
			8				3									3			4	3	5	40d
			9				3									3				3	5½	50d
																					6	60d

227—Number and Diameter of Wood Screws.

No.	Diameter.	No.	Diameter.	No.	Diameter.	No.	Diameter.
0	.056	8	.162	16	.268	24	.374
1	.069	9	.175	17	.281	25	.387
2	.082	10	.188	18	.293	26	.401
3	.096	11	.201	19	.308	27	.414
4	.109	12	.215	20	.321	28	.427
5	.122	13	.228	21	.334	29	.440
6	.135	14	.241	22	.347	30	.453
7	.149	15	.255	23	.361		

228—Seating Capacity of Theatres, etc.

Gilmore's Garden, New York, 8,443
Stadt Theatre.............. 3,000
Academy of Music, New York 2,526
Academy of Music, Phila... 2,865
Carlo Felice, Genoa........ 2,560
Opera House, Munich...... 2,307
Alexander, St. Petersburg... 2,332
Adelphi Theatre, Chicago... 2,238
Music Hall, Boston......... 2,565
Academy of Paris.......... 2,092
Imperial, St. Petersburg..... 2,160
La Scala, Milan............ 2,113
Covent Garden, London.... 2,684
Boston Theatre............ 2,972
Grand Opera Hall, New Orleans................ 2,052
St. Charles Theatre, New Orleans................ 2,178
Grand Opera House, New York 1,883

Booth's Theatre, New York.. 1,807
Opera House, Detroit....... 1,790
McVicker's Theatre, Chicago, 1,786
Grand Opera House, " 1,786
Ford's Opera House, Baltimore.................. 1,720
National Theatre, Washington..................... 1,709
Debar's Opera House, St. Louis.................. 1,696
Grand Opera House, San Francisco.............. 1,650
Euclid Avenue Opera House, Cleveland.............. 1,650
Opera House, Albany....... 1,404
Hooley's Theatre, Chicago... 1,373
Coulter's Opera House, Aurora, Ill.............. 1,004

229—Heights of Towers, etc., in the World.

	Ft.		Ft.
Proposed Tower at World's Fair................	1,100	St. Peter's Church, Rome.....	448
Eiffel Tower, France........	1,000	St. Martin's Church, Germany,	411
Washington Monument, D. C.	555	St. Paul's Church, London...	365
Rouen Cathedral, France....	495	Salisbury Cathedral, England..	400
Pyramid of Cheops, Egypt....	486	Cathedral at Florence, Italy..	386
Antwerp Cathedral, Belgium..	476	Church at Fribourg, Germany,	386
Strasburg Cathedral, France..	474	Cathedral of Seville, Spain....	360
Pyramid of Cephrenes, Egypt,	456	Cathedral of Milan, Lombardy,	355
Vienna Cathedral, Austria....	449	Cathedral of Utrecht, Holland,	356
		Pyramid of Sakkarah, Egypt..	356

HEIGHT OF TOWERS, ETC., IN THE WORLD.

(Continued.)

	FT.		FT.
St. Mark's Church, Venice, Italy	328	Bunker Hill, Monument, Massachusetts	221
Assinelli Tower, Bologna, Italy,	272	Leaning Tower of Pisa, Italy..	179
Pantheon, Paris	274	Opera House, Paris	183
Trinity Church, New York	284	Washington Monument, Baltimore	175
Column at Delhi, Hindoostan..	262	more	175
Porcelain Tower at Nankin, China	260	Trajan's Pillar, Rome	151
Notre Dame Church, Paris	224	Obelisk of Luxor, Paris	110

230—Force of the Wind.

DESCRIPTION.	MILES PER HOUR.	FEET PER MINUTE.	FEET PER SECOND.	FORCE IN POUNDS PER SQUARE FT.
Hardly perceptible	1	88	1.47	0.005
Just perceptible	2	176	2.93	0.02
	3	264	4.4	0.044
Gentle breeze	4	352	5.87	0.079
	5	440	7.33	0.123
Pleasant breeze	10	880	14.67	0.492
	15	1,320	22.	1.107
Brisk gale	20	1,760	29.3	1.968
	25	2,200	36.6	3.075
High wind	30	2,640	44.	4.428
	35	3,080	51.3	6.027
Vey high wind	40	3,220	58.6	7.872
	45	3,960	66.	9.963
Storm	50	4,400	73.3	12.300
Great storm	60	5,280	88.	17.712
	70	6,160	102.	24.108
Hurricane or Cyclone	80	7,040	117.3	31.488
	100	8,800	146.6	49.200

231—Length of the Largest Bridges.—Brooklyn Bridge, 3475 feet; Forth Bridge, Scotland, 8,290 feet; Louisville, over the Ohio, 5,218 feet; St. Louis, over the Mississippi, 2,045 feet; Cincinnati, over the Ohio, 2,220 feet; Cantilever Bridge at Niagara, 910 feet; Victoria, Mon-

treal, 9,144 feet; High Bridge, Harlem, 1,460 feet; Suspension Bridge, Niagara, 1,268 feet; Bridge at Burton, England, 1,545 feet; Holy Trinity Bridge, Florence, 322 feet; Havre de Grace, over Susquehanna, 3,271 feet.

Rialto Bridge at Venice, a single marble arch, is 98 feet long.

The largest cantilever bridge in America is over the Colorado River at The Needles. The main span is 660 feet; length of each arm, 165 feet; viaduct, 120 feet; total length, 1,110 feet.

232—To Find the Tonnage of Vessels.—CARPENTERS' RULE.—For single-decked vessels multiply together the length of the keel, the breadth at the main beam and the depth of the hold (all in feet), and divide the product by 95. The quotient is the tonnage. For double decked vessels take half the breadth at the beam for the depth of the hold and proceed as before.

GOVERNMENT RULE.—If the vessel be double decked take the length from the fore part of the main stern to the after part of the stern post above the upper deck; the breadth at the broadest part above the main wales, half of which breadth shall be accounted the depth of the vessel, and then deduct from the length three-fifths of the breadth; multiply the remainder by the breadth and the product by the depth and divide this last product by 95. The quotient shall be deemed the true contents or tonnage of the vessel. If the vessel be single decked take the length and breadth, as above directed, deduct from said length three-fifths of the breadth and take the depth from the under side of the deck plank to the ceiling in the hold; then multiply and divide as before and the quotient shall be deemed the tonnage.

233—Rules for Extracting the Square Root.—
1. Point off the given number into periods of two figures each by putting arcs over each two figures, commencing

to space from the right. When there are decimals in the figure space the decimals from the whole figure, as

$$\overline{17}\overline{69}.\ \overline{1}\overline{26}\ .$$

2. Find the greatest square in the left-hand period and write its root in the quotient ; subtract the square of this root from the left-hand period, and to the remainder bring down the next period for a dividend.

3. Double the root already found for a divisor, ascertain how many times the divisor is contained in the dividend, excepting the right-hand figure, and place this figure in the quotient and also in the divisor. Multiply the divisor thus increased by the last figure in the quotient and subtract the product from the dividend, and to the remainder bring down the next period for a new dividend.

4. Double the root already found for a new divisor and continue to operate as before until all the periods are brought down. If to run it into a fraction bring down two ciphers for a new period.

EXAMPLE.—Extract the square root of 110.24.

$$\overline{1}\overline{10}.\overline{24}\ \big|\ \underline{10.49}$$

		1	
First divisor,	2.	10	First dividend.
Second divisor,	20.	1024	Second dividend.
	204.	816	
Third divisor,	208.	20800	
	2089.	18801	
		1999	Remainder.

CHAPTER XX.

Agreement of Partnership—Form of Contract for Building—Contractor's Notice of Lien—
Notice of Lien from Other than the Contractor—Mechanic's Time Slip—
Schedule of Charges of the American Institute of Architects—
Glossary of Terms Used in Architecture and
Building Construction.

AGREEMENT OF PARTNERSHIP.

This agreement made this   day of ...., 189 , between
.................., of ....
...., State of
party of the first part, and
of ...., State of ....
, party of the second part:

Witnesseth, That the said parties agree to associate themselves together as copartners for a period of ten years from the date hereof in the
business of contracting and building, the name and style of the firm to be

...

For the purpose of conducting the business of the above-named partnership the said party of the first part has at the above date of this agreement invested .... dollars as capital stock, and said party of the second part has invested a like sum of .... dollars, both of these
amounts to be expended and used in common for the mutual advantage of
both parties and their business. It is further agreed by the parties hereto
that so long as they are associated as partners they will not follow any
avocation or trade to their own private interest, but will throughout the
entire period of their copartnership put forth their best efforts for their
mutual advantage and increase of the above named business and capital
stock. That the business may be fully understood by each of the parties it is
further agreed that during the period of this copartnership full and accurate books of accounts shall be kept, in which each partner shall record or

cause to be recorded all moneys received by him and expended by him, as well as all articles sold or bought for the use of said firm. The gains, expenditures and losses to be equally divided between them. It is further agreed that once every year, or oftener should either party desire it, a full and accurate exhibit shall be made each to the other, or to the executors, administrators or assigns of either of the parties hereto, of losses, receipts and profits made by reason or arising from said copartnership business. And after such exhibit is made the surplus, if there be any, shall be divided equally between said parties. And, furthermore, should either partner desire, or should the death of either of the parties make it necessary, then they, the said copartners, will each to the other, or in case of death of either, the surviving partner to the executor or administrators of the party so dying, make a full, accurate and final account of the condition of the partnership, as aforesaid, and will fairly and accurately adjust the same; and also take an inventory of the said capital stock, with increase and profit thereon which may appear or be found to be remaining. All such remainder shall be equally divided between said copartners, their executors, administrators or assigns. It is also agreed that in case of a misunderstanding arising with the partners, which cannot be settled between themselves, such difference of opinion shall be settled by arbitrators upon the following conditions: Each party to choose one arbitrator and these two thus chosen shall choose a third; the three thus chosen to adjust the difference, which shall be a final settlement between the parties hereto.

In witness whereof the parties aforesaid hereunto set their hands and seals the day and year first above written.

.... [SEAL.]

.... [SEAL.]

Signed in the presence of·

GEORGE ANDERSON.

JAMES DICKINSON.

FORM OF CONTRACT FOR BUILDING.

Articles of agreement made this ....   day of   , between
————————————— , of
in the County of   .... and State of
———————— , of the first part, and ....

........................, of .... in the County of
.... and State of..

Witnesseth, That the said ...., party
of the first part, for the considerations hereinafter named, contracts, bar-
gains and agrees with the said ...., of the
second part, his heirs, assigns and administrators, that he, the said
...., will within .... months
from this date erect and finish in a good and workmanlike manner accord-
ing to his best skill a .... house on Lot No...........
(Here describe the lot.) Said house to be of the following dimensions,
with all material and labor as described in the plans and specifications
hereto annexed. (Here describe building material, plan, etc.)

In consideration of which the said ....
does for himself and legal representatives promise to pay to the said
...., his heirs and assigns, the sum of
.... dollars in the following manner: ....
dollars when the building is under roof, ... dollars
when the building is ready for plastering, ... dollars
when the building is completed. .... dollars.

It is also agreed that the said .... or his
legal representatives shall furnish at his or their expense all material to be
used in said building.

In witness whereof we have hereunto set our hands the year and day
first above written.

....

Contracts should be made in duplicate so that each party may hold one.

CONTRACTOR'S NOTICE OF LIEN.

To ...., Town Clerk of the Town of
..............., in the County of ....

Take notice that I, a resident of said town, have, or claim to have, a lien
upon the building hereinafter described, and the appurtenances, and the
lot upon which the same stands, as security for the amount due me in pursuance of the statute in such case made and provided. That the said
building is known as No. .... in
...., or stands on the lot bounded and
described as follows (insert description), and said house is owned by
.... That the claim against said lot
or the owner thereof is for work, labor and services as carpenter and

builder, and for the materials furnished by me as the contractor with the said .... for the building, altering or repairing of said house, under and in pursuance of an agreement made with .... , that .... days have not elapsed since the performance and completion of such labor (or furnishing the materials). Yours, etc.,

Date, ...

NOTICE OF LIEN FROM OTHER THAN THE CONTRACTOR.

To ...., Town Clerk of the Town of ...., in the County of .... Take notice that I, a resident of said town, have, or claim to have, a lien upon the building hereinafter described, and the appurtenances, and the lot upon which the same stands, as security for the amount due me in pursuance of the statute in such case made and provided. That the said building is known as No. .... in .... or stands on the lot bounded and described as follows (insert description), and said house is owned by That the claim against is for work by me performed as a .... for .... months, labor performed by me on said building in pursuance of an agreement with .... , the contractor, amounting to .... (or is for building material furnished for and used in the erection of said building in pursuance of an agreement with said ...., amounting to ....) and that . days have not elapsed since the performance and completion of said labor (or since the said materials were furnished). Yours, etc.,

, 189

[The number of days, etc., must be filled in in accordance with the requirements of the lien law in each State, as well as the names of the towns and county.]

When a person contracts to build a house and is prevented by sickness from finishing it, he can recover for the part performed if such part is beneficial to the other party.

MECHANIC'S TIME SLIP.

WORK DONE THIS DAY.

————————, 189

FOR WHOM.	DESCRIPTION OF WORK.	TIME.

————————, 189

MECHANIC ————————

FOR WHOM ————————

DESCRIPTION OF WORK ————————

SCHEDULE OF MINIMUM CHARGES OF THE AMERICAN
INSTITUTE OF ARCHITECTS.

Adopted by the American Institute of Architects, October 23, 1884.

Adopted by the Western Association of Architects, November 14, 1884.

*Reaffirmed by the American Institute of Architects upon the consolidation of the West-
ern Association of Architects and the American Institute of Architects, November 20, 1889.*

For full professional services (including supervision) FIVE PER CENT.
upon the cost of the work.

In case of the abandonment of the work the charge for partial service is
as follows: Preliminary studies, 1 per cent.; preliminary studies, general
drawings and specifications, 2½ per cent.; preliminary studies, general
drawings, specifications and details, 3½ per cent.

For works that cost less than $10,000, or for monumental and decorative
work, and designs for furniture, a special rate in excess of the above.

For alterations and additions an additional charge to be made for sur-
veys and measurements.

An additional charge to be made for alterations and additions in contracts and plans, which will be valued in proportion to the additional time
and services employed.

Necessary traveling expenses to be paid by the client.

Time spent by the architect in visiting for professional consultation, and
in the accompanying travel, whether by day or night, will be charged for,
whether or not any commission, either for office work or supervising work,
is given.

The architect's payments are successively due as his work is completed,
in the order of the above classifications.

Until an actual estimate is received the charges are based on the pro-
posed cost of the works, and the payments are received as installments of
the entire fee, which is based upon the actual cost.

The architect bases his professional charge upon the entire cost to the
owner of the building when completed, including all the fixtures necessary
to render it fit for occupation, and is entitled to extra compensation for
furniture or other articles designed or purchased by the architect.

If any material or work used in the construction of the building be already upon the ground, or come into the possession of the owner without
expense to him, the value of said material or work is to be added to the
sum actually expended upon the building before the architect's commission
is computed.

SUPERVISION OF WORKS.

The supervision or superintendence of an architect (as distinguished
from the continuous personal superintendence which may be secured by

the employment of a clerk of the works) means such inspection by the architect, or his deputy, of a building or other work in process of erection, completion or alteration as he finds necessary to ascertain whether it is being executed in conformity with his designs and specifications or directions, and to enable him to decide when the successive installments or payments provided for in the contract or agreement are due or payable. He is to determine in constructive emergencies, to order necessary changes, and to define the true intent and meaning of the drawings and specifications, and he has authority to stop the progress of the work and order its removal when not in accordance with them.

CLERK OF THE WORKS.

On buildings where it is deemed necessary to employ a clerk of the works the remuneration of said clerk is to be paid by the owner or owners, in addition to any commission or fees due the architect. The selection or dismissal of the clerk of the works is to be subject to the approval of the architect.

EXTRA SERVICES.

Consultation fees for professional advice are to be paid in proportion to the importance of the questions involved, at the discretion of the architect.

None of the charges above enumerated cover professional or legal services connected with negotiations for site, disputed party walls, right of light, measurement of work, or services incidental to arrangements consequent upon the failure of contractors during the performance of the work. When such services become necessary they shall be charged for according to the time and trouble involved.

DRAWINGS AND SPECIFICATIONS.

Drawings and specifications, as instruments of service, are the property of the architect.

GLOSSARY OF TERMS USED IN ARCHITECTURE AND BUILDING CONSTRUCTION.

Abaciscus—One of the tiles or squares of a tesselated pavement.

Abacus—The uppermost member or division of a capital.

Abutment—That part of a pier from which the arch springs.

Acroteria—Small pedestals for statues and other ornaments placed on the apex and the lower angles of a pediment.

Alternate—To place by turns. To follow each other in the order of every other one.

Anchor—A piece of wood or iron built in the wall to hold joists.

Angle—A point where two lines meet.

Amulet—A small flat fillet, encircling a column, etc.

Angle Iron—An iron bent the shape of an angle and used to tie corners, etc.

Apartment—A room.

Apex—The top.

Aqueduct—An artificial channel for conveying water.

Arcade—A series of arches supported by columns.

Arch—Primarily a construction of bricks or stones, so arranged as by mutual pressure to support each other and to become capable of sustaining a superincumbent weight.

Architrave—The casing and mouldings about a door or window. That part of the entablature which rests upon the capital of a column, and is beneath the frieze.

Archway—A passage under an arch.

Ashlar }
Ashler } —A stone used for the facing of a wall.

Askew—Twisted or crooked.

Astragal—A small semicircular moulding encircling a column, etc.

Attic—A low additional story immediately under the roof of a building.

Back of Rafter—The top edge.

Backing Joist—Planing the top edge, giving them a slight curve.

Balcony—An open gallery projecting from the front of a building.

Baluster—A small pillar or pilaster supporting a rail.

Balustrade—A range of small balusters connected by a rail.

Battens—Strips of timber used to nail over joists or cracks.

Batter—A term applied to a wall when its face slopes inward.

Bead—A circular moulding.

Bearer—Anything used to support another.

Belfry—That part of the steeple in which the bells are hung.

Belt Course—A band of stone, etc., which runs around the exterior of a building.

Bent—A name given to a truss after it is put together.

Block and Tackle—Blocks with pulleys in them, and ropes used for hoisting.

Boom—The arm of a derrick.

Bow Window—A window projecting in curved lines.

Boss—A piece of wood in the top of a steeple or tower to which the top of the rafters are nailed.

Brace—A piece of timber extending across a corner from one timber to another.

Bracket—A support of wood or iron.

Breast—A timber framed in front of a chimney or stairway to receive the tail joist.

Bridging—The pieces nailed between joists in the form of an X.

Broach—A small spire or steeple springing from a tower without any intermediate parapet.

Broken Ashlar—When the stones are of various sizes and heights, but with parallel joints.

Bull's-eye—A small window.

Button—A knob for fastening.

Buttress—A projection from a wall to create additional strength and support.

Butts—A name given to hinges.

Camber—To give a convexity to the upper surface of a beam.

Cant—To tilt.

Capital—The top or head of a column, pilaster, etc.

Carry Up—A term used by masons to indicate the building up of a wall.

Chamfer—The beveled edge of anything originally right angled.

Chord—A right line connecting the two extreme parts of an arch. The base or tie of a truss.

Clapboards—Boards used on the exterior of a house which are thinner on one edge than on the other.

Cleat—A piece of wood nailed to something to strengthen it.

Collar Beam—A horizontal piece of timber bracing two opposite rafters.

Column—A cylindrical pillar.

Concave—A surface sloping inward, as the in circumference of a circle.

Concrete—A mixture of cement, stone and sand. Where lime is used it is called lime concrete.

Consoles—Trusses employed as an apparent support to a cornice upon the flanks of the architrave.

Composite Arch—An arch made of more than one curve.

Convex—A surface swelling externally into or toward a spherical form.

Coping—The top or cover of a wall. To fit one moulding to another.

Corbel—A short piece of timber in a wall jutting out to carry an arch.

Corner Strip—A strip used to finish the corner of a building.

Cornice—Any moulded projection which finishes the part to which it is affixed. Generally applied to the moulded finish of a wall.

Crane—A machine for lifting.

Cripples—The short rafters which meet on a hip or valley.

Crockets—Foliaged ornaments placed along the angles of pediments, pinnacles, etc., in Gothic architecture.

Cusps—The pendants of a pointed arch.

Datum—A line on a plan from which points are reckoned or measured, as the datum line in leveling.

Degree—The 360th part of a circle.

Dormer—A window placed on the roof of a house.

Dovetail—To unite with a tenon in the shape of a spread dovetail.

Dowel Pins—Pins of wood or iron used to fasten timber joints together.

Drop—A turned ornament put on the bottom end of newel posts, etc.

Eaves—The edge of a roof.

Easmond—A circle moulding on a stair string.

Ellipse—An oval figure bounded by a regular curve.

Escutcheon—A shield over a keyhole, or a heraldic shield containing a coat of arms.

Facade—The principal front of any building.

Facia—The board forming the face of a cornice.

Fall—A line leading from a block and tackle to which the power is applied.

Fillet—A small flat face or board used principally between mouldings.

Finial—The top or finish of a tower or steeple.

Flashing—The metal used when shingling around a chimney or wall or in the valleys of a roof.

Flutes—Upright channels on the shafts of columns.

Fore—The front part of the building.

Frame—Anything put together in pieces, as the timbering of a building.

Frieze—The middle division of an entablature which lies between the architrave and the cornice.

Furring—Strips used to lath to or to block studs, etc., out to a line.

Girder—The principal beam in a floor for supporting the binding and other joists whereby the length of bearing is lessened.

Girth—A small horizontal beam or girder.

Goose Neck—A piece of wood or iron in the form of a goose neck.

Groin—The line formed by the intersection of two arches.

Grounds—Strips used as a guide in plastering, etc.

Guy Line—A rope used to steady or hold anything

Hammer-beam—A portion of an open timber roof forming a truss at the foot of the rafter, which gives strength and elegance to the construction.

Header—A stone or brick laid lengthwise through a wall.

Heel-board—A board used to hold the foot of rafters.

Herring-bone Bridging—The bridging or cross pieces of a partition placed diagonally.

Hip—The angle formed by the intersection of two sloping sides of a roof.

Hog Chain—A chain used to strengthen girders and joists.

Horse—A string to support stairs; a support for scaffolding.

Impost—The capital of a pier or pilaster which supports an arch.

Inlaid Floor—A floor composed of small pieces of different woods.

Jack Rafters—Rafters that fill in between the principal rafters of a roof. Also called *common rafters*.

Jack-screw—A screw for raising weights.

Jambs—The vertical sides of an aperture.

Joist-bearer—The narrow board framed into the studs to carry the joist.

Joists—The timbers to which the boards of a floor or the laths of a ceiling are nailed.

Kerf—The cut made by a saw or other tool.

Keystone—The highest central stone of an arch.

Kiln—A place or building used to dry or burn certain materials deposited within it.

King-post—The centre post in a trussed roof.

Latticework—Any work made by crossing strips of wood or iron and forming open squares.

Lavatory—A room or place for washing.

Lean-to—A small building or part of a building which stands or leans against a larger building.

Ledger—A piece of timber used in a scaffold placed at right angles to the uprights.

Lintel—A horizontal piece of timber or stone placed over an opening.

Lookout—A piece of timber run out on which to build the cornice.

Mansard Roof—A sloping roof named after the inventor, Francois Mansard.

Margin—A border. The flat part of the stiles of framework.

Mast—A long, round piece of timber raised perpendicularly.

Member—A moulding. The term is also applied to the subordinate parts of a building.

Mesh—The openings in a screen or latticework.

Modillion—Projecting brackets under the corona of the Corinthian and Composite and occasionally also of the Roman and Ionic orders.

Monitor—A ventilator on a rolling mill or machine shop.

Mortise—A hole cut into a piece of wood into which a tenon or corresponding portion of the wood of another piece is inserted.

Muntin—The central vertical piece that divides the panel of a door.

Mullion—The upright post or bar dividing two lights of a window.

Needle—A timber used in raising houses, etc.

Newel Post—The principal post in a stair balustrade.

Niche—A concave recess in a wall in which to place a statue or any similar ornament.

Ogee—A moulding in the form of the letter S.

Outrigger—A piece of timber projecting out to hoist timber, etc.

Oval—Oblong and curvilinear. Resembling the longitudinal section of an egg.

Panel—An area or compartment sunk from the general face of the surrounding work, as a wainscot or a wall.

Parting Strip—The bead between two sashes in a window frame.

Parapet—A breastwork or low wall used to protect the gutters, roofs, etc., of churches and houses.

Parget—Plaster for plastering the inside of flues.

Pediment—The triangular termination used in classical architecture at the ends of buildings, over porticoes, etc.

Pedestal—A substructure used to elevate and sustain a column, statue, etc.

Pendant—A hanging ornament.

Pilaster—A square column or pillar sometimes disengaged, but generally attached to a wall, and projecting only a part of its thickness.

Pintle—An iron pin or bolt.

Pivot—A pin or short shaft on which anything turns.

Plancher—The under side of a cornice.

Plinth—A block forming the base of a column or finish to receive the baseboard.

Plumb Rule—A straight board used with a plumb bob to plumb studs, etc.

Pole—A stick used for measuring.

Porch—An exterior appendage to a building forming a covered approach to one of its doorways.

Purlin—A piece of timber placed horizontally on the principal rafters of a roof to support the common rafters.

Putlog—A piece of timber for supporting the planks of a scaffold, one end of which rests on the ledge of the scaffold and the other in a hole left in the wall.

Quicklime—Lime unslacked.

Quirk—A twist or turn from the straight or right course.

Queen-post—One of two vertical timbers in a truss of a roof.

Rafter—One of the timbers of a roof extending from the plate to the ridge.

Rake—The slope of a roof.

Range—To place in a row.

Relief—The projection of a figure or ornament from the ground or plane on which it is formed.

Ribbon—A narrow board framed into the studs to carry the joist.

Ridgeboard—A board at the top of a roof placed between the ends of the rafters.

Rosette—An ornament resembling a rose.

Rubble Wall—A wall built of rough, irregular stones.

Sag—To sink or bend.

Segment—One of the parts into which any body naturally divides.

Scribe—To mark and adjust with compasses; to fit, as one edge of a board, or one piece of timber or wood to another.

Scuttle—An opening in a floor, a roof, etc., and closing with a lid.

Shore—To support by a shore; to prop up.

Skew—Awry, askew.

Sleeper—A beam or timber which supports the joist of a floor.

Sling—An endless rope to be passed around a cask or other article to be hoisted or lowered.

Spandrel—The triangular space formed between the outer curve or extrados of an arch, a horizontal across its apex and a perpendicular line from its springing.

Staging—A stage or platform for support.   A scaffolding.

Stile—The vertical piece in framing or paneling.

Stoop—A porch with steps; a balustrade and seats.

Stirrup—An iron shoe made for carrying a joist.

Strut—A piece of timber placed obliquely in a framed part of a building, serving to keep a main beam in its proper situation.

Stud—The timbers used in the walls of a building.

Stuff—A mass of indefinite matter.   The material out of which anything is made.

Sweep—To strike a curve.

Tag Line—A line fastened to anything being hoisted to guide and steady it.

Tail Joist—Joist framed into a trimmer.

Tangent—Touching a curve or surface at a single point.

Tenon—A projection cut on the end of a piece of timber to fit into a corresponding cavity or mortise cut in another piece of timber for joining them.

Threshold—A plank or a piece of stone, iron or timber beneath a door, particularly a door of entrance to a house or other building; a door sill.

Tie—A piece of timber or metal serving to bind two bodies together which have a tendency to separate or diverge.

Trammel—An instrument used by carpenters for constructing an ellipse.

Tread—The horizontal part of a step on which the foot is placed.

Trimmer—A piece of timber inserted in roof, floor, wood partition, etc., to support the ends of any of the joists, rafters, etc.

Trunnions—Pivots used to hang transoms in the centre.

Truss—A framed assemblage of pieces of timber or iron for tying up or suspending a principal beam or piece for supporting a roof, etc.

Turn-buckle—A link, with a thread cut in each end, used to tighten stay rods.

Valley—The internal angle formed by two inclined sides of a roof.

Veranda—A light external gallery, with a sloping roof, supported on slender pillars.

Vibrate—To move or play to and fro, as a pendulum.

Wall Plate—A piece of timber placed along the top of a wall to receive the ends of the roof timbers, or placed on a wall to receive the joists of a floor.

Warp—To twist out of shape.

Wind—To turn, as one flexible substance round some other body; to twine; to coil; to wreathe.

Windlass—A machine for raising weights.

MINIATURE OF PLATE XXXIX. SIZE OF PLATE, 9x12 INCHES.

CONTAINING

FORTY-FIVE PLATES

Showing designs for houses of moderate cost, with descriptive letter-press, contributed by various architects, together with the following articles:

Suggestions on House Building,

BY ALBERT WINSLOW COBB, ARCHITECT,

AND

How to Plumb a Suburban House

afely, Economically and Effectively, together with Plans and Specifications.

BY LEONARD D. HOSFORD.

One oblong quarto, handsomely bound in cloth, $2; in paper, $1.

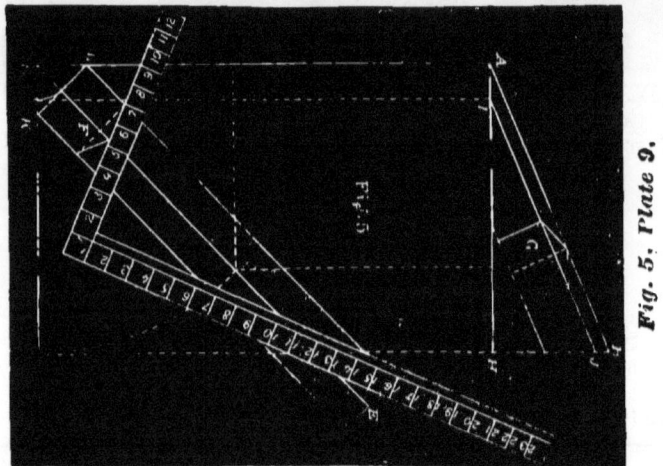

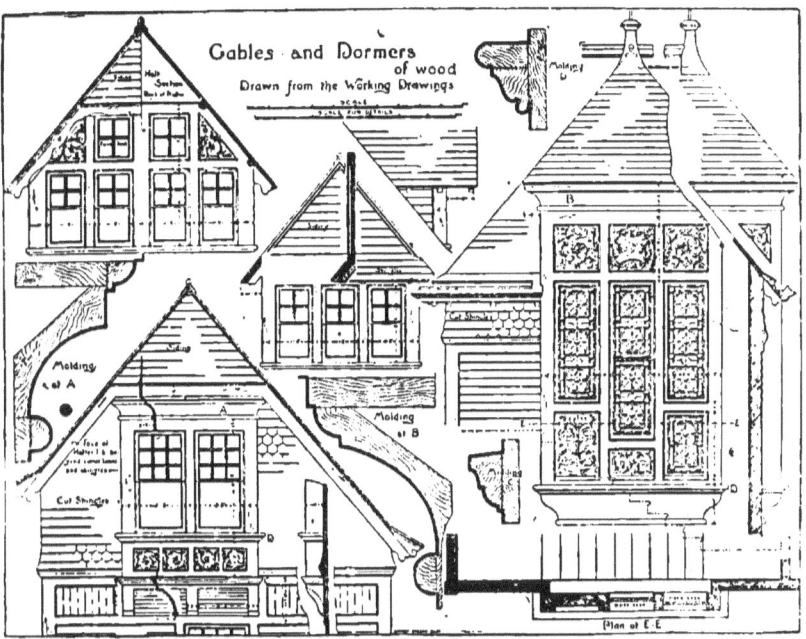

Miniature Plate II, Selected Details.   Full Size, 12 x 16 Inches.

SELECTED DETAILS

— OF —

INTERIOR AND EXTERIOR FINISH

— FOR —

ARCHITECTS, CARPENTERS AND BUILDERS.

Containing 32 Large Folio Plates and 365 Details, all Drawn to Scale.

This collection is the result of a careful selection from a large number of plates published in "Building" and "Architecture and Building," together with the plates on Store and Bank finish in "Interiors and Interior Details," now out of print, as well as special plates of mantels, doors and interior finish from the San Mateo House of Bruce Price, all of which are published from the original drawings and on a large scale.

One large oblong folio size, 14x18½, handsomely bound in boards.

Price postpaid, Boards, $2.50; Paper, $1.50.

PRACTICAL PAPER HANGING.

A Handbook for the Practical Man, giving a full description of the tools
used and the method of hanging all kinds of wall decorations.

100 Handsome Engravings.

By ARTHUR SEYMOUR JENNINGS,

Editor "Painting and Decorating." Formerly Associate Editor of "Scientific American" and of the "Builder and Decorator."

CONTENTS.

CHAPTER I.—The tools employed in paper hanging, cutters, trimmers, rotary trimmers, seam rollers, corner rollers, straight edge, paper hangers' tables, paste brushes, smoothing brushes, etc., etc.

CHAPTER II.—The different varieties of wall hangings, buff blanks, brown blanks, white blanks, flats, bronzes, gilts, embossed gilts, tints, micas, satins, flocks, felts, granites, tapestries, leather hangings, Lincrusta-Walton, Venetian leather papers, Anaglypta, Lignomur.

CHAPTER III.—Hanging paper on side walls; measuring quantity of paper required; table showing number of pieces required; trimming wall paper; paper hangers' paste; to make paste that will keep; sizing. How to paste the paper and how to hang it; turning the corners; papering old walls; removal of old paper; papering over whitewash, rough and broken walls; hanging paper on damp walls. Papering on boards; papering over paint; re-papering over varnished paper; varnishing wall paper. How to clean wall paper; the bran method, stale bread and other methods.

CHAPTER IV.—Dadoes, friezes and borders. How a dado should be hung up a staircase; hanging friezes.

CHAPTER V.—Ceiling decorations; how to hang the paper; designs for ceilings in wall paper canopy ceilings; repairing defective ceilings.

CHAPTER VI.—How to hang burlap or buckram; how to hang Lincrusta-Walton; composition for fixing Lincrusta; directions for decorating Lincrusta in antique ivory, in ivory and gold and in antique metal. Instructions for hanging Anaglypta; decorating Anaglypta; ceiling decorations in Anaglypta. How to hang Lignomur; precautions to be taken. Flax hangings; silk hangings.

CHAPTER VII.—Hanging drapery; hanging tapestry and cretonne. How to put up tufted tapestry; how to do pleated work, lace decoration, shirred or gauged work.

CHAPTER VIII.—Wall paper from the dealer's standpoint; prices; wall paper as a selling article; tendency to amalgamate the businesses of paper hanging and painting; how to show wall paper; numbering patterns.

CHAPTER IX.—Wall paper specialties, etc., etc.

A PRACTICAL WORK FOR PRACTICAL MEN.

Bound in Illuminated Boards. Price, $2.

A GREAT BARGAIN.

To close out our stock we offer balance on hand (7 instruments) at

$15.00 EACH.

AN IMPROVED LEVELING INSTRUMENT.

Adapted to the use of Architects, Engineers, Masons, Builders,
Farmers and Others.

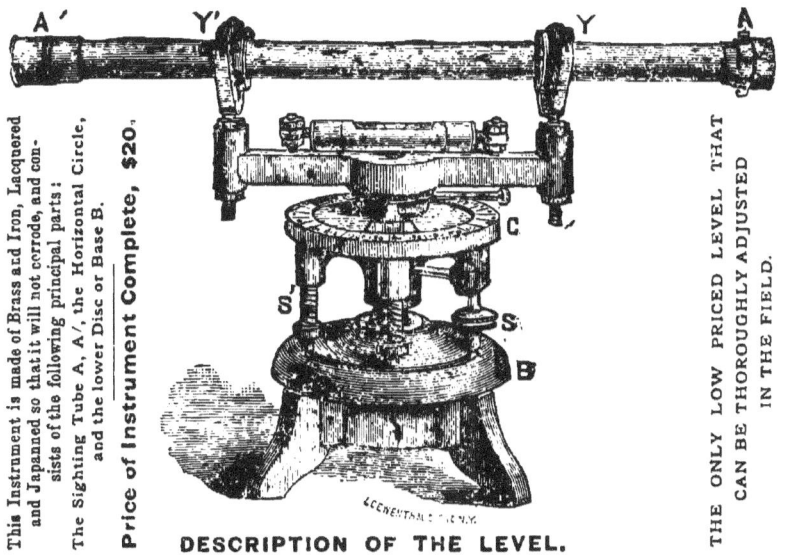

This Instrument is made of Brass and Iron, Lacquered and Japanned so that it will not corrode, and consists of the following principal parts:
The Sighting Tube A, A′, the Horizontal Circle, and the lower Disc or Base B.

Price of Instrument Complete, $20.

THE ONLY LOW PRICED LEVEL THAT CAN BE THOROUGHLY ADJUSTED IN THE FIELD.

DESCRIPTION OF THE LEVEL.

THE sighting tube AA′ is 14 in. long and has at the end A′ a pin-hole looking through the tube, and at the other end A a small ring inside the brass shield or outer ring, shown in cut, holding the cross wires. A cover is provided as shown in cut to protect the cross wires. This tube rests in the Ys, Y and Y′. On this tube at the Ys are two rings with flanges, like car wheels, and it is held in its place by the latches on the top of the Ys. By loosening these latches this sighting tube may be revolved to test the adjustment of the cross wires.

At the feet of the Ys will be seen the nuts, one above and one below the end of the cross bar, which may be turned, thus raising or lowering the end of the tube and adjusting the line of sight to the line of level. The circle C is graduated to 1·° and the pointer marked to degrees, so that the instrument may be used in laying off angles, squaring foundations &c. The pointer is movable and can be fixed in position by the set screw shown in the cut just below the cross bar. The cross bar carries the glass bubble which is seen in the cut. The bubble itself may be adjusted by the screws. To the circle are attached the two thumb-screws and springs opposite to them, by means of which the instrument is brought to a level.

In the outer edge of the base B is a smoothly turned groove in which the feet of the screws and springs may slip easily whenever it may be necessary to revolve the circle on the base. The center of the base is formed into a socket for the ball referred to above. The under surface has a solid cylinder which screws in the collar of the tripod. The cord suspending the plumb-bob drops from the center of the instrument to which it is attached by a loop not shown in the cut. From this description it will be seen that this instrument can be *adjusted* in every way possible in the highest priced instruments, and has besides the additional feature of a horizontal circle, making it in reality a plain transit, as well as level.

Every instrument will be completely adjusted before it is shipped.

The instrument is put up in a handsome wooden box, with strap for carrying, and furnished with a surveyor's tripod and a short or mason's tripod.

Price of Instrument Complete, $20. Reduced to $15.

Forwarded by express on receipt of price. The charges of transportation in all cases to be borne by the purchaser, we guaranteeing the safe arrival of all instruments to the extent of express transportations, and holding the express companies responsible for all losses or damages on the way.

NEW YORK AND CHICAGO.

DEVOTED TO

Art, Architecture, Arhæology, ∴
∴ Engineering and Decoration

PUBLISHED ONCE A WEEK.

Subscription, $6.00 per Year.   **Fifteen Cents per Copy.**
Foreign Subscription, $7.50.

Sample Copy Free.

BOUND VOLUMES.

"BUILDING."

Vol. II., Price $2.50.   Vol. III., Price $2.50; Special Edition, $8.00.   Vol. IV.—XI., $4.50 each.

"ARCHITECTURE AND BUILDING."

Vol. XII.—XIX..Price, $4.50.

These bound volumes comprise a large number of examples of current architecture, such as Residences, Cottages, Churches, Public Buildings, Large Office Buildings, Club Houses, Hospitals and all the varied classes of buildings being erected throughout the country, making a compendium of architectural designs not otherwise obtainable.

WHAT SUBSCRIBERS SAY.

Adler & Sullivan, Architects, Chicago, Ill.: "We have been subscribers to ARCHITECTURE AND BUILDING for many years, and have always found its contents interesting and instructive."

Henry Ives Cobb, Architect, Chicago, Ill.: "I have been a subscriber to your magazine for a number of years, and have found it a useful and progressive periodical. I take pleasure in recommending it as a valuable acquisition to any collection of architectural periodicals or library."

D. H. Burnham, Chief of Construction, World's Columbian Exposition, Chicago, Ill.: "I am a subscriber to ARCHITECTURE AND BUILDING, a weekly magazine published in New York and Chicago, and find it valuable in many ways. I can recommend it heartily to those needing such a periodical."

Holabird & Roche, Architects, Chicago, Ill.: "In reply to your inquiry as to our opinion of your paper, ARCHITECTURE AND BUILDING, would say that we have taken the magazine for the last three years and are entirely satisfied with it."

Francis J. Norton, Architect, Chicago, Ill.: "Being a thorough reader of all the leading architectural papers, I feel justified in saying that I consider ARCHITECTURE AND BUILDING the most modern and practical architectural paper published."

Frank Niernsee, Architect of the State House, Columbia, S. C.: "I take several architectural publications, and I find your journal second to none—always keeping fully abreast of the times. You have a wide circulation in the South."

WILLIAM T. COMSTOCK, Publisher,

23 Warren Street, New York.

Monadnock Building, 260 Dearborn Street, Chicago.